J

PRAISE FOR *Until We Meet Again*

"Moonlight, mystery, and murder make for a thrilling combination in this lush tale that bridges the present day with the Gatsby era on a time-crossed beach. *Until We Meet Again* is tragically beautiful with twists you won't see coming."

—Martina Boone, author of the Heirs of Watson Island trilogy

"Suspenseful, poignant, and romantic: well worth the read."

—*Kirkus Reviews*

"A beach house, a mystery, and time-travel love make *Until We Meet Again* a romantic, engaging read."

—Deb Caletti, author of *The Last Forever* and National Book Award Finalist for *Honey, Baby, Sweetheart*

"Time stood still as I read this breathtakingly story. I didn't want it to end."

—Kasie West, author of *The Fill-In Boyfriend* and *The Distance Between Us*

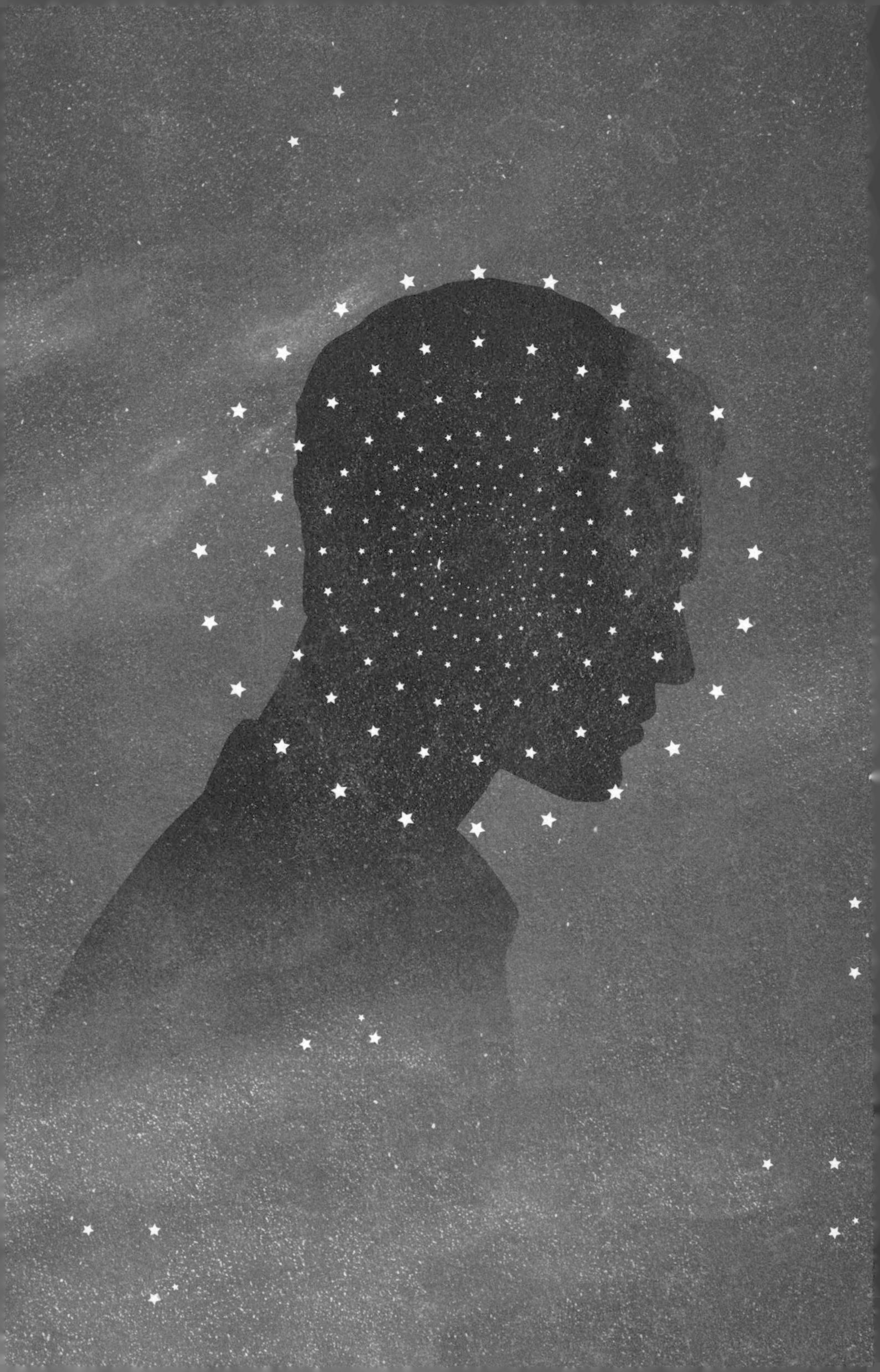

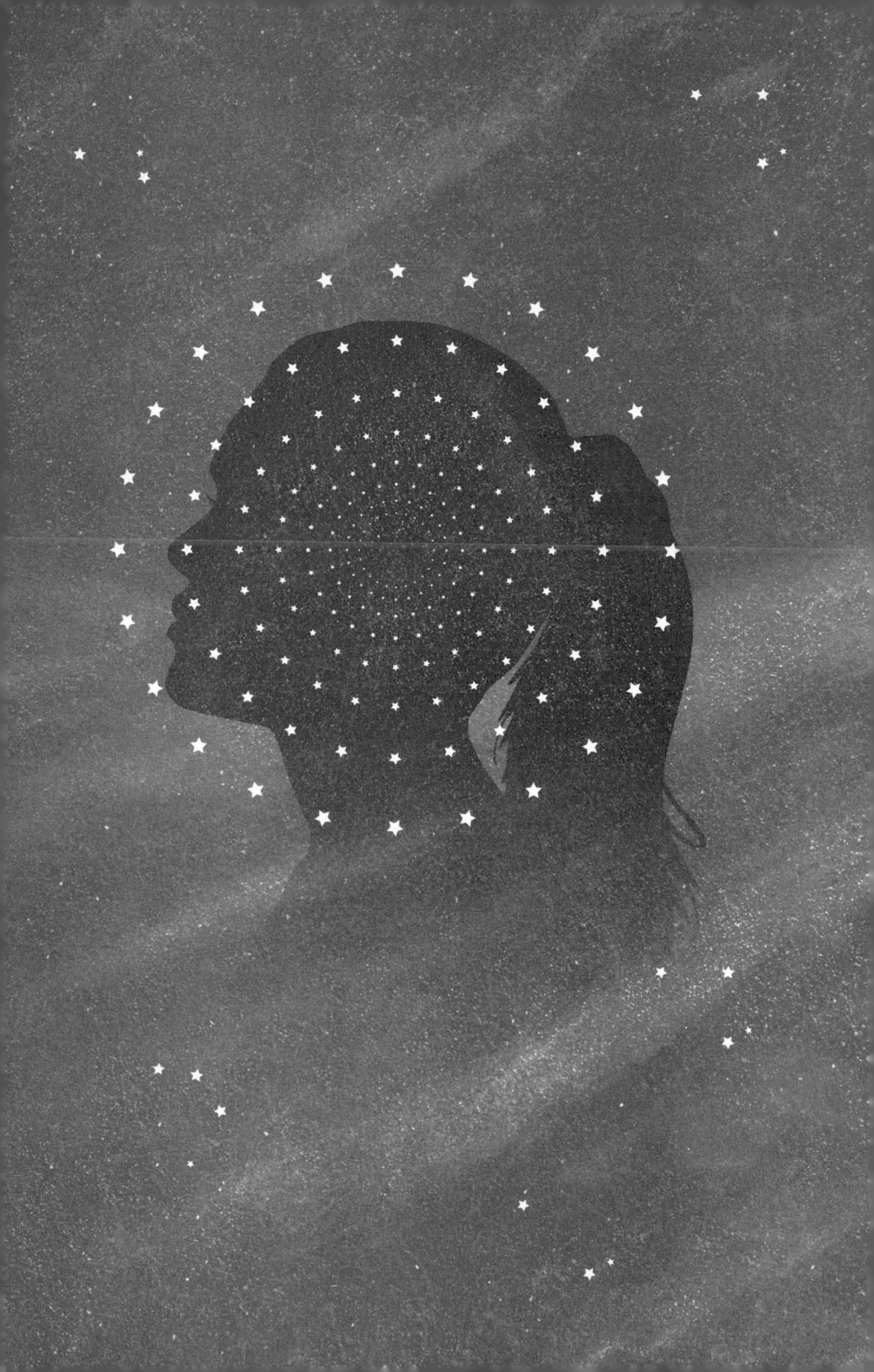

RENEE COLLINS

Cover and internal design © 2015 by Sourcebooks, Inc.
Jacket design by Faceout Studio, Jeff Miller
Cover images © PeskyMonkey/Getty Images;
Christine Schneider/Getty Images;
Arman Zhenikeyev/Shutterstock
Internal images © Viktora/Shutterstock;
Ostill/Shutterstock

Sourcebooks and the colophon are registered
trademarks of Sourcebooks, Inc.

The characters and events portrayed in this book
are fictitious or are used fictitiously. Any similarity to
real persons, living or dead, is purely
coincidental and not intended by the author.

Published by
Sourcebooks Fire,
an imprint of Sourcebooks, Inc.
P.O. Box 4410, Naperville, Illinois 60567-4410
(630) 961-3900
Fax: (630) 961-2168
www.sourcebooks.com

Library of Congress Cataloging-in-Publication Data
is on file with the publisher.

Printed and bound in the United States of America.
WOZ 10 9 8 7 6 5 4 3 2 1

For Ben,

because I like our love story best of all.

Prologue

The beach is empty. In the fading glow of twilight, the waves roll up to the rocks in sweeping curls of white foam. The sand glistens like wet steel. The grass bends low in the briny night wind. Always changing, yet always the same. I imagine the beach has looked like this since the beginning of time.

Stepping onto the soft terrain, I feel transported to some ancient evening, eons ago. Long before my uncle claimed this land as his own. Long before man even dared to taint these shores.

I wish the fleeting vision were true.

My gaze falls to the full moon's reflection on the water. It's broken into shards on the black sea, tossed about with each wave. A small, white shape catches my eye. It's in the glare of the reflection, so I nearly miss it.

I step into the wave break. A seabird, dead and limp, is rolling back and forth in the foam. Her wings are spread open, her white-and-brown-speckled breast exposed.

I lift the small creature into my palm. *What killed her?* I wonder. There's no sign of injury. Did she drown in the sea? Pinching her brittle, fragile leg gently between my fingers, I notice a small metal band snapped around her ankle. The sight of it startles me. Examining it closer, I catch the faint impression of numbers and letters etched into the band, but something in me resists reading them. I can't say why.

What does it matter, anyhow? The poor creature is dead. And she reminds me that there is no going back. Time howls on, like the wind. And it is not only weaker creatures like this bird that succumb to it. Even the strongest man will fall before its crushing forward push.

I set the bird out into the water. As the tide pulls her away, I accept this truth. Soon the summer will be over. Too soon.

CHAPTER 1

Cassandra

Date: July 8.

Days at my mom and stepdad's new summer home: 22

Hours spent at the froufrou country club: 0

Hours spent on the fancy private beach: 0

Hours spent lying on the couch bemoaning my lack of a life: somewhere in the 100s.

Number of times Mom has told me to make some new friends and stop moping around: also somewhere in the 100s.

To paraphrase Shakespeare: Oh, for a muse of fire to convey how utterly and completely bored I am.

Given the circumstances, it should be clear that I have no choice but to try to sneak into my neighbors' yard and swim in their pool at 2:00 a.m.

My two accomplices are less than ideal. Travis Howard and Brandon Marks are local royalty of this ritzy, historic neighborhood slapped on the coast of Massachusetts's North Shore. Both have the classic all-American look—tall, sparkling blue eyes, and a crop of blond hair that's been gelled to scientific levels of perfection. But given the circumstances, they'll have to do.

Brandon can barely keep pace as we cut along the tailored brush that adorns the Andersons' back fence. Maybe because he's too busy shooting nervous glances behind us.

"We're being followed," he says.

Travis and I exchange a look.

"Chill out, dude," Travis says.

I sigh. "Seriously. I didn't pack my smelling salts, so try not to faint."

Travis holds out his fist for a bump.

Brandon is resolute. "At the very least, we're being watched. You think these people don't have security cameras?"

"No clue," I say brightly.

"Well, that's reassuring."

"I try."

I probably should have come on my own. Trouble is, I need a pair of hands to boost me over the fence. My little brother, Eddie, couldn't do it, since he's three. And for obvious reasons, I couldn't ask Mom or Frank. That left the only other person I know here: Travis.

He and I met at a garden party. How bourgeois is that? I was so bored, I was ready to claw my eyes out. Then I saw this crazy guy doing a chair dance, to the utter shock of the local hens, and I decided he might be okay. Travis is pretty cool. He reminds me a little of my friend Jade back in Ohio—a delightful troublemaker. Having Travis's buddy Brandon tagging along, however, has proved to be an unwelcome change of plans.

It's late, but humidity still hangs in the air. Not as oppressive as during the day, but enough to make the hair against my neck damp. Crickets chirp loudly in the surrounding brush, which makes me uneasy somehow, as if their incessant noise will draw attention to us. As if they're crying, "Look! Look! Look! Look!" to some unseen guard. Brandon's nerves must be contagious.

Luckily, I spy the edge of the fence before I can dwell on my uneasiness for too long.

"We made it," I say.

Gripping the bars, I look for a good spot to grab midway up. Travis helps me with the inspection.

"Right over here," he says, motioning. "The ground's a little higher on the other side, and those bushes will break your fall."

"Nice," I say, impressed. "You have a lot of experience breaking in to private property?"

"Yeah, except we usually go for cash and high-value items. Breaking in to go swimming should be a nice change of pace."

I smirk and he gives me a Mr. Teen USA wink.

"All right then," I say. "Hoist me up."

Brandon steps in between us. "Are we seriously doing this? You know, your stepdad's house has a huge private beach. If you want to swim so badly, can't we go there?"

"You're missing the point, Brandon."

"You never explained the point."

"Only a fool asks to understand that which cannot be grasped," I say, pretending to quote some ancient philosopher.

Travis blinks. "Dude. That was deep."

"I know, right?" I turn back to Brandon. "See? He gets it."

"This is really stupid," Brandon says, unamused.

I pull out my phone. "So, I guess you don't want to be in the group shot then?"

Travis comes to my side and puts his arm around me. "Sweet! Selfie time."

I hold out my phone, and he and I make an overly enthusiastic thumbs-up pose.

Brandon folds his arms impatiently across his chest. "Can we get on with this?"

"Well, look who's eager to have some fun," I say, giving him a hearty slap on the back. "About time you came aboard."

Brandon shakes his head and holds out his interlocked hands. Travis stands across from him. Together, they form the perfect ladder. Pushing off of their shoulders, I reach for the top of the fence. One push and my leg tips over the edge.

"Got it!" I shout. Perched on the top of the wall, I survey my target. The pool is lit, even with the Andersons away for the week, and it gleams an appealing turquoise blue in the dark night. If I had time and my stuff, I'd paint the scene. For now, however, an immersive, performance-art type of scenario will have to suffice.

"Let's do this," I say, hopping onto the grass below. I land firmly on my feet and unlatch the side gate.

Brandon remains frozen at the threshold. "Cass…"

"Let me guess. You don't think this is such a good idea."

Travis laughs. "Seriously, dude, don't be such a pansy."

He starts through the gate when Brandon grabs his arm. "Trav. You know why we can't."

Travis says nothing, but a shadow crosses his expression. I frown. "What?"

When Travis doesn't reply, Brandon exhales. "We could go to jail."

"Oh, don't be so dramatic—"

"No, seriously. We're both…kind of on probation."

He officially has my attention. "Explain."

Travis shakes his head. "It's not that big of a deal. Brandon's freaking out."

"Then tell me," I say.

His eyes shift away from mine. "It was me and Brandon and some of the guys from the lacrosse team. One night a few weeks ago, we were a little drunk. It was late. And we sort of…broke into a liquor store."

Brandon scrambles to explain before I can react. "It wasn't my idea. We never would have done it—it was really stupid, okay? Anyway, we got caught, but Austin's dad pulled some strings and got us off with a warning."

I nod slowly. "I see. So, you got Daddums to skirt the law for you?"

"It's not like that," Travis says, but I can tell he's really embarrassed.

Brandon sighs. "I can't get into trouble. I've got a lacrosse scholarship on the line, and my parents would murder me if I screwed that up. Trav's the same."

I'm not sure which is more irritating, the sham justice system in these ritzy areas or the fact that there's actually a legitimate reason to cut our little excursion short.

I fold my arms. "So after all this, we're leaving?"

"I never said that," Travis says, defensive.

Brandon glares. "Don't be an idiot, Trav. It's not worth it."

I can tell by the look Brandon gives Travis that he actually means *I'm* not worth it. Irritation flares up in me.

"Well, I haven't come all this way to wuss out now. You boys and your lacrosse scholarships are free to go back home."

"Fine," Brandon says. "I'm out of here."

He storms off without a glance back. Travis lingers, but I can tell he's seen the error of his ways and wants to go as well.

"Go ahead and leave," I say. "I'm over the fence. I don't need you anymore."

Travis sighs. "Brandon's right. We should probably get out of here."

I plant my fists on my waist. "Nope. I'm going to swim."

"Cass."

"Seriously, go. I can take it from here."

"I'm not leaving you alone at two in the morning. It isn't safe."

I laugh. "How very gallant, Travis."

"I'm serious. It isn't safe."

With only a smile, I turn and head for the pool. He calls my name in a sharp whisper, but I ignore him.

Little garden lights illuminate the path and surround the flagstone patio. The pool shimmers. You've got to hand it to the Andersons. They have a nice place here.

I circle the pool thoughtfully, then dip one toe in the water. "Ideal temperature."

No simple entrance into the pool will do. It's got to be diving board or nothing. With determination, I march to the elaborate diving area and grip the ladder.

Travis calls my name again. I glance over my shoulder with a sigh. He's in the shadows by the shrubs.

"You're crazy," he whisper-yells.

"Guilty as charged, Travis, my dear." I blow him a kiss and climb the diving-board ladder. My nerve ends tingle as I approach the long plank. It's a stupid little thing, but I feel more alive now than I have all summer.

"Okay. Here goes nothing. One...two..."

The porch lights snap on with the fury of midday sun. It startles me so much that I throw my arms up to block it and almost fall backward into the pool.

"All right, kids," a man's voice booms. "Fun's over."

Who knew an über rich, gated community would have twenty-four-hour guards on staff? Oh wait. I knew. I just didn't care.

A big man in a bouncer-type jacket strides in by the side of the deck, right near where I entered. To my left, Travis flattens against the house, trapped. If he runs, the guard will notice for sure.

The beam of a high-powered flashlight blasts in my face.

"Get down from there."

I shoot a look to the gently rippling pool water, then to Travis, then back to the guard. He's clearly not in the mood to screw around.

Something about this situation feels so symbolic of this whole summer. There I was, about to plunge into that film internship in New York. Or go to Paris with Jade. Or maybe the acting camp. I hadn't really decided. Either way, I was ready to start living and get out of Nowhereville, Ohio. And what happens?

Mom and Frank get the crazy idea to rent a beach house in Massachusetts. And because Frank can work remotely with his finance job, they don't rent it for a week like a normal family. They rent it for the entire summer. And of course, they insist on dragging me and Eddie down with them. To sit on my butt all day and to go to garden luncheons.

"Where are the two guys I saw you with?" the guard calls out.

Cameras. Of course there are cameras. The beam of the flashlight cuts from me to scan the yard. Travis's whole body tenses, and guilt washes over me. As much as I initially wrote him off as a rich jock, I actually kind of like the guy. He's been cool and willing to play along with my ridiculous little shenanigans. I can't let him suffer serious, long-lasting consequences.

Meeting Travis's eyes, I mouth the word "go" and then wave to the security guard with both arms. "It's just me, big guy. Me all by my lonesome."

The flashlight snaps up to me. My pulse races. What I'm doing, I'm not exactly sure. But the recklessness feels good.

"I thought I saw someone else," the guard says.

He starts to pull the light away to search the yard. I have to act quickly. Drawing in a breath, I pull my sundress over my head and toss it on the patio. For a single, humiliating moment, the guard's flashlight illuminates my red bra and underwear for all the world to see. Travis better be halfway home by now.

The guard's voice is calm but laden with warning. "Miss..."

"Last one in the water's a rotten egg!"

Drawing in a breath, I give one good bounce on the diving board, leap into the air, form the perfect swan position, and plunge into the water.

CHAPTER 2

Cassandra

Few things can compare to the humiliation of standing on your doorstep at 2:00 a.m., dripping wet, with a security guard holding your arm. As he knocks, I'm suddenly not sure which is worse, facing jail time or Mom's wrath.

In a rare stroke of luck, it's Frank who answers. He's blinking groggily, his hair mussed from sleep.

"Cass?" he says, frowning with confusion. "What is this?"

The guard releases his grip on my arm, presenting me for the slaughter. "Your stepdaughter thought it would be a fun idea to go for a swim in the Andersons' pool tonight."

Frank blinks, still trying to wake up, and stares at his watch. I shift uncomfortably in place.

"It was an accident. I was confused. I was…sleepwalking."

The guard shoots Frank a grimace, but Frank says nothing. After an excruciating pause, he sets a hand on the security guard's arm.

"Thank you for bringing her back…" He reads the security guard's name tag. "Jim. I certainly appreciate it. I can take it from here."

The guard grimaces. "I ought to bring her in. We take trespassing very seriously in these parts."

Frank nods. "As you should. And I can assure you, her mother and I will not let this go unpunished."

The guard's frown deepens. "I don't know…"

Frank smiles warmly. "Tell you what, Jim. You turn her over to us, with the promise that she'll be thoroughly taken to task, and in the morning, I'll talk to Mike Anderson about getting you the weekend off. We can have Braden cover for you."

My throat tightens. This can either go very well or very, very bad.

The guard analyzes Frank, silently weighing the pros and cons of his next move. But then, in seemingly slow motion, he nods and gives me a little push forward.

"If it happens again—if anything like this happens again—she's in for it."

I could explode from sheer relief.

Frank gives the guard's arm a friendly squeeze. "Much appreciated, Jim."

Smiling cheerfully, he escorts me into the house and shuts the door. The smile drops as he turns to me.

"I can explain," I rush to say.

"Tomorrow. You can and will explain everything in the morning. Right now, I suggest you go put on some dry clothes and try to get some sleep."

My face burns with shame at how nice he's being about all this. "Thanks, Frank."

He waves my words away with a half smile and shuffles back toward his room. I make my way to mine with a sinking feeling. Mom's going to kill me when she finds out.

Phase One of my Punishment Reduction Plan involves Eddie. By the time I wake up, it's past ten, and by now I know Frank has told Mom what went down last night. The relative quiet coming from downstairs is a bad sign. They're talking about me, waiting for me to emerge. I need an adorable little boy to soften the blow.

Creeping on tiptoe, I make my way to the playroom first. Eddie is nowhere to be seen. Not in his room either. That leaves only two other places: either he's with Mom and Frank, or he's watching cartoons in the den. Hoping for the latter, I slip downstairs.

Low but tense voices drift in from the dining room. Still talking about me. Clenching my jaw, I edge my way to the den.

Success.

Eddie is sitting crossed-legged on the couch, watching his favorite cartoon about an orphaned robot alien and his robot puppy. He looks up as I come in. He's unreasonably cute. It's lucky, really. I had the typical preteen issues when Mom got remarried. Don't get me wrong, for everyone's sanity, it was the right thing for my parents to get divorced, but I definitely had my issues when Frank came into the picture. And then Eddie was born, and slowly I began to realize how we'd work as a family. So much so that I can't imagine life if Frank hadn't come along. Eddie is the glue that holds us all together. Smiling, I plop down at his side.

"Hey, buddy. Can I watch your show with you?"

Eddie points to his chest with a chubby toddler finger. "I be the robot. You be the puppy."

"Fair deal." I nestle beside him, and he pets my hair.

"Good puppy."

I make my best dog sound and sniff Eddie's face, which smells distinctly of Cinnamon Toast Crunch.

"That tickles!" he says, laughing.

I give his cheek a quick kiss and then lay my head next to his little shoulder. "Puppy is nervous. Puppy thinks Mommy Dog is mad at her."

Eddie pets my head again. "Don't worry, Puppy. Mommy Dog is nice."

Ah, the safe, easy world of a kid. Almost makes me wish I could go back to being three again, when things were so simple.

"You okay in there, buddy?"

Mom's voice makes me sit up, and a moment later, she steps into the doorway. When she sees me, her arms immediately cross over her chest. She's calm but prepared. This isn't going to go well for me.

"So you're up," she says. "Have a good sleep?"

I pull my arm around Eddie. "Yep. Just playing a little robot alien and puppy with my bro."

"Cassandra. Kindly make your way into the dining room. We're going to have a talk."

"Why can't we talk in here?" I know they won't be as hard on me in front of Eddie.

In response, Mom raises a single eyebrow in that "I mean business" way. Sighing, I slide from the couch.

"Say good-bye to your sister, Eddie," I mutter. "Remember me as I was."

"Move it, Cass," Mom says.

I march into the dining room, my head held high like a martyr being walked to the chopping block.

Frank sips coffee at the table. He casts me a look as I pull up a chair. A look of sympathy? Apology? It's too subtle to tell. As Mom sits down across from me, I brace myself for the full gamut of parental clichés:

"What on earth were you thinking?" (I wasn't thinking. Clearly.)

"Didn't I raise you better than this?" (Apparently not.)

"This is about me not letting you stay the summer with your father, isn't it?" (Nope. Way off.)

"You're going to be grounded for a very long time, young lady." (And that's different from the status quo…how?)

However, Mom says nothing. Only the ticking of the French-chef clock on the wall invades the silence. Each moment puts me more on guard. Then finally, she releases a slow sigh. Okay, here it comes.

"What's going on, Cassandra?" Mom asks, her voice alarmingly gentle. "What's happened to you this summer?"

I shift in my chair, choosing to pick at a small fleck of dried milk on the table rather than look at her. She goes on, relentless.

"You seem lost. And it's hard to watch. You're so smart and talented. You could have the whole world at your fingertips if you focus. But you're spinning your wheels. You say you want to be a filmmaker, so I send you to directing camp. When was the last time you made a film, Cass? Then there were acting lessons.

"Then you told me you wanted to paint. I gave you private art instructions for six months, and I haven't seen you so much as pick up a brush all summer. And I suppose I wouldn't mind if you'd been off making new friends and having fun. But you haven't done anything this summer. Nothing but become angry and reckless. What's happening to you, Cass?"

Heat pulses to my face. I dig harder at the fleck on the table.

"You need to find yourself, young lady. You're going to be a senior in the fall. It's time to learn who you are and what you want out of life."

Frank sets a hand on my arm. "We're here for you, kiddo. We just want to help."

I don't look up. Can't look up. I feel exposed. Yelling, punishments—those I can handle. But this? It needs to end right now.

I sit back in my chair with a "ho-hum" shrug. "What can I say, Mom? I guess I'm going through an adolescent phase. Puberty. Hormones. That kind of thing. "

"Cassandra."

"I know," I say, holding up my hands as I stand. "I know. I'm grounded."

"Cassandra."

I back toward the door, to my room. To safety. "Grounded for life. Got it. I guess it's time to take up harmonica and start scratching a tally of days on my bedpost."

Mom calls my name again sharply, but I've turned for the hallway. I run up to my room and slam the door.

The Battle of the Dining Room Table isn't over. Both sides have merely regrouped at their respective camps. Mom's next offensive comes via Frank, shortly after dinner. He knocks on my door to cheerfully inform me that Mom says I'm allowed to go to the party tonight.

"Allowed to go." Clever wording, since she knows that being barred in my room all night would be infinitely more enjoyable than going to that party. Getting all dressed up in a white eyelet-lace dress and floral scarf. Playing the role of pretty daughter for the guests. Nodding and smiling my way through a dozen dull conversations. Well played, Mother. Well played.

Slumped in the wicker deck chair that night, I glare at Mom as she chats with the other guests. Another mind-numbing party. Rich, middle-aged people grasping desperately at the final threads of youth, blabbing, and drinking cabernet sauvignon.

Frank pulls the cork off another bottle, laughing at what was most certainly a lame joke. With as much money as these people have, they're shockingly dull. The only person I care to spend any time with is Travis, but his parents are here with him, and even though he got off scot-free last night, their piercing glares warn me not to move any closer.

So I stay in my chair, drinking a Sprite and watching a moth swirl around the white Chinese lanterns that have been strung out over the deck.

At ten o'clock, Mom gives me a nod. My time has been served. I contemplate going inside to my room, but since I'll be cooped up there for the next few days while I'm grounded, I decide to stay outside.

Ripping off the floral scarf and leaving it on a bush in a weak sign of rebellion, I wander onto the grounds. This house is too fancy for a backyard. It has grounds. For the millionth time, I wonder what possessed my mom to come here. Yes, it's a gorgeous old home in a gorgeous location, but we don't belong. And we never will. No matter how much money Frank has. We are Middle American, live-in-the-suburbs people. We don't have soirees out on the veranda. We have barbecues in the backyard, where the men drink too much beer and the kids play truth or dare in the den.

Illuminated by an orb of lantern light on the deck beyond me, the party group is laughing and talking about empty things. The obnoxious truth jabs at me. I always smugly assured myself that I didn't belong in Ohio, that I was meant for greater things. Now here I am, and I still feel like I don't belong. Maybe I'm just a hopeless snob who will be unhappy everywhere I go.

The impulse to do something stupid once again prickles through me. A small act of harmless vandalism, perhaps. Maybe I'll rip off my clothes and stroll back into the party, naked as the day I was born.

I kick a rock near my foot, sending it skidding over the path. What am I, twelve? Am I secretly trying to get Mommy's attention because I'm worried she loves her new husband more than me? Properly shamed, I try to jam my hands into my pockets until I remember I'm wearing a dress and don't have pockets.

I find myself wandering past the lit water feature, past the rosebush-adorned gazebo, over a brick-colored path of flagstones, and across the meticulously maintained back lawn. By default, I head to the estate's private beach. It's not a great swimming beach—too rocky—and I don't expect anyone from the party to have wandered out there.

At the edge of the grass, a row of high, trimmed bushes acts like a natural wall. Walking along the edge, I find my secret shortcut to the water. I happened across it a few weeks ago. At one point, perhaps someone had intended for it to be a paved path to the beach, but that never materialized. Now the lawn crew lets the branches grow just enough to hide the gap but maintain the access.

The soft pound of surf reaches me before I see the water. The tang of salt is thick on the air. Growing up in Ohio, I didn't get much exposure to the ocean. The community pool was the extent of my experience with water. Maybe because of that, something about the size and constant motion of the sea both intrigues and terrifies me.

A few more strides through the thick bushes, and I see the water ahead. It's black and vast and in what seems to be in perpetual motion. The white tips of breaking waves roll onto the beach, lapping the gleaming sand. It's a surprisingly long stretch of beach. A cove, really. Perfectly enclosed by brush to the back and rocky points to either side. Big rocks are scattered in the water and along the shore, but there's enough sand to sit. It's quiet and rugged and starkly beautiful. I draw in a breath of night ocean smell and immediately decide that I should have taken my brooding here from the start. This place is clearly much better suited for the job than some stuffy party.

I flop on a sandy patch near a crop of rocks and stare out at the gently crashing waves. A salty breeze feathers my hair across my face. I decide not to move it. I bet I look more pensive this way. What I'm pensive about, I don't really know. How pathetic is that? I don't even know why I'm angsty and sad. I just am.

I pull out my phone. Maybe I'll send another text to Jade.

Hey. I'm at a lame party. Bored. I hope you're bored too.

She won't reply until sometime tomorrow. If at all. She's certainly not bored. She's too busy in Paris, "sucking the marrow out of life." Relishing the challenge and excitement of the art museum internship that I clearly would have applied for if I'd known about it. Probably. I push my fingers into the cool sand, grimacing.

I don't know why it annoys me that Jade seems to have her five-year plan all worked out. I mean, can't an artist just love to create art? Why do we suddenly have to make a job out of it? Part of me wishes things were simple. Like they were three years ago, when Jade and I were stoked to be going to high school. Then Jade wouldn't have gone to Paris, and I wouldn't have come here with Mom and Frank. We would have stayed with my dad, had slumber parties, and talked about boys, and we wouldn't have cared about anything.

Light catches my gaze. There, at the black-on-black line of the ocean's horizon, is a wide, glowing band. It takes a moment for me to realize what it is. The beginning of the moon's rise. I pull up the Farmers' Almanac on my phone. Apparently the moon will be full tonight.

I look back to the shimmering light. It's magical and eerie at the same time. Hugging my knees, I nestle to watch. The first golden line of the moon emerges, huge and trembling in the residual summer heat, out of the dark water. And then, something inexplicable happens.

A flash of light. A brilliant pulse of white emanates from the rising moon and soars across the ocean, touching the shore like a kiss.

I sit up with a start, eyes wide. It was so fast—faster than a blink. So fast that I'm almost not sure if I saw it. Maybe it's my eyes. Flashes of light are early indications of retinal tearing. Or is it glaucoma? Jade's dad is an optometrist, and she's always worrying about some intense eye problem that could happen to her. But before I can grab my phone to call her, I notice a shape.

There's a figure on the beach. Standing over near the shoreline.

How did I not see him come out onto the beach? Was I too busy staring at the moon?

I squint against the darkness. The figure is definitely male. And young. Even from this distance, I can tell that. I watch him, not moving. I probably should be nervous, alone on a beach with a stranger, especially a stranger who is possibly a ninja. Mom gave me a handy travel-size canister of pepper spray to carry on my key chain for just such an occasion. I always thought she was a touch paranoid. She'd probably be furious with me for not running at the first sight of this guy.

But I think I'm safe. Studying him, I deduce that he's a party guest. The slacks and dress shirt give that away. He's even wearing a tailored jacket. A little overdressed. Trying too hard. I can't tell for sure from this far away, but I'd peg this guy at about my age—seventeen—maybe a year or two older. I don't remember seeing anyone my age at the party, other than Travis and Brandon. More compelling evidence that he's a ninja.

Not noticing me, the stranger steps down to the shoreline. Tucking his jacket behind him, he stuffs his hands in his pockets and gazes out at the ocean. I feel the impulse to make him aware of my presence, but something stops me.

Maybe it's his oddly fancy clothes. Or something about the way he's standing there. Maybe it's because he looks as lonely as I feel.

He walks a step into the water, kicking a rock. He's tall and lean, and even his walk is pensive. What's he thinking about so intently? Maybe tragic, impossible, first love? I hope so.

He bends to pick up the rock and throws it into the ocean. I should stop staring. When he notices me, it's going to be pretty awkward to explain why I didn't make my presence known. I should sneak out while his back is turned.

Or maybe I could watch him a little longer…

It's almost as if I'm waiting for him to pull out a notebook and start to write exquisitely sad poetry. Is it pathetic how quickly I assign a persona to a complete stranger and then start imagining what it would be like to fall in love with him? In real life, he's probably a snotty rich kid, obsessed with his souped-up Camaro or getting laid in the backseat of said souped-up Camaro, or both.

I sigh. A little too loudly. Ninja Boy whips his head around and looks right at me.

My spine straightens. I contemplate running. Or perhaps feigning blindness. Anything's got to be better than owning up to the fact that I've been creepily watching him for the past five minutes.

Great. He's walking over.

"Sorry," he calls out. "I didn't see you there."

I open my mouth to sputter some fumbling apology, but then a stab of rebellion cuts through me. What's the point? I don't owe this guy an apology for sitting on my own property. So what if he thinks I'm weird or psycho? After this summer, I'm never coming back to Crest Harbor, which means I'll never see this guy again.

My pulse speeds up in spite of my resolve, but I stand my ground.

"Don't mind me," I say. "There's plenty of room on this beach for all brooding loners."

A half smile pulls at his lips. "That so? Well, is there a required distance between brooders or can I take this spot here?"

He's pointing to the sand right beside me. Without waiting for a reply, he sits down and smiles. It's a pretty fantastic smile. Add to that sandy-blond hair that's been slicked back and deep brown eyes, and it's settled. He's too gorgeous to be anything but a rich jerk looking to get laid.

Sad, really. I almost don't want to talk to him and have my perfect construction ruined. Couldn't he have stayed in the distance, looking mournful and poetic?

He bends back on his hands and looks out over the water. "Some moon, huh?"

I follow his gaze. The moon is now a huge, golden circle of light.

"Yeah, pretty spectacular."

"Very interesting moonrise too." The boy shoots me a sidelong glance. "Did you by chance see…?"

I tense. "See what?"

Looking suddenly self-conscious, he shakes his head. "Nothing. Never mind."

I narrow my eyes. He didn't see the flash of light too, did he? I'm about to ask him when he stretches his arms out and inhales deeply.

"Ned was right. It's the perfect night for a party."

"I suppose," I say dryly.

He sits up, folding his arms across his knees. "So what are you doing out here all alone?"

The feeling of reckless abandon spreads in me again, drowning out any socially acceptable small talk I could offer. I have nothing to prove and no one to impress.

"Not much. I'm just pondering the subtle anguish of life."

He raises his eyebrows. "Well." He studies me, probably thinking I'm some crazy emo girl. Then he nods, turning his gaze back to the ocean. "That makes two of us."

He doesn't seem to be mocking me. In fact, he looks rather lost in his own thoughts. A little smile comes to his lips.

"For each ecstatic instant, we must an anguish pay."

The words are oddly familiar, and then I remember. "Emily Dickinson."

"That's right," he says. "You seem surprised that I would quote her."

"I am."

He lets out a single laugh. "And why is that?"

"You don't look like a ponder-the-anguish-of-life-and-quote-Dickinson kind of guy."

He seems amused. "Don't I? Tell me, what does *that* kind of guy look like?"

He'd look like Mr. Perry, my balding, spindly English teacher. Not a young, stylishly dressed, uncomfortably good-looking ninja.

"Let's say you look like you fit right in at the party, not a poetry reading."

His smile fades a bit. "I suppose it was rude of me to leave the party. But I couldn't think with all that noise. I was standing there and I realized I'd had quite enough. You know?"

"So you left because it was too loud? That's not exactly a typically accepted reason to brood, but I suppose I'll allow it."

"It's more than that."

"Okay, so what then?"

He sighs. "Have you ever been in a room full of people and felt completely alone? And everything around you, the lights, the champagne, the people, it all feels so…"

"Empty?"

"Exactly."

He studies me so directly that my skin starts to tingle.

"I've felt that," I say, holding his gaze.

"Is that what brought you out here to the beach?"

This guy is either well rehearsed at wooing angsty, artistic girls, or he isn't quite the jerk I had him pegged to be. Adrenaline pushes aside my usual wall of sarcasm.

"I think I wanted to do something crazy, but I chickened out and came here to sulk instead."

"What would you have done?"

"If I hadn't chickened out, you mean?"

He nods, watching me.

"I don't really know. That's part of the problem."

He laughs a little. "You're different. I could tell by the way you sat here looking out at the shore."

"You're pretty strange too, you know."

"Guilty as charged," he says with a wink. "So what do we do about it, you and I? A pair of odd ducks searching for meaning."

"I guess we have to do something crazy."

"Let's," he says. "What will it be?" Then he springs up. "I know." He grabs my hands, pulling me to my feet. "We'll jump into the ocean!"

I laugh at the irony of his suggestion. "No thanks. I had a nice swim last night, and that got me into enough trouble."

"Aw, come on. It'll be fun."

"Nope."

A sly smile creeps onto his face. "You didn't come out here to talk. You could have done that at the party."

Without warning, he bursts into a run down the beach, pulling me along with him. We run into the rush of stormy ocean wind. I can barely stay on my feet to keep up with him.

"Hey!" I shout, my hair streaming behind me. "Stop!"

"Enough talk! Now we act!"

"I said no swimming!"

He keeps running. "We'll dive off the point, see if we can catch a mermaid."

"No! I'm too young to die."

He laughs, and I can't help laughing too. We run until we reach the base of the rocky point, where we both stop, bending over to catch our breath.

"Push me in that water and I'll drown you," I say between gasps of air.

He grins. "I thought you wanted to do something rash."

"I do. I'm just not into dying with a complete stranger. Not quite what I had in mind."

"I am getting a little carried away, aren't I? I don't even know your name."

"No, you don't."

"Well, are you going to tell me or have I lost my chance to know you?"

My breathing has calmed, but something about the way he looks at me keeps my heart pounding.

"Cass," I say. "Cassandra."

He holds out a hand. For a handshake, I guess? Quaint. I give his palm an awkward tug.

"And you are?"

He blinks. "Lawrence," he says, looking mildly surprised I asked.

"Sorry, I'm not from around here. I don't know all the cool kids."

His brow furrows a little.

"You're honestly shocked I don't know your name," I say with a scoff.

"No, but since this silly party sort of centers around me, I thought you'd—"

"Excuse me, what? The party centers around you?"

He shrugs, looking cornered. "Easy. It wasn't my idea."

"Oh, so you're claiming that my mom and stepdad randomly decided to make you the star of *their* party at *their* house? You're either outrageously narcissistic or delusional. Right now, I'm thinking probably both."

He frowns. "We must be talking about two different parties. I mean the one right there through those bushes."

"Uh, yeah. That's my mom and stepdad's house."

He stares at me. "You're mistaken."

My face burns. "I know we don't exactly fit in, but they rent the place fair and square, so it is, in fact, their house."

He furrows his brow as if straining to understand my words. "I don't believe I know your parents."

"Oh, of course not. They only invited you into their home for a party, which is apparently in your honor. No, no reason to bother knowing who they are."

He scratches the back of his neck. "I didn't mean—"

"Whatever."

"Are your parents related to my Uncle Ned somehow?"

"Uncle Ned?"

Again, he looks surprised that I don't know the who's who of Crest Harbor. "Ned Foster."

"I suppose he's another big-name, fancy person in this area who I need to know and worship? I'm not that girl, okay? I couldn't care less about Ned Foster."

Lawrence looks at me like I'm crazy. Shame ripples across my face. This is what I get for letting my imagination run away with me. For thinking this guy was somehow different. I start to march up the beach.

"I'd better get back."

"Wait." He runs up after me. "I didn't mean to offend you. I'm just...very confused."

"Well, I'm not. I had you pegged the minute I saw you."

Before he has a chance to reply, I run the rest of the way up the sand and through the bushes. Once I'm on the lawn again, I slow down. But there are no footsteps rustling behind me. I come to a full stop, hating my weakness, and glance back toward the beach.

But Lawrence isn't following me.

CHAPTER 3

Lawrence

She runs off, back to the party. Angry? Embarrassed? I wish I could understand what just happened. I rush after her through the brush, but she's somehow managed to dissolve into the crowd on the lawn.

"There you are, Lon!"

Charles claps a hand on my back. His breath reeks of the cheap hooch Uncle Ned had brought in from New York.

"There's the birthday boy," he slurs.

"Charles, did you see a girl come in from the beach?"

"You mean Fay?"

My words halt. It wouldn't sound great that I've been out on the beach alone with another girl. I cast my eyes around the manic crowd. The jazz band jangles and crashes like some crazy, delirious music box. Everywhere, arms raise, glasses glinting with frothy drinks in hands. A sea of bobbed hair, dark and platinum alike, bounces and dances as if of its own accord.

But I don't see the strange girl from the beach anywhere.

Aware of Charles watching me, I nod vaguely. "Sure. Where is Fay?"

"She's over by the band. She was looking for you earlier. I tried to get her to dance with me, but she wouldn't have it. She only has eyes for you, lover boy."

I swat him away, grinning as I walk past, but the smile fades the moment he's out of view. A woman with a glittering headband and feather boa crashes into me, giggling, before she runs off to join her friend. To the left, several swells are laughing it up and slapping their knees. I want to go back to the beach. To the soft, cool sand. The breezy quiet of the surf.

At the top of the patio, I scan once more for the girl. For Cassandra. She should stand out pretty well—her unique dress, her hair, all long and golden brown.

"Looking for someone?"

Fay Cartwright's voice curls up like a purring cat on my shoulder. I turn and she's standing beside me with that half smile that suggests a dozen secrets. The dark lining around her lashes brings out the hazel of her eyes in a sultry, sleepy way. She always looks like she knows something I don't want her to know. For a moment, a flicker of fear lights in me that she somehow spotted me on the beach talking with Cassandra.

She moves a little closer and her arm grazes mine. I can smell the perfume she's dabbed on her slender neck. Her raven hair falls in a sharp angle against her cheek. The Cartwright family is hardly a fixture in North Shore society—I've never even seen her folks at any of these parties—but Fay's beauty is enough for most to overlook her new money.

"Big crowd tonight," she murmurs.

"Ned shouldn't have."

"Sure he should. It's not every day a boy turns eighteen."

"Maybe so. But I would have been happier with a simple dinner, a few friends. Maybe going to a talkie in Crest Harbor."

Fay smirks a little. "Not a fan of the crowds?"

"Not exactly."

"They rather excite me," she says, a glint in her eye. "But tell you what, why don't you and I go somewhere a little more secluded? I can help you relax."

Her finger traces my jacket sleeve and brushes ever so slightly against my hand. She turns and walks slowly toward the house, her gold dress shimmering with the gentle sway of her hips. It's like a siren's song, and I find myself drawn after her.

Just before I enter the house, Uncle Ned calls my name. He's sitting on the patio with his neighborhood cronies. The gleam of burning cigar ends light their genial smiles. Ned is by far the largest man in the group. He's tall and broad, with a belly to beat them all. His crop of black hair is the only physical trait he and my father share.

"Lon, my boy, come over here."

I cast a look at Fay, who's paused at the base of the marble staircase. She shrugs a little and grabs a drink from a passing waiter's tray. Lifting it, she winks and takes a sip. She'll wait for me. I hope.

Ned pours a round of brandy as I approach.

"Here, son. You take a drink. You're a man now, by George."

He speaks with genuine affection. Ned's wife, Stella, died before she could give him any children and he's always treated me like a son. I think that's why, when Mother died last year, Ned became more involved in our lives than ever before. Because he understands the loss.

"Thanks," I say to him.

Orson Baker gives me a slap on the back. "Little Lonnie's all grown up. Who could believe it? When are you going to college, kiddo?"

"His pop back home has it all set up," Ned answers for me, his smile positively brimming with pride. "He starts Harvard in the fall."

The middle-aged men all nod with approval and lift their brandies to me. I want to tell them to save their breath. I want to tell them that my father may have it all set up, but that doesn't mean I'm going. But I offer as genial a smile as I can manage.

Aunt Eloise joins us. She's Ned and my father's older sister. She lives an hour or so away and acts as Ned's mother hen, always keeping an eye out for the lonely old bachelor. Tonight, she's wearing her gaudiest dress, a knee-length number with sewn-on pearls and crystals. She wants to look like the wildest flapper in the room—anything to hide her graying hair and sagging face. I try my best to compliment her. Aging does vex her so.

"Lonnie," she says loudly, already tipsy. "There you are. Fay was looking everywhere for you."

"I'm all right, Aunt Eloise," I say, giving her a quick peck on the cheek.

"You lovely boy." She laughs, touching my face. She turns to her companions. "Such a treat to have him so close by for the summer. We begged and begged. Didn't we, Ned? And he's having a fine time. You're having a fine time, aren't you, Lonnie?"

"Sure am." I check to make sure Fay's still waiting for me. She is, but she's passing the time chatting with some tall, grinning joe who can't keep his eyes off Fay's bosom. My left hand tightens into a fist.

"I better run," I say. "Fay's waiting for me."

"Of course," Ned says, giving me a pat on the back. "You have fun. But be back by midnight to blow out the candles! There may be a surprise waiting for you."

He winks at his friends. There's a dancing girl in the cake. I've already heard from Charles. With a weary smile, I remind myself to act surprised.

"See you later."

I weave my way past the jubilant partygoers into my uncle's house. When Fay spots me approaching, her lips curl in an irrepressible smile. I come up beside her. The fellow gives me a dumb look.

"You got a problem, pal?" he asks. "I was talking with the lady."

"You were trying. Here's a hint for next time: her eyes are up here."

Fay laughs behind her hand. The rube bristles, but he can read the writing on the wall.

"Ah, keep her," he says. He fiercely smooths his hair back and sulks off. When he's gone, Fay folds her arms.

"Well, I had to get your attention somehow."

"Believe me, you have it."

She smiles and straightens my tie, even though it's perfect as is. "Now," she murmurs. "Where were we?"

"I believe you wanted to help me relax."

"That's right." She turns and glides up the stairs with the grace of a cat. I take a step after her, but something makes me pause. The thought of the strange girl on the beach. Silly, perhaps. I don't even know her. But even that brief encounter reminded me of everything I've let myself fall into this summer. The parties, the gang of friends, even Fay. They seem to be everything I want. And yet...why do I feel like I'm floundering and doing nothing to stop it?

Fay pauses on the stairs, looking back at me. She tilts her head just so, beckoning. Maybe it's because I'm a weak man, but I accept what Ned and Fay and my father place before me. Self-loathing settles in my gut like a coiled snake. Thrusting my hands into my pockets, I follow Fay into the whispering shadows beyond the party.

CHAPTER 4

Cassandra

By the time I've dragged myself into the kitchen for breakfast, the omelet Frank made me is cold. Mom's wiping the counters and calling for Eddie to pick up his race-car track. When she notices me, her eyes shadow with an inscrutable look.

"I'm surprised you slept in so late. You went to bed pretty early."

I shrug and slump up to the bar. I stab a fork into the rock-solid omelet.

"Have one of these instead," Mom says, sliding a raspberry pastry across the granite bar. I accept the olive branch with a smile. A half smile, really. It's the best I can manage with the mood I'm in this morning.

Frank glides in, the Wall Street Journal tucked under his arm.

"Mornin', Sassy Cassie. Have a good rest?"

I shrug, hoping my mouth full of pastry will excuse me from having to make small talk.

Frank pours himself a glass of orange juice. "So, did you have a nice time at the party last night?"

"Mmm," I mumble noncommittally through my food. My

mind is pulled once again to my strange, ultimately frustrating conversation with Lawrence.

"Keep getting to know the folks around here," Frank says, giving an optimistic wink. "Lots of really great people."

"Mm-hmm." I say again. I mentally calculate my fastest tactful exit from this conversation.

"Some really important people too," he goes on, thinking I'll be impressed. But his words do spark a question.

"That reminds me," I say. "Someone at the party was talking to me about Ned Foster. I'm guessing you know who he is."

"Ned Foster," Frank says, pondering the name. "Huh. Can't say that I do. But there is a Foster family over near Weston. Old stock. They've had relatives here since the eighteen hundreds, if I'm not mistaken."

Just as I thought. Crest Harbor royalty.

Mom points at Frank suddenly, her memory jolted. "Didn't a Foster build this house back in the nineteen twenties? I think I remember the real estate agent telling me something about that."

"Could be," Frank says, sipping his orange juice. "You know I don't pay attention to that kind of stuff, Cuddle Bug."

I'd normally roll my eyes at Frank's nicknames, but my mind is too busy turning over what Mom said.

"So do the Fosters still own this land or something?" I ask. "Are we renting from them?"

"Oh no," Mom says. "No, the Fosters sold the property not long after they'd bought it. Rather suddenly, I guess. Can't remember why."

I stab my fork into the raspberry center of what's left of my pastry. What was Lawrence talking about then? Is he some kind of expert on the old homes of Crest Harbor or something? I sure hope not. That would make him both stuck-up and pretentious.

And intriguing.

And stupidly attractive.

His smile lingers in my mind like a dull ache. I puff out a breath. *No, he's a jerk. Don't forget how he acted last night.* Like he owned the whole town.

So why do I still want to find out more about him?

Because I'm stupid. I accept this fact.

"Can I hang out with Travis today?" I ask, looking up at Mom hopefully. He'd know more about Lawrence, I'm betting.

"Not on your life. Your butt is grounded, Cass."

"He can come here."

"Nope. You have chores, then summer reading, and then, if I'm feeling generous, I'll let you have your laptop after lunch."

I sigh loudly. "Fantastic."

Mom's face is an iron wall of indifference to my plight. "You made your bed; now you have to lie in it."

I flop off the bar stool and march toward the stairs. "Actually, I didn't make my bed yet this morning. But I think I will go lie in it."

"I'm so proud," Mom calls as I stomp up the stairs.

Being grounded isn't the worst punishment Mom could have given me, if only because it's almost no different from the rest of this summer vacation. But somehow I'm in my worst mood yet. As two uneventful days lurch by, the restlessness morphs into bitterness, soured like old milk.

By the third day, I'm in such a lousy mood that the sound of Frank slurping his watermelon after dinner sends me to the edge of hysteria. I need to get out of here fast. I grab two dripping slices of watermelon and announce that I'm going to get some fresh air. Mom and Frank can barely mask their relief. I'm sure I've been an absolute treat to be around.

Munching the watermelon, I tromp out onto the lawn. As I walk, I realize I'm headed to the beach. Of course. I hesitate for a moment. How pathetic is it to go back there? Very. But then again, at this point, I think I'm about as pathetic as they come.

Setting my jaw and chucking the watermelon rinds into the bushes, I press ahead. I need to see the beach again. I need to get its association with Lawrence out of my system. As I approach the pathway, the sound of surf drifts toward me, making my heart skip a little. Which is ridiculous. Glaring, I push through the bushes and burst out onto the sand.

And there he is.

Lawrence. Emerging from the water. Shirtless. Wearing funny, little swim trunks. He smooths the water from his tousled hair and his eyes lock on mine.

I would chalk this up to a really pathetic daydream on my part if not for the equally stunned expression that crosses his face. For a split second, we stare at each other. "Cassandra?" he calls over the pound of surf.

He takes me in, as if checking if I'm real. I'm at once aware of the watermelon juice on my chin, of my too-short, shredding jean shorts, of my hair in a scraggly bun. I scrape my arm over my mouth.

"What on earth are you doing here?" I demand, marching down to the grass so he can hear me.

"I'm…swimming?"

My eyes unavoidably go to his bare arms and chest. His body is firm, but not in the gross, too-much-weightlifting kind of way. He's not buff but clearly strong. As I stare, a trickle of water slides down his bare chest, like liquid gold in the early evening sun.

I snap my gaze back up to his face. *Focus, Cass.*

"Um, yeah," I say. "I can see that you're swimming. I mean, what are you doing here? On private property."

"I could ask you the same thing," he says, laughing a little.

These rich people really are too much. There's probably a path to this beach somewhere over by the point, which makes it as good as public property, right?

"It's quite an unexpected surprise to see you," Lawrence says, his smile derailing my train of thought.

I brush a windblown strand of hair from my face and fold my arms. "Listen—"

"I'm glad you came back," he says, stepping forward to grab his towel. "We ended on such a bad note the other night. I thought for sure I'd never see you again."

His words throw me off. Suddenly, the crisp response I had vanishes on my tongue. He gives his hair a quick rub with his towel, giving it that perfectly sexy tousled look. Then he smiles, putting the final seal on my tongue-tied state.

"Did you come for a swim?" he asks. "The water's excellent."

"Uh, no. I was...brooding again, I guess."

"Seems to be a favorite pastime of yours. What burdens you so, Cassandra?"

I roll my eyes. "I told you already."

"That's right," he says, pointing. "The subtle anguish of life."

I nod, though I'm surprised he remembered. "Something like that."

"I hoped you were simply trying to get a laugh out of me." Lawrence looks into my eyes, his gaze piercing. "I'd be sad to know you truly are unhappy."

My stomach flutters. I look away from him. "Don't worry. I'll live."

"You know, brooding can only get you so far. You really ought to try a swim. The ocean's good for the soul."

"I'm okay just looking at it."

Lawrence turns a glance to the waves beyond, sparkling in the golden evening sun. "True. It's undeniably lovely. The second most beautiful thing to look at on this beach."

"Oh gosh. You really are a player."

"I'm a man bound by truth." He drapes the towel around his neck. Then he lifts his chin, as if trying to remember something.

"Of truth and sea, her eyes become

Bound, endless in the vast beyond.
And morning starlight's milky shine
Reverberates her soul in mine."

I bite back what certainly must be a dopey grin. I'm a sucker for a boy who recites poetry. "Is that…Byron?" I ask, uncertain.

Lawrence laughs. "No, though I'm quite flattered. That's my poetry."

I raise an eyebrow. "Your poetry? As in, you wrote it?"

"Tried to." When I offer nothing more than skeptical silence, Lawrence says, "Is it really so hard to believe?"

This information still needs processing. After a restless three days trying very hard not to think about Lawrence, seeing him again, shirtless and reciting poetry, is seriously throwing me for a loop. I start to walk along the shoreline. He keeps pace beside me.

"Well," I say carefully. "You don't meet many guys that write poetry. And those that do are…" I start to say "not as hot as you," but thankfully stop myself.

"Are what?" Lawrence asks. "Drunks?"

"Not exactly the word I was looking for."

"I'm not. Just so you know."

I smirk. "I'll believe that when I see it."

We walk in comfortable silence. Lawrence bends his head a little to meet my gaze. "So, what did you think? Of my poetry, I mean. Did you like it?"

"Not bad." This downplayed response takes some effort.

"I'll accept that." Judging by his smile and the way he keeps his eyes on me, I can't help but feel that he's well aware of the effect he has.

"Don't you have a shirt or something?" I ask, trying my best not to look at him.

"Am I making you uncomfortable?"

"No," I say with an incredulous laugh that comes across as trying way too hard to sound incredulous. Lawrence holds a smile, and I feel my face flush. *Get on your game, Cass.* This is ridiculous.

Lawrence walks up the beach and grabs a white linen shirt that had been hanging on the bushes. He pulls it over his head and jogs back to me. I'm ready for him.

"So," I say, as he comes to my side, "I assume you write poetry to help convince ditzy blonds that you're deep and interesting, and then they'll want to sleep with you."

Lawrence presses a hand over his heart. "She strikes to kill!"

"I'm calling it as I see it."

"Well, in this case, you happen to be wrong."

"I don't think I am. I've got you pegged."

"Not quite." The corners of Lawrence's smile fade. That distant, pensive look returns. "Actually, I've never shared my poetry with anyone else. Other than my father. And he made it quite clear how useless he thought it was."

This slows my pace. If Lawrence is playing me, he actually deserves serious props, because, holy crap, he's convincing.

"It's not useless," I say softly. "What I heard wasn't, anyway. I mean…maybe the other stanzas suck."

Lawrence doesn't reply. I bite my lip. I don't want the conversation to end. Not yet. I need to investigate more. Time to lower the wall of sarcasm a bit.

"For what it's worth," I say, "I think it's pretty awesome that you write."

"Thanks," he says, but he still seems distant.

A particularly large wave rushes up, the white foam lapping our feet. I turn to dodge it and notice that the sun has slipped behind the house and out of sight. The clouds burn red and purple. It's a hot, humid night, and the wind carries the scent of sea and fresh-cut grass. As I breathe it in, a warm, buzzing sense of well-being spreads over me. For the first time in a long time, I feel the strongest urge to get out my canvas and brushes. That sky represents everything that's perfect about summer.

"Beautiful sunset," Lawrence says, following my gaze.

"It's flawless."

Our eyes meet, and there's something in his expression that I can't put my finger on. I get reckless when I'm happy, so I decide to fish it out of him.

"So"—I start to walk again—"you say you've never let anyone read your poetry."

"That's right."

"Then why did you recite some to me?"

"A good question," Lawrence says, nodding. "Why did I?"

"Do you not know, or are you trying to be cute?"

"I really don't know," he admits. "There's something about you..."

It's the kind of line every artsy girl wants to hear. And as clichéd as it might be, I melt a little inside. This guy is good.

We walk down closer to the shore. The cool water skims against our toes. Lawrence bends to pick up a rock and gives it a firm toss into the ocean.

"What is it?" he asks. "What is it that makes you so different?"

"I've always been weird. It's kind of my thing."

"That's not what I meant. It's not every day you meet a girl who knows poetry."

I shrug. "I guess not, though I don't know a ton. I'm more of an artist. Painter."

Lawrence stops, staring at me. "That so?"

"Yes, but I'm not the drunk kind either. Only during my blue period."

He nods, impressed. "I think that's swell," he says earnestly.

I laugh at his choice of words. "Yeah. It's really swell."

"What do you paint?" He seems genuinely interested.

"Well, I'd paint that sunset, for one thing."

"Ah, yes. You do landscapes then?"

"Sometimes. I paint a little of everything. Whatever reaches out and grabs me by the collar."

Lawrence hasn't taken his eyes off me. His smile of unmasked admiration makes my heart blossom in my chest.

"I knew there was something different about you."

"Oddly enough, I feel the same about you." I'm getting dizzy trying to figure this guy out. It's exciting and puts me on alert at the same time. "Can I ask you a random question? Were you raised in a foreign country? Or maybe a hippie commune? A friendly cult?"

Lawrence looks amused. "No. Why?"

I shake my head. "No reason."

"We really are a pair of odd ducks, aren't we, Cassandra?"

"The fact that you use the phrase 'odd ducks' illustrates that perfectly."

He looks at me again in that way of his—bold, unassuming, and curious, as if he's taking me in and not afraid to show it.

"I want to know more about you," he says. "If you'll give me the chance."

Heat rushes to my cheeks. "I might be open to that."

"Why don't you come in the house? Our cook can get you some ice cream while I change. And then we can talk more."

"You live close to here?" I ask.

Lawrence points toward my house. "I'd say it's pretty close."

I perk up. I thought all of the neighboring houses were empty, their owners off in Europe or the Maldives or whatever obscure, luxury vacation spots the wealthy flock to. But he's close? We can actually see more of each other? I'm grounded, but I can get around that.

I cast a glance down at my ragged, watermelon-juice-dripped shorts. Maybe it's vain, but if we're really going to hang out I want to look cute.

"Give me five minutes to change?"

"Sure, unless you were hoping to go for a swim."

Does he think this is my bathing suit or something? "No," I say. "That's your thing, remember?"

I start toward the house. I don't want to give him a reason to change his mind. "Meet me out front by the street, and then we'll walk to your place?"

A flicker of confusion crosses Lawrence's face, but he shrugs. "I guess, if you want, but—"

"I know it's lame, but I'm a girl. Humor me."

I turn back to the house before he can respond. Leave them wanting more, Jade always says. I roll my eyes at my own thoughts. It's ridiculous how excited I feel right now. I prance, literally prance, back into the house.

Mom and Frank are chatting in the living room. In a single bound, I fly over the back of the white leather couch, drop at Mom's side, and latch my arms around her in a bear hug.

"What on earth?" Mom asks. "Who are you, and what have you done with my mopey teenage daughter?"

"I'm still her," I say, batting my eyelashes sweetly. "Only now I want a suspension of my grounding."

Mom smirks. "I should have guessed."

I jump to my knees beside her to properly beg. "Okay, so I met this guy the night of your party—"

"Oh dear," Mom says, taking off her reading glasses.

"He's really nice. He's very polite. We're going to hang out for a little while." I grab her hand and press it to my cheek. "Pleeeeeeease?"

Mom turns a skeptical look to Frank, but he's already sold. "It's nice to have our happy Cass back."

"True," Mom says. "You have been a pill lately."

I nod. "I know. But I swear I'll stop. I'll be better. I'll be an absolute delight."

Mom and Frank laugh—a promising sign—and then Mom sighs. "Fine. But you'd better be back by curfew, kiddo."

"Absolutely," I vow.

Mom rolls her eyes, but she's smiling. I throw another hug around her. "You're the best!"

As I gallop up the stairs to my room, I catch them exchanging amused and exasperated whispers. Doubtless, a conversation about the tempestuous nature of teenagers will ensue. And rightfully so. But I don't mind. Right now, all I care about is finding a cute outfit, brushing my hair, and getting my butt out to the street.

Digging through the tangled mess of my closet, I manage to find a cool blue T-shirt and a less shabby pair of shorts. A high ponytail masks my unwashed hair, and a cute pair of earrings finishes the look. I purposefully don't spend too much time getting ready. I don't want to seem like I'm trying too hard. Even though I kind of am…

As I run back downstairs, I can't suppress my smile. It's silly to be so excited, but my excuse is that I'm not excited about seeing Lawrence, per se; it's more that I'm just happy something interesting is happening in general.

I force my pace to a slow, casual stroll as I walk the long driveway. I pass the gate and look down both directions of the street. In the twilight, only the lampposts show any indication of civilization. Cicadas buzz loudly in the surrounding hedges. The glint of fireflies flickers in the woods beyond. And then, somewhere in the distance, like in a horror movie, a dog barks.

But there's no sign of Lawrence.

My lips purse in a little frown. I took longer than five minutes to get ready, but not that much longer. I peer down the street again. Nothing. My mind starts to tick through possible scenarios. Did he wait and think I wasn't coming? Did he get detained at home? Maybe his parents are holding him up. Maybe he's getting ready himself? I'll give him five minutes.

Ten minutes pass.

Then fifteen.

Twenty…

A knot sits heavy in the pit of my stomach. I've been stood up. Was this all some kind of sick joke? The thought makes me queasy. He doesn't seem like the type. Or does he? Didn't I see the warning signs right from the start? But I ignored them because I was attracted to his brooding, poetry-reciting self. Which is probably exactly what he'd planned.

Feeling sick, I stare up the street yet again, hoping against hope that I will see his dark outline appear. My pathetic hope fills me with a surge of shame. He's not coming. I must look so stupid waiting here on an empty street. My face goes hot, and I dash back to the house. I can't get inside fast enough.

As I head upstairs, I hear Mom's voice.

"Cass? You're back?"

My promises of sweet, cheerful behavior taste like salt on my tongue. I want to yell at her. I want to act out. I want her to know I'm in pain. But I swallow the words down.

"We've decided to meet another time," I call, trying my best to sound normal.

"Oh." Mom's voice is unbearably gentle. "You okay?"

"I'm fine. Just tired. I'm going to go to bed."

"Okay… Good night."

I don't respond. I drag myself up the stairs to my room and push the door closed.

CHAPTER 5

Cassandra

I feel inexplicably calm when I wake in the morning. Maybe "numb" is a better word for it. Either way, I'm absolutely determined not to waste another ounce of emotion or thought on Lawrence Foster. I glide down to breakfast with my head high. I am calm. I am relaxed. I am unmoved.

As I approach the table, the glance Mom and Frank exchange does not pass my notice. Is that a glint of pity I see on Mom's face? I sigh and flop down at my seat. Even Eddie seems to be tentative as he munches his sugary cereal. There's only the sound of hesitant chewing. I roll my eyes.

"Mom," I say calmly. "I have a request."

"Sure, dear," she says overly cheerfully. "What's up?"

"Let's do something. Something that will take up the whole day. Something fun."

Frank sets a hand on my shoulder. "Anything you want to talk about, Sassy—"

"Nope. Not even remotely."

"Right," Mom says. "I know what we can do. Shopping. Shopping fixes everything."

"There's nothing to fix," I say in a swift, defensive way that negates what I actually said.

Mom plays along anyway. "Let's go shopping. And take the convertible."

I lift my glass of orange juice. "Cheers to that."

My diversion plan works perfectly. It's not as if it's hard. Lawrence was an intriguing (and okay, fine, very good-looking) guy that I knew for about three seconds. Nothing more. The sting of humiliation passes fairly easily.

Or so it seems. The crack in the facade comes two days later. Eddie and I are playing catch in the backyard while Mom and Frank clean up after a barbecue. Project Cheer Up Moody Teenager has included all manner of diversions. And I'm not complaining. In fact, I kind of love my family for it.

I help Mom and Frank finish cleaning. They bring in the last of the plates, and I'm going out to make sure we haven't left any watermelon rinds for the yellow jackets to swarm over when Eddie runs up to me, dismayed.

"Cassie! I can't find my football!"

With an eyebrow raised, I point to the red toddler-sized football in his hands, and he sighs with exasperation.

"My green one, Cassie. I lost it!"

I ruffle his curly, little mop top. “Easy, kiddo. I’ll help you find it.”

Mom’s voice drifts out from inside the kitchen. “Who wants ice cream?”

Eddie’s eyes brighten like twin comets. I can’t help but laugh. The kid has got to be the most easy-to-excite human being on earth.

“Go get some ice cream,” I say. “I’ll find your green football.”

He trundles off, nearly falling over in his eagerness. Shaking my head with a smile, I survey the lawn. It takes a minute of looking before I spot it. A small, neon-green football sitting near the back hedge. Right by the path to the beach.

I exhale. Walking calmly to the path, I keep my thoughts firmly in check. This is not giving in. I’m just grabbing Eddie’s toy. I have no intention of…

As I bend to retrieve the toy, the smell of salt and sand brushes past me on the wind. The soft pound of surf whispers in the distance. My throat feels dry all of a sudden. Standing, I tilt my head to peer down the narrow, overgrown corridor. I can see blue. The ocean. The sand. And I’m pulled toward the beach.

It’s beyond insane, but he’s sitting on the sand. Just sitting there on the beach, reading a book.

In a single moment, a series of emotions fly through my mind in rapid succession. First, a tangible thrill at the sight of him. Then confusion at how he could possibly be here again. Then shame, the desire to turn and run before he sees me and can laugh in my face. Then rage. Pure, trembling rage.

I stomp out, and he whips around. His eyes go wide. He springs to his feet.

"I don't believe it," he says, his face ashen.

Rage still has a hold on me.

"Seriously. Seriously? You're really showing up here again? You're either a bigger jerk than I could have imagined, or you're secretly a bum and don't have anywhere else to sleep at night."

He shakes his head. "How did you…"

"Why are you here?" I demand. "To gloat? To mock me? Are you secretly recording this all on your cell phone so that you can make fun of me to all of your snobby friends?"

"Cassandra—"

"I want you to leave, Lawrence. I have nothing to say to you."

He takes a step toward me. "Why are you acting like this?"

I laugh, incredulous. "Why? Hmm, gee, that's a good question. I don't know… Maybe because you stood me up."

"What?"

"I waited for twenty minutes, which is, I'm sure, exactly what you wanted. You probably would have preferred a half hour or forty-five minutes for optimum humiliation, but hopefully the twenty minutes will satisfy you."

Lawrence stares at me, blinking, as if I'm speaking incomprehensible words. He takes a breath.

"Cassandra," he begins slowly. "I waited for you for a solid hour on that street."

The sincerity, the anger in his tone throws me for a moment.

"Don't lie," I say. "There wasn't a living soul out there. It was just me and the fireflies."

Lawrence throws up his hands. "I'm telling you, I waited for an hour. I would have rung you on the telephone, but I don't know where you live. I don't even know your last name. I have no idea how to contact you."

I put my hands to my temples. "What are you talking about? Of course you know where I live!" I jab my hand toward my house. "Hello?"

Lawrence scoffs. "Is this some kind of joke? That house?"

"Umm, yes. That house right through those bushes. You came to our party. You've been swimming on my beach. I'm going to have a hard time believing that where I live somehow slipped your mind."

He pinches the bridge of his nose. "My Uncle Ned's house is through those bushes, Cassandra."

"Not this again!" My voice raises, bordering on shrill, but I don't care. "What are you talking about? I've never even heard of this Ned guy. Look, I don't care who lays claim to this town or who owned the land a thousand years ago or whatever. This is where I live. This is the house my stepdad is renting, fair and square."

"I'm trying very hard to figure out why you're acting this way."

"It's not complicated. That's my house."

"Why do you keep saying that?" he asks with a frustrated growl. "That house. This beach. It's all Ned's. How could you be mistaken about that when the only way to get here is through his front door?"

"You're crazy."

And then it dawns on me. What if he really is genuinely crazy? Gorgeous but crazy. Maybe Ned is a manifestation of acute schizophrenia.

"I have no idea who this Ned guy is, but he certainly doesn't live here."

"I'm sorry. You're mistaken."

"I don't think so."

"This house belongs to Ned Foster," he says, his anger now matching my own. "He built it three years ago."

I stare at him. "Seriously, you're insane."

"I'm starting to think *you* are, lady."

"Brush up on your history before you try and lie. The house was built in the twenties."

"Exactly," he says. "Nineteen twenty-two."

"So…you're bad at math then?"

"What?"

"Uh, nineteen twenty-two was a little more than three years ago, wouldn't you say? More like ninety-three."

He gives me a blank look. "Ninety-three…"

"Years ago. Nineteen twenty-two was at least ninety years ago." I repeat.

"This is nineteen twenty-five, Cassandra," he says, speaking slowly as if I'm the crazy one. "How could 'twenty-two be ninety years ago?"

I nod with exaggerated interest. "Oh, it's nineteen twenty-five, huh? That's fascinating."

He says nothing. Only stares. And I've officially had enough.

"That's it. I'm not going to stand here and play games. I'm leaving."

"Cassandra," Lawrence calls as I stride back toward the house. "Wait."

He runs up behind me, but I refuse to turn around. He falls in step with me as I stomp up the beach.

"It's like you're a character in some play," he says, scraping a hand through his hair. "You show up at my birthday party and now at my house without an invitation. You wear the strangest, most daring clothes. And now you're telling me nineteen twenty-two was ninety-three years ago..."

I push through the bushes. "I don't know what role-playing game you're trying to get started here, but—"

As I turn to shoot him my most imperious parting glare, the words halt in my throat.

His face, his whole body is...fuzzy. I blink, but he's still covered in blur. It's like someone has thrown a thin muslin screen around just him. As if I'm seeing him through a lens with a smudge over the exact place he's standing. I smash my fists against my eyes and look again. But he's looking at me funny too.

"Cassandra?"

I back away, still blinking to get the crazy blur out of my eyes. Is this an early symptom of a heart attack or something? Am I going blind thanks to some sudden, undiagnosed vision problem?

He walks toward me, speaking, but I only hear a muffled garble of words. And if possible, he's getting even more transparent. He's blending in with the bushes, the ocean, the sunset behind him. Speechless, I retreat, stumbling onto the back lawn.

Lawrence sets a foot on the grass. I see his almost translucent lips form my name, and then he's gone. Dissolved into the background.

CHAPTER 6

Cassandra

I stare at the spot where Lawrence disappeared. It didn't happen. It couldn't have happened. I must really be going blind. Or I'm having a stroke.

Maybe I'm dying. Or dead.

I move closer to the lawn where Lawrence had been standing.

One step.

Another.

And then a faint haze of color takes shape in front of the bushes. My heart is beating against my rib cage as if it's trying to escape. I move closer and the colors darken a shade. The shape takes a recognizable form. Human. A dull mumble reaches my ear.

"Lawrence?" My voice shakes.

I run toward the bushes and push past the scratchy branches lashing my skin. The shape ahead of me grows darker and more vivid with each passing second. The mumble becomes strained, like bad reception on a cell phone.

"Cassandra?"

"Lawrence!"

I push past the final, overgrown hedge. My foot touches sand. And I run smack into Lawrence's chest.

My eyes meet his. He grips my arms, his face pale as a sheet. "Cassandra!"

I can't get a good breath. I pull out of his grip, staring at him, terrified. "What was that? What. In the world. Just happened?"

He says nothing, his eyes wide.

"What happened?" I demand. "You disappeared. You vanished. You…"

"Dissolved into the background?" he asks, his voice trembling.

"Yes…"

"I didn't disappear," he says. "You did. I was shouting your name. Didn't you hear me?"

"I did until you melted into nothingness."

He shakes his head, dazed. "I was here the whole time."

"So was I!"

"Then what happened?"

"I don't know!" I shout. "I have no idea. I'm freaking out here as much as you."

We're both quiet for a moment, breathing hard and waiting for the other person to figure this all out. Lawrence looks toward the hedges, and I follow his gaze.

"Maybe it was an entirely random event," he says. "A heat wave. A pulse of energy."

He starts toward the bushes. I grab his hand. "What are you doing?"

"I want to see…"

"Don't get too close!" I insist, pulling him back.

He taps his fist to his mouth, his brow furrowed with concentration. "What if...what if we try it again? See if the same thing happens?"

"Are you crazy?"

"It's worth a try."

"No," I say firmly. "What if you disappear, only this time you don't come back?"

Lawrence considers this. Then, without answering, he steps toward them again.

"Don't!" I shout.

"I have to see."

His hands brush along the coarse leaves. He bends to examine the trunks and roots, grinding a pinch of sand between his fingertips.

"It looks normal to me," he says. "I think we need to try again." He stands and holds out his hand. "Come on."

"You're insane," I say, folding my arms. "I'm not going anywhere near that path."

"So you're planning to spend the night on the beach? We have to go through there sooner or later. We might as well try it together."

I shake my head, but somehow my feet move toward him. This is stupid. This is Russian roulette. Something seriously weird is going on, and we're asking for a second helping.

"One test," I say. "And we come right back to the beach if anything weird starts to happen."

He nods, taking my hand. His palm is sweaty. His eyes glint

with nervousness and excitement. I don't know why he's so eager to dematerialize again.

"On three," he says. "This is crazy. You are crazy."

"Whatever you do, don't let go of my hand."

For as long as your hand exists. "We're crazy."

"One...two...three."

The pathway ahead of me blurs as we step through the narrow corridor. Within three steps, Lawrence starts to go fuzzy. I gasp. "It's happening."

"Do you feel anything?"

"Why would I? You're the one disappearing."

"Keep going," he says, though his voice is becoming more muffled.

"We should stop."

Even though he's fading before my eyes, I can still feel his grip on my hand. He pulls me toward the lawn.

"Lawrence, I'm freaking out. I want to go back."

"Keep going!" His voice is garbled and faint. Vanishing.

I stumble into the yard, pulled by the fading shape in front of me. His grip lightens, like sand sifting through my fingers. My pulse is pounding in my head. My ears are ringing.

"Stop!" I shout. I make out the slightest suggestion of his silhouette before he's gone.

"Lawrence! Go back to the beach! Hurry!" Frantic, I smash through green branches until, gasping for breath, I collapse onto the sand.

What is happening? I'm losing it. I am legitimately losing it.

Or maybe I'm not. Maybe this is the end of the world. Not a big bang but a whimper. Everyone just vanishes. It would make a fantastic sci-fi novel.

Two hands clamp down on my shoulders. "Cassandra."

Screaming, I whirl around. Lawrence is on his knees before me, panting and pale but flesh and bone.

"Did you see Ned?" he asks.

"What?"

"Ned."

I blink. "What are you talking about?"

"Ned was on the back lawn. You didn't see him?"

I stare at him, my brain unable to handle all of this. I feel sick, light-headed. I bend forward to keep from throwing up. Lawrence's shoulders rise and fall with his breath. His eyes scan my face, as if searching for answers embedded somewhere in my eyes.

"Are you a ghost?" he whispers.

"What? No! What are you—? Of course I'm not!"

He cocks his head, unsure. My jaw sets. "If I were a ghost, would you feel this?" I punch him in the arm.

"Say!" He rubs the spot, grimacing. Then his eyes narrow. "It could be a trick. I'm not familiar with the supernatural."

"I'm not a ghost, Lawrence."

"Well, neither am I. So what's the explanation?" He taps his fist to his mouth, deep in thought. "What if it's the pathway that's haunted?"

"But we've both walked it a hundred times and nothing

strange has ever happened," I say. "Whatever is going on, it has something to do with you."

"Or you."

"Or us together…"

Our eyes meet. Lawrence pushes his fingers into the sand, absently carving a line as he thinks. Then he looks up hesitantly.

"I say we try it again. Maybe if we run, we can make it to the house together."

I shake my head, but he grabs my hands.

"Once more. Please."

We try it three more times. Running at full speed the first time, crawling on hands and knees the second, and pausing in the middle the last time to examine the bushes and surroundings. But each pass brings the same result. The person in front vanishes, as if some otherworldly force is determined to blot them out.

As the sun dips low, the sky orange and purple with the coming twilight, Lawrence and I sit on the beach in silence, staring out at the waves like the first time we met. But I have no words this time. No witty punch lines. What can you say when faced with the inexplicable?

Lawrence pinches the bridge of his nose, exhaling. And then suddenly he snaps his head up. "What?" I ask.

"What year is it?"

"Excuse me?"

"What year do you think you're from? You said nineteen twenty-two was more than ninety years ago."

"Because it was."

He swallows hard, says nothing.

"Do you dispute this fact?"

For a long pause, he only stares at me. Then he releases a shaky breath and rubs his face.

"Is it possible?" He mutters to himself. "From the first time I met her, all the confusion, all the strange insisting."

"What are you talking about?"

He bites his lip, as if preparing his words carefully. "Cassandra…this is my uncle's private beach. At his home. He built it three years ago. It's never belonged to anyone else. The year is nineteen twenty-five."

Now it's my turn to stare.

Is he trying to be funny? Or is he truly crazy? Schizophrenic? Or…

The image of Lawrence vanishing into the air like a cloud of steam returns to me. An undeniable event. Tested five times.

A terrible thought pierces my mind. What if he's the ghost? Haunting this beach for the last ninety-plus years? That would explain why he thinks it's 1925, why he acted so strangely the first time I saw him.

But…he's a solid entity. I can feel him. He breathes. He gets wet. He's changed clothes. I'm not well acquainted with ghost rules and decorum, but I'm pretty sure they don't change outfits. I take his hand in mine. Warm flesh. The firmness of bones beneath it.

"Cassandra…what are you doing?"

I don't respond, but instead press two fingers to the smooth inside of his wrist. My head and body are in too much turmoil.

I can't get a read on his pulse. He stares at me but doesn't move, as if he's watching me in a strange dream.

I set my fingertips on the base of his neck, where the jawline and the throat connect. And there it is. The soft, warm movement of blood passing through the carotid artery.

"You're definitely alive," I say softly.

His eyes, still latched onto mine, flicker with a strange intensity, and I retract my hand, suddenly self-conscious.

"Which is a good thing," I add. "Because you would make a lousy ghost. Not scary in the slightest."

We share a smile, and then all too quickly, return to reality. I sit back and try to gather my thoughts.

"So…you really think it's nineteen twenty-five."

"It *is* nineteen twenty-five," he says. "But I gather you don't agree."

"I don't. Because it's two thousand fifteen."

Lawrence raises an eyebrow. "You believe you are living a hundred years in the future. When your parents own Ned's house. When Ned is long gone. When…I'm long gone."

His words send a chill through me.

Lawrence squints at the gap in the bushes. "Is it possible?" he whispers.

I'm asking myself the same question. Is it possible that he actually is from 1925? That he's traveled here somehow? Or did I travel back to 1925?

Lawrence's voice trembles slightly. "I gather that you are living your life as usual in this house, in your time."

"And you're doing the same thing. In nineteen twenty-five…"

"Yes," he says. "Exactly. And yet, somehow, we intercept on this beach, and this beach alone." His eyes get wide. "This would explain why you thought I didn't meet you the other night, why I waited and waited but you never came. I did wait on the street, but it was in nineteen twenty-five."

I massage my temples. Too many thoughts in my brain. It feels like a balloon that has been overinflated, sure to pop any second.

"I don't know what to think right now," I say. "I feel…kind of sick actually." Nausea has crept into my stomach. I'm dizzy. Weak. I just want to lie down.

I stand, and Lawrence jumps to his feet. "Where are you going?"

"In. I…I need some time to process this."

"Will you come back? Will you meet me here again?"

"Why? I don't know if that's a good idea."

"Why wouldn't it be?"

I back away from him. "Because it's insane. Because you can't possibly be from nineteen twenty-five. It can't be real."

"But it is," he insists. "And we have to try and understand it."

"My brain can't handle any more right now."

His eyes plead with me. "Tomorrow. Please. Meet me here on the beach."

I bite my bottom lip. Inside, past the tangle of confusion and fear, a thrill spreads through me.

"Sometime after lunch," I say, nodding. "Mom and Frank are going to an art gallery in the afternoon, so I'll have some alone time."

"I'll wait for you," Lawrence says. "I'll be here."

CHAPTER 7

Lawrence

Two a.m. finds me at my desk. I haven't even tried to lie down. I know I won't sleep. Not tonight. Not after what I've seen. My hand grips the pen, trembles against the page, and words flow. They pour from me like a rushing tide, breaking against the paper in waves of unquenchable fervor. I don't think, don't try to construct a perfectly formed phrase reflective of my thoughts. I just write. And this feeling, to finally have the freedom of words I've craved all summer, is nearly as exciting as my discovery on the beach.

When I've filled the last of the paper in my desk drawer, sweat beads on my upper lip and temples. My pulse pounds all the way to my fingertips. I set the pen down and sit back. I leaf through a few of the pages, and the impulsive wish to share my writing with someone burns through me. Cassandra's face appears in my mind. I push through the sheer linen curtains hanging in the doorway to the balcony and go out to grip the stone rail. The salty tang of the ocean glides on the evening breeze, and I can hear the faint crash of surf, but the blackness of night covers the sight of it. Closing my eyes, I picture the ocean, the beach, Cassandra vanishing in a shimmering glint of color. Thinking about it makes me shiver all over.

I feel as though I'm on the precipice of something incredible, something beyond rare. I have to capture everything about this moment. If I can crystallize it with words, then perhaps, when I'm shipped off to Harvard and a life of carefully planned obedience, I'll have at least one moment of amazement to hold on to. I tighten my grip on the pages. There's more. More I need to say. I'll write all night if I have to.

There's fresh paper in Ned's study. I move quietly down the hall and main stairs, hoping not to wake anyone. As I pass the foyer, however, a flash of lights catches my eye.

Headlights.

At this hour?

Frowning, I step up to one of the thin, glass windows alongside the door. There's an automobile outside, but it's not in the driveway. It's parked on the lawn, off to the side, partially hidden by bushes. If there had been a party tonight, I wouldn't think anything of it. But there was no party. And no guests.

So what is that jalopy doing out there in the middle of the night?

A door slams. The engine roars to a start. I strain to get a look at the driver, but he turns a hard left and peels out of the driveway.

I watch until the lights vanish behind a row of trees in the distance. It's not that I don't trust our watchman, Porter, but I can't help feeling uneasy. True, a house like this has a constant flow of people coming and going. Caterers, maintenance workers, and servants. But still…I make a note to talk to Porter about the car in the morning.

Thinking of notes, excitement resurges in my chest. I head for the fresh ream of paper in the study and forget about the strange automobile.

The sultry murmur of a woman's voice pulls me from heavy layers of sleep. A softness of flesh brushes against my cheek. Exhaustion fights back hard, but I pull myself into the dewy sunshine of consciousness.

She speaks my name. "Lawrence."

A glimmer of long, golden hair comes to me. Her face. Her probing blue eyes. Cassandra. In the overbrightness of light streaming in through those linen curtains, I can see her standing over me. She's come back.

I sit up, inhaling sharply.

Fay is perched on my bed beside me. Her slender eyebrow rises. "Morning, Lonnie."

I strain my eyes, and Cassandra's face vanishes as she did last night on the beach. For a sharp, fleeting moment, the terrifying thought that it was all a dream cuts into my lungs. But I catch a glimpse of the frantic writings stacked on my desk and my stomach relaxes. It was real. It happened.

Fay smiles a little and pulls at my loosened shirt. I'm still fully dressed, lying on top of the blankets where I collapsed sometime last night.

"Up late studying, I assume?" she asks. "Getting ready for college?"

My eyes dart to the papers on my desk once more, but this time with a surge of panic. I can't remember much of what I wrote, but the words on the page seem to shine like a beacon, exposing my secret to Fay. I slide off the bed and grab for them as casually as I can, stuffing the pages into the drawer.

"Something like that."

Fay takes my spot, reclining on my bed and curving her hips to expose just a touch of her lace stockings at the thigh.

"You'll make one heck of a lawyer, Lonnie, though I pity the woman who marries you. Lying all alone in bed at night as you study up for your next case."

"I suppose it will take a patient gal," I say distractedly, still feeling nervous that she read the pages while I was sleeping. She has that knowing smile, but it's her trademark. She makes sport of pretending she knows something you'd rather she didn't.

Fay stretches out her arms in a lazy yawn that makes her dress strap slide down her shoulder. She runs her fingertips along her décolletage.

"I'd never put up with such a man," she says. "I demand to be adored above everything else. I must be worshiped."

I met Fay here at the house at a party celebrating my arrival. She's been appearing at social events all summer. She's like a phantom. She never comes with anyone else, never speaks of a life outside the noise and frivolity of Ned's parties. She exists only to haunt me with her sly laugh. And I still can't quite figure out what she wants. Moments like these, I'm certain she's trying to seduce me. But other times she seems aloof, even resentful of me.

I glance at the door. "I suppose it's rather late. Ned's probably waiting for me."

Fay watches me and then sits up, brushing her sleeve back in place. "He gave that up hours ago. It's almost noon, you know."

"Ah."

Fay's still analyzing me, though she's trying to hide it with a casual, almost bored expression. "As a matter of fact, you slept right through my visit. I have to go now."

"Must you?"

She stands, and I catch a hint of hurt on her face. "I have an appointment in town." She smooths her hair and breezes past. "Do ring when you're ready to give me the time of day."

I grab her hand. "I'm sorry."

She forces a laugh. "What for?"

"Fay."

All at once, she presses her lips to mine. Her kiss is short, but slow and tempting. The tip of her tongue brushes lightly against mine. It's indecent and intoxicating in a way only she can manage. When she breaks off the kiss, a curl of triumph pulls at her smile. She pats my cheek.

"Enjoy your studying."

With that, she glides out of my room, her hips swaying ever so slightly, like they always do.

Feeling flushed, I loosen my collar. I have half a mind to run after her. But then my eyes fall to my desk. I slide open the drawer with a tug. I pull out my notes and scan over the words. Almost like a portal, they draw me right back to the emotions of yesterday. It's afternoon now. Cassandra might be waiting for me. I set the pages down and soar out of my room.

Uncle Ned is in the library, sipping a brandy and reading the paper. As I rush by, he sits up abruptly.

"There you are, Lonnie! Being the slouch today, are you? You know, you missed Fay coming by."

"Don't worry. I saw her." I make a motion to the door. "Have to run, Ned."

Without waiting for his reply, I continue on to the back patio. Each step over the back lawn feels longer than the last. My breath is as fast and short as my heartbeat. Breaking into a full run, I crash through the bushy path.

But the beach is empty.

Waves lap against the shore in slim, white lines. Gulls screech overhead and dip in the salty wind. But no Cassandra. A line of doubt cuts into my heart. She should be here. I don't want to even approach the what-ifs, but they creep up on me all the same.

What if the doorway that allowed us to see each other has closed? What if she's gone forever? What if she can come back, but she doesn't want to? I stare at the shabby green bushes, which quiver in the ocean wind.

She'll come back. She has to come back. I plant myself on the sand, facing the pathway. I'll wait all day and night if I have to. I'm not leaving until I see her one more time.

CHAPTER 8

Cassandra

I stand at the entrance to the pathway. My eyes are closed. My hand brushes against the bushes. The smell of ocean and greenery hangs on the wind. The gentle repetition of breaking waves pulses in my ears. I'm here. I'm awake and very much alive. This moment is real. So whatever happens when I walk through these bushes will also be real.

Exhaling deeply, I open my eyes. *Let's do this.*

One step follows another, each growing more confident. And even before I set my foot on the sand, I catch sight of him. He's sitting on the beach, both hands pressed together at his lips, watching the bushes with a look of deep concentration. When he spots me, his eyes light up. He jumps to his feet.

As he walks toward me, his enthusiasm shifts to a satisfied nod. "So it wasn't a dream then."

"No. Not unless this has been the longest, most elaborate dream in human history."

"It's good to see you," he says. "For a while there, I thought you might not come."

"That was definitely a possibility. Last night left me pretty shaken up."

"I barely slept," Lawrence concedes.

"That makes two of us."

Standing here with him feels surreal and oddly normal at the same time. I don't know what it should feel like to be honest.

I realize I've been staring at Lawrence for at least thirty seconds in complete silence. He doesn't seem to mind, but I look away quickly.

"So," I say awkwardly. "What happens now?"

Lawrence shakes his head. "I confess. I don't really have a plan. I just…knew I wanted to see you again."

I narrow my eyes. "Has this whole thing been an elaborate plot to date me? You know, you could have just asked me out."

He lifts his hands like he's been caught. "Was it so obvious?"

I try to hold my serious expression, but his badly hidden smile makes us both laugh.

"No, but seriously," I say. "You're really from nineteen twenty-five? Like, for real?"

"Afraid I am."

"You walk into that house, and it's nineteen twenty-five?"

"Correct."

I rub my forehead. "It's so weird."

"You said it," he murmurs in an adorable 1920s style of agreement.

The nineteen twenties. It might be my imagination, but the length of the beach we're standing on has taken on an almost eerie change. What was once a simple coastline is now host to an unbelievable truth. How is it possible that Lawrence and I are here together? How is this happening? Why this beach? And why now? My eyes move from the rocky point on one end of the cover to the other. An idea bubbles up.

"What if we tried going down one of those paths?" I ask, pointing. "Do you think the same thing would happen?"

"It's a good question."

"We should test it," I say.

"It's certainly worth a try."

We start to climb out to the closer point. It's windy, but the heat of the afternoon spreads down in brilliant white light. The crash of waves against the rocks fills the air with a salty mist that almost sparkles in the sun.

"I'm almost afraid to try this," I say, looking ahead at the rocky, bush-speckled path.

"Afraid it might work?"

"I guess so. I mean...what if I can travel into nineteen twenty-five?"

"Or what if I can come into the future?" Lawrence asks.

"I say we go to your time first. You're living in the cooler era."

"That so?"

"Definitely. I mean, I'm a fan of women's rights and smartphones, but you have flappers and speakeasies and Fitzgerald."

"So you know a little about my time, then, I guess?"

"Sure. We had a whole unit on the Roaring Twenties in English when we read *The Great Gatsby*."

Lawrence's brow wrinkles, as if I just spoke in Chinese. I realize those phrases are probably all modern iterations. And *The Great Gatsby* probably isn't widely known yet, if it's even published yet.

"Things were much more exciting in your time," I say. "More pure. More honest. More, I don't know…alive, I guess."

His laugh carries a hint of bitterness. "I'm not so sure about that. But here's hoping things change in the next few years for the better."

Like the Great Depression? The Dust Bowl? World War II? All right around the corner. And Lawrence is going to live through them. My heart sinks a little. I give him a quick, sidelong glance, envisioning him in a soldier's uniform, storming the beaches at Normandy. Chills run over my skin and I shudder involuntarily.

"You okay?" Lawrence asks, his brow lowering.

I look away from his gaze. "Fine. Just got cold for a second."

Should I warn him? Maybe toss out a subtle "I wouldn't do much investing in the stock market, if I were you." Or, "Keep an eye on the Germans. They're still pissed about World War I, and it's not over yet. Not even close."

I follow the thought through a few scenarios. If I told him, would anyone believe him? "Hey, I met this girl from 2015 on the beach, and she said we should assassinate some German guy named Adolf Hitler."

Yeah, right.

Would it even help Lawrence? Maybe knowing all the crap

he's about to face would make him go crazy. If the world were about to end, would I want to know about it?

"What's wrong?" Lawrence asks, breaking my train of thought. "You look scared all of a sudden."

I rub my arms, unable to shake the cold. "It's…really weird to know some of the things that are going to happen in America in the next few decades."

Lawrence perks up. "What kind of things?"

"I feel like I shouldn't tell you."

"Aw, come on! You can't tease like that."

"I'm serious," I say. "It seems unethical somehow."

"All right then. Have it your way. If you won't tell me about your time, at least tell me more about you. I can't help but wonder if you're related to my Uncle Ned through the generations."

"I don't think so. My mom and stepdad rented this place a few months ago. Apparently, it had been sitting empty for forever."

"So, you're not from the North Shore?"

"No. I hail from the most boring town in the most boring state in the Union."

A smile tugs at Lawrence's lips. "Ohio?"

I laugh. "How did you guess?"

"I'm from America too, you know, albeit a slightly earlier version."

"Maybe not as much has changed as you think."

"Maybe," he says, his brown eyes shining. "So, what do you do in Ohio? I take it from your clever conversation that you're being educated?"

"I guess. When I actually make it to class."

"I think that's swell. A lot of girls I know have no interest in learning. They don't see the point."

"Thank goodness for progress."

"You said it. I admire a gal who likes to learn."

I shrug, but I feel undeniably light inside at his compliment. We walk in comfortable silence. I steal another glance at him. He looks sharp in his slacks and linen button shirt with the sleeves rolled up to the elbows. That's probably as casually as they dress in the 1920s. His hair is feathered by the wind in a way that's effortlessly sexy. I swallow hard.

I've been so preoccupied thinking about this whole 1920s thing that I can tell I'm not being myself.

"So," I say, going for casual banter. "You write poetry, huh?"

"I suppose. A few scribbles. I'm not too swell at it."

"You're pretty swell. I mean, you're no Whitman, but I liked what I heard."

"Well, thank you. Like I said, my old man thinks it's a waste of time. He says I should focus on preparing for college and then law school."

"A five-year plan, eh? Sounds familiar."

"Something like that." There's an edge of sadness to his voice. "It's not that I don't want to go, necessarily. I just…I never had the choice, you see. My path has been laid out for me since I was born. Harvard, like my father. Law school, like my father. Work in corporate law, like my father. Marry a society girl my father approves of. Have sons. Throw polite parties at my summer home on the North Shore."

"What if you just tell him you don't want to do all that? Tell him you want to find your own way."

"If only it were that easy," he says, shoving his hands in his pockets.

"He can't force you."

"You don't know my father. He's a powerful man. Ever since my mother died last year, it's like I've become his employee, rather than his son."

I'm starting to see why Lawrence was brooding on the beach that first night. "I'm so sorry," I say softly. "I can't imagine what it must be like to lose a parent."

He concentrates on the ground as we walk. "I don't mean to bring the mood down."

"After what you've gone through, I'd say you have every right."

"I'm fine. I just wish I could talk to him, you know? And that he'd actually listen to what I want. Of course, you understand having little choice in life, being a woman."

I feel a twinge of guilt at moping over my First World Problems. "Actually, things are pretty equal between men and women in the future. I can do anything I want."

"Sounds wonderful."

"I guess. Sometimes I think that's part of the problem—too many choices."

"I wish I had your problems."

"Yeah, well, part of me wishes I had yours. I wish someone would just tell me what I'm good at and what I should be."

"You're good at painting," he offers.

"Am I? You've never even seen my stuff."

"I want to see it. I'm sure you're excellent."

"That's sweet, but for all you know, I royally suck." I kick at a pebble in front of me. "Maybe if I knew where I truly had talent, I'd know what I wanted to do with my life."

"It's official then," Lawrence says. "If we find a way to travel into each other's time, we'll swap places."

"Sounds like a plan."

We shake on it. Then Lawrence points to the sandy path ahead. "Here's our chance. There's the trail." He extends his hand for mine. "Shall we?"

I pause at the foot of the dirt path, then set my hand in his. "Let's do this."

A few steps on the trail, and nothing has changed. Our eyes meet.

"This is scary," I whisper.

Lawrence smiles. "Well, you're still here."

A few more steps. Still a solid entity.

"Dude," I say, eyes wide. "It's working."

His face bright with excitement, Lawrence breaks into a run down the path, pulling me along behind him. But before we've gone six feet, a fuzzy shimmer falls over him. His grip goes soft. We run a little farther, and the effect intensifies. Lawrence meets my gaze, crestfallen, and then disappears.

Though the first test of his theory failed, Lawrence is determined to test every angle. We even walk out to the tip of the point, but it doesn't change the outcome. We make our way over to the other point too. I don't think it will be any different, but I don't say as much. Maybe because a part of me wants to keep up our conversation, and the long hike along the shore will do just that.

But as I'd thought, the other trail is no different. After more than two hours of walking, we end up back on the beach. Lawrence brings some sandwiches and fruit from his house—or my house, I guess—and we eat on the sand.

"So, I guess this is it," Lawrence says, taking a bite of apple. "I can only see you here on this beach. Nowhere else."

I nod. "It's weird. Like some cosmic force is trying to keep us apart. I guess this is the universe's way of telling me I'd make a really awful flapper."

In spite of my joking around, the strange sadness of the situation pricks at me.

Lawrence rotates his apple in front of him, examining it. "Who knows? Maybe the universe is trying to bring us together."

I look at him sidelong. His dark-brown eyes, unembarrassed by his words, meet mine. I try to play it cool.

"Saying stuff like that doesn't do anything to refute my 'this is all an elaborate scheme to ask me out' theory."

He raises a sly eyebrow. "So far, I'd say my plan is working pretty well."

I bump him with my elbow, pressing down a smile.

He grins and takes another bite of his apple. "I do have one other theory to try out… I don't know if you're up for it."

"If it involves me taking off my clothes, you can forget it."

He looks both shocked and amused by my words. I guess it's a pretty racy joke for a 1920s kid.

"Tell me your theory," I say, redirecting the conversation.

"Well...what if this all has something to do with the ocean? The currents. The tides."

I look out at the water, considering this. "It does have a certain logical symbolism to it. What are you thinking?"

"What if we swim out and see how far we can go?"

"You really like swimming, don't you?"

"Yes, but it's not that. I really think there might be something to this."

I consider for a moment. I'm not the strongest swimmer. But something about his theory intrigues me.

"It's worth a try, I guess."

"Excellent." He stands. "Let's run to put on our swim clothes. Meet you here in five minutes."

"Aha! So it does involve me undressing!"

Lawrence laughs. "Aw, go change, would ya?"

We walk together through the bushes until he vanishes. My stomach twists as I watch him fade to nothing. Even though we've tested it a dozen times, I can't help but worry that this dematerializing was the last, and that this weird crack in time will close forever.

I rush up to my room, wanting to get back to the beach as soon as possible. Tugging out my overstuffed drawer, I survey my pathetic selection of swimwear. I settle on a black bikini, toss on my swim dress, and run downstairs. As my hand brushes down the banister, it sinks in that Lawrence is here. Right now. Separated by almost a hundred years. The thought quickens my heartbeat. I try to calm down on the walk back to the beach.

Lawrence is waiting for me in those adorably short, vintage swim trunks of his.

"Ready?" he asks.

"Yep." I pull off my swim dress. "Ready."

Lawrence's eyes widen a little. "Holy Toledo," he says breathlessly.

I guess a bikini is also scandalous for the 1920s. This awareness pleases me.

"Fashion changes a lot over the next hundred years," I say.

"You ain't kiddin'."

"Okay, Lawrence, eyeballs back in sockets."

He grins. "For some reason, I'm more anxious than ever to try to travel to your time."

I whack his arm.

We wade out together, wobbling a little on the rocks under our bare feet, but soon it's deep enough to swim. The water is cold and goose bumps rise on my skin. The current pulls against me like a promise. Waves bob us up and down, slapping lightly against our shoulders.

"This probably isn't the best time to say that I'm not a great swimmer," I call over the rush of surf.

A warm, firm hand wraps around mine. Lawrence smiles. "I'll watch out for you."

We swim on. Soon my feet can no longer touch the bottom.

A dark feeling settles over me. This is not good. Who knows what could be swimming around beneath my feet, watching me from below?

"Do you know if there are any sharks in these waters?"

Lawrence laughs. "Don't worry, Cassandra. I've got you."

"You didn't answer my question."

The waves grow stronger the deeper we go, the closer we move to the breakers. Lawrence makes a few strong strokes, letting go of my hand for a moment.

"You haven't disappeared yet," he calls. "This is the farthest we've gotten from the beach. I think we might have found the solution!"

I strain to see him over the white peaks of waves. Water keeps splashing against my face. But every time I rub it away, I sink a little. I don't like feeling so powerless, so vulnerable. Then, one particularly large wave engulfs my head completely. I thrash to the surface, coughing and sputtering.

"Lawrence, I want to go back."

No answer. Nothing but the crash of surf.

"Lawrence?"

Wiping my eyes, I look in every direction. Combined with the up and down of the waves, it's a dizzying, chaotic feeling. But the only thing I can see is the surface of the water. He's gone. Panic seeps into my chest like ink. I'm alone out here in the middle of the ocean. My legs are tired. The waves are too strong. I'm going to go under.

"Lawrence!" I shout. "Lawrence!"

Another wave smacks against my head, dragging me down. Startled, I release the air in my mouth in a burst of bubbles. The water is an opaque indigo. Salt burns my eyes. My lungs ache for breath. I feel my body sinking like a stone.

CHAPTER 9

Cassandra

My body twists. I don't know which way is up and which is down. I flail my arms and legs, searching for some semblance of balance. But that only seems to drag me down farther.

And then, just as my lungs are about to burst, a pair of arms wraps around my waist. My body rights itself and I kick up as hard as I can. My head bursts out of the water and I gasp. Wet hair covers my face. I wipe it aside, coughing.

"Cassandra! Are you okay?" Lawrence's voice crackles, soft and distant. And yet I still feel his arms. I nod, panting for breath. I can hardly make out his face.

"How did you see me?" I ask, shaking from the whole experience.

"I don't really know," he admits. "Are you sure you're all right?"

"I'm okay. Let's just go back."

We swim a few strong kicks. The thrust of the waves propels us. As we draw closer to the shore, the blurry, translucent Lawrence fills in with color and form until he's back to himself. We swim hard—not speaking. Then finally we reach the shore. I crawl up on shaky limbs and collapse onto the sand.

I lie there for a moment, my cheek pressed to the sand. Waves rush over my feet and legs, but I don't move. Lawrence lies on his back beside me.

"Well," he says, his voice halted and tired. "That's that, then."

When we've caught our breath, we wrap in the towels Lawrence brought and sit back in our spot on the beach.

"I still don't know how you saw me under the water," I say, hugging the warm towel close to me. "I could barely see you even above the surface."

Lawrence shakes his head. "I'm so sorry to put you through that."

"It's not your fault I'm a crappy swimmer."

He rubs his temples. "When we got that far out, I was so sure we'd discovered the solution. I got excited and let go of your hand. But then, I couldn't see you… I thought you'd drowned."

"I was worried about that myself for a minute."

He puts his hand on my back. "Cassandra, can you forgive me? If I'd known, I never would have suggested that we—"

"Don't apologize. The waves were stronger than I thought, that's all."

"But I am sorry."

"It's not your fault, Lawrence."

He sighs. "Well, I feel awful grummy about it anyhow."

This makes me smile. "You say the weirdest words."

The corner of his mouth turns up. "You're one to talk."

I bump him with my shoulder, and we both laugh.

We're sitting close. Little more than a few inches apart. The impulse to scoot closer and rest my head on his shoulder tugs at me, but I resist. I wonder if he's thinking what I'm thinking: that we've run out of scientific reasons to stay on the beach. It's clear—there's no way around it. This beach and this beach alone is where our worlds overlap. So what now?

Lawrence draws a line in the sand with his finger. "So I guess the day's over."

I swallow hard. "Yeah, it is."

"And we know all we can know about...this." He motions to me and the beach.

"I suppose so."

"I don't know what to make of it," he says with a sigh. "I really don't. What does it mean? Why did this happen? What are we supposed to do about it? Maybe we should tell someone."

"And who would believe us?"

"We can prove it. We'll show them how you disappear on the path."

I imagine myself telling Mom or Jade. How could that possibly go well? "I don't know," I say. "That seems like a bad idea. I say we keep it to ourselves for now."

Lawrence nods. "You're probably right."

I exhale heavily. "Maybe we should be more careful."

"What do you mean?"

"I don't know. What if it's dangerous somehow?"

Lawrence turns to face me. "You mean...you think we should stay away from each other?"

"I don't know what I think, okay? This whole scenario freaks me out."

"What if we try and forget that then," he says.

"What do you mean?"

His gaze is intense. "What if we forget that I'm from nineteen twenty-five and you're from two thousand fifteen."

"How can we forget that?" I point toward the bushes. "How can I forget that you dissolve into the air if you try to leave this beach?"

He grabs my hand. "Because it doesn't matter. Because, when all is said and done, we're just two people. Are we really so different, despite the decades between us?"

My stomach flutters like crazy. It's almost impossible to meet his gaze. "I guess not."

He says nothing but keeps his eyes fixed on me. I release a slow breath. "Maybe…it would be okay to meet one more time."

An irrepressible smile breaks across his face. "Sure. No harm in that."

"But we have to be careful."

"Absolutely."

I puff out a sigh. "I think we're probably crazy."

"Crazy's not always a bad thing," Lawrence says with a grin. "Let's meet tomorrow night. After the others settle down for the evening."

"I can probably do that. What do you have in mind?"

He raises his eyebrow in a mischievous way. "You'll see."

I point at him. "If it has anything to do with swimming, I will punch you."

Luckily for Lawrence, when I arrive at the beach the next evening, just after sunset, he's dressed and seems to have no intention of jumping into the ocean. He's built a small bonfire and set up four green-and-white-striped beach chairs.

"Hello!" he calls as I approach, waving cheesily.

I suddenly feel embarrassed. I got ready like this was a date or something. I put on my cutest jeans, a black tank top, and a chunky beaded necklace. I even curled the ends of my hair. Lawrence looks sharp and slightly fancy, as always, but that's just how he dresses. Those two other beach chairs make me think he doesn't intend for this to be romantic though.

"Did you…invite some friends?" I ask, approaching with hesitant steps.

Lawrence follows my gaze to the chairs. "Oh that? No, no, I was just trying to make Ned think I was having some others come tonight. Didn't want him to get suspicious. You know."

A twist of pleasure tightens in my stomach. So we will be alone.

"What did you tell your parents?" Lawrence asks, pushing a fresh log onto the fire.

"It was just my stepdad who was home. Frank's pretty easygoing. I told him I'm taking a walk."

Lawrence examines me and smiles. "I like your trousers. They're very avant-garde."

"Not so much in my time," I say. "Though they are skinnier jeans than I normally buy."

"Well, you're a dish either way."

The nervous-but-happy feeling crackles inside me again. "Thanks."

"Have a seat," he says, motioning to the chairs.

I sit down and Lawrence takes the chair beside me. We're quiet, both mesmerized by the orange glow of the fire. I guess first-date awkwardness transcends time. I cross my legs, searching for some shred of conversation.

"So, are we going to roast some marshmallows?"

Lawrence grins. "Sure. If you want."

"You know what's really good is roasted Starburst."

"Is that a type of marshmallow?"

"No. Starbursts. You know...the candy?"

He gives me a shrug.

I sit up. "Get out! Are Starbursts not invented yet in nineteen twenty-five?"

"I've never heard of them."

"Oh man! That's just sad. They're infinitely superior to the marshmallow, as far as roasting is concerned."

"What on earth are they?"

"I have to show you. Words can't really do them justice."

Lawrence lifts an eyebrow. "I think you might be overselling them a tad."

"Okay," I say, standing. "Now I have to go get some. My credibility is on the line."

Back at the house, it takes some ransacking, but I find a pack tucked in Mom's "secret" candy stash behind the flour container. I'll repay her later. I grab some roasting sticks and head to the bonfire again.

"Do you have them?" Lawrence asks.

With dramatic flair, I present the Starbursts. "Ta-da!"

He picks up the slim rectangular pack, looking somewhat disappointed. "That's it? It looks like chewing gum."

I laugh and pat his head. "Oh adorable, nineteen-twenties Lawrence. You have so much to learn."

He folds his arms with a smirk. "I'm waiting to be impressed. You're stalling."

"Just wait, just wait. Let the fire do its magic."

Lawrence watches me as I prepare the stick with two gleaming, square candies and search for the hottest part of the coals. Then I begin my time-crafted process of achieving the perfect caramelization.

"You're quite intense about this," he says.

"You'd better believe I am. I take my treats very seriously."

"I can respect that."

I give him a sidelong glance. In the soft glow of firelight, he looks as warm and gorgeous as ever. It seems so strange to be sitting here with him—a guy from 1925. I shouldn't think about it. That's what we agreed on yesterday. But it's not the sort of fact that slips from your mind.

"Okay," I say, bringing the perfectly roasted Starburst away from the red embers. "It's ready." I present the gooey deliciousness to Lawrence with both hands, formal Asian style. “Be careful. It’s hot.”

With a skeptical eyebrow raised, Lawrence examines the admittedly strange-looking candy creation. Then he pops it in his mouth. He winces at the heat and then chews thoughtfully. I watch him, biting a fingernail with anticipation. He chews with unnecessary care. Then swallows.

“Well?” I ask.

“You shouldn’t have let me taste that,” he says. “Now I’m more determined than ever to travel to your time.”

I laugh. “Starburst pushed you over the edge, huh?”

He smiles wryly. “You’re not a bad motivator yourself.”

And like that, the magic of the Starburst has made the first-date awkwardness disappear. The rest of the night only gets better. We laugh, talk, gorge on candy, and then, when the fire is low and the stars blaze bright, we wrap ourselves in blankets and search out constellations above us. Everything is so perfect that I don’t want to ever leave.

But I know that can’t be. Real life—boring, frustrating 2015—is waiting just beyond those bushes. As Lawrence and I fold up the blankets and chairs, despair cuts into me like a blade. I try my best to keep things light, to squeeze out the last bits of pleasure from this first and final date of ours. Lawrence lingers as well. Does he not want the night to end either?

“Well,” he says, looking around the beach. “I guess that’s that.”

“Yeah.” I let out a breath that sounds a lot like a sigh. “I had a good time.”

"I did too. Those Starbrights were ginger peachy."

I chuckle. "Sure were."

"Of course, they have nothing on my Aunt Eloise's lemon meringue pie." He digs the tip of his shoe into the sand. "You ought to come back tomorrow so I can bring you a piece. One treat for another. Seems only fair."

"Oh, you're sneaky, Lawrence."

"Nothing sneaky about it. I ought to return the favor, that's all."

I should refuse. I know this. I'm being careless with my heart. This is a guy I can never really date. Not even close. And yet…

"One more day. That's it."

Lawrence beams. "Swell. Meet me here for lunch? I'll bring us out a picnic."

"Sounds ginger peachy."

CHAPTER 10

Cassandra

Aunt Eloise's lemon meringue pie lives up to the hype. At the picnic with Lawrence, we pick up right where we'd left off the night before. We're so absorbed in conversation that a sudden clap of thunder makes us both look up at the sky with a start. A blanket of rain-laden clouds hang above us. Droplets turn to sheets of cold wetness in a matter of seconds.

Lawrence and I jump to our feet.

"Where did this come from?" I ask, holding my hands over my head as a weak shield.

"Snuck up on us," he says. "If you weren't so darn interesting, I might have seen its approach."

The compliment makes my heart swell. I want to keep talking, but the rain pours harder. Lawrence isn't running inside either. Our eyes meet. It's as if neither of us wants to be the one to leave. I wipe the rain from my face, though it doesn't help.

"Well," I say, "I guess we'd better..."

Lawrence sets his hand on my arm. "Wait."

His touch sends a ripple of energy down my arm. He bends down and collects our plates and forks. Then he lifts the blue wool blanket, gives it a firm shake to loosen the sand, and sweeps it over the tops of the bushes.

"I'm not ready to go in yet," he says, ducking beneath his makeshift tent with a grin.

I slip under the blanket and join him. "Not bad," I say, examining our little shelter. "Well done, Boy Scout Lawrence."

"It won't keep us very dry, but it ought to help. It's a warm rain anyway."

"And now that you've said that, we'll both catch pneumonia and die."

Lawrence laughs. "I'm fairly certain that won't happen. But then, I'm headed into law, not medicine. Maybe they're writing our death certificates as we speak."

I shake my head. "Sorry, but if we both catch pneumonia, I'd be significantly better off than you. One of the few perks of my era."

I expect Lawrence to carry on with the banter, but when I look at him, he's watching me with an unexpectedly soft smile. His eyes drift down to my lips.

"I wouldn't mind dying today," he says. "Might as well end on a high note."

A current of electricity runs through my body, but hearing him talk about death pulls me back to reality. Technically speaking, whenever I leave this beach, Lawrence already is dead. In my world, in the real world, he's probably been dead for at least twenty years. The thought spreads through me like ice. I rub the chill from my arms. "No more talk about dying. It's too…creepy."

"You're trembling," Lawrence says, noticing my shiver. He puts his arm around me. "Better?"

You have no idea, Lawrence. I try not to let him see me flush with pleasure. "Isn't this what they call getting 'fresh' in your era?"

"My intentions are innocent!"

"Suspect."

"Only sometimes." He brushes a hand across the roof of our dripping shelter. "We should probably go in and get dry."

My heart sinks a little. "I guess so."

"Do I need to concoct another excuse to see you again, or will you meet me for meeting's sake?"

"You're welcome to concoct an excuse. For my amusement."

"All right then. Cassandra, will you meet me tomorrow morning so that I can give you a surprise?"

"A surprise, huh?" I tap my chin, pretending to mull over the pros and cons. "Intriguing…"

Lawrence winks. "I promise it will be worth it."

"Tomorrow it is, then."

I'm up early. I feel silly admitting it to myself, but I'm too excited to sleep. It's probably better to get out of the house before everyone is up though. I'm sure Mom has noticed how much time I'm spending on the beach. Better to minimize her awareness. I'll meet Lawrence and be back before she even notices I was gone.

After picking out my favorite blue cotton dress, I pull my hair back into a curly ponytail and head downstairs. But Mom's in the kitchen, pouring Eddie some cold cereal. I freeze in the doorway, my plan foiled. Then I feel a pair of big, brown eyes latch on me.

"Cass," Eddie says, pointing his chubby toddler finger at me.

Traitor.

Mom looks surprised. "What are you doing up this early? I thought teenagers were clinically dead before ten a.m. during the summer."

"Funny. You should consider a career in comedy."

"One day I'll live my dreams." She motions to the kitchen. "Do you want some breakfast? Frank's going to fry some eggs."

I shoot a darting glance to the backyard. "Actually, I was thinking I would go for a run. Clear my head a little."

Mom's eyebrows rise. "You're going for a run?"

"Yes. Don't sound so incredulous."

"Hey, I think it's a great idea. Definitely. Give it a try. See how you like it."

I fold my arms, feeling defensive, even though we both know I'm the least likely person on this planet to be a runner. "I really am going to do it."

"Wonderful. Then before you start, you should have some breakfast. Let me make you some oatmeal."

"Can't. Don't want to exercise on a full stomach."

"At least take some fruit."

Seeing that I must appease her motherly concern, I grab a banana from the counter, peel it, and cram three bites into my mouth.

"Satisfied?" I ask, my cheeks full of banana.

She smiles and I head off.

"Aren't you going to change out of that dress?" Mom calls as I disappear around the corner.

I could smack my forehead. Instead, I yell back in my most confident voice, "I like exercising in dresses."

I wince, waiting for her radar-like senses to pick up on the abnormality of this. There's a tense pause.

"Just make sure you have your pepper spray," she calls.

I release a silent breath of relief. "Yep. I've got it. Love you. Bye."

When I finally hit the cool, salty air of the back patio, my stomach does a little backflip. I'm way too eager. It's truly lame. But I'll own that lameness today. Quite proudly. I jog down the path. In spite of Mom's skepticism, I probably could run a marathon today. I have all the energy in the world.

But when I arrive at the beach, it's empty. I scan down the shore for any sign of him, but only the crashing waves move in the stillness. I go down to the shore and touch the cool water. The wind blows my hair and dress back lightly. This is good. Now I'll look ethereal and romantic when he comes.

After a few minutes, however, I start to get impatient posing there. Where is he? I walk back up to the pathway, peering through the green branches. But there's nothing.

A sudden rustle of the branches makes my stomach leap into my throat. A white seagull pushes out of the bushes and flutters away. I frown. It seems strange to see a gull there.

A sinking feeling comes over me. Something's wrong…

Maybe it's over. Maybe whatever anomaly of science or nature allowed us to see each other has finally repaired itself. I stare down the empty path, not breathing, as if I could will Lawrence to come out with the sheer intensity of my desire. As if I could call to him across a hundred years with only my heart.

Lawrence.

The bushes shiver with movement. Drawing in a sharp breath, I rush forward.

"Lawrence?"

But then, right in the middle of the brush, I feel the strangest tingle down my spine.

My ears prick up. The sound of faint footfalls and voices pierce the wind. The hairs on the back of my neck stand on end, and I spin around. My gaze canvasses the path behind me with swift strokes. And then I see it. The muted glimmer of two forms.

They're obviously from Lawrence's time, but I'm not sure it's him. It could be anyone.

I have a split second to decide. Trying to pass them and run back in the house seems like the safest option. But then the forms get more defined and I impulsively dive back toward the beach. Being seen by these strangers would be bad enough, but having them see me materializing out of thin air would be even worse.

I tumble forward onto the sand and scramble to get back on my feet. My heart's racing in my throat. I'm turning for the point when a deep, male voice snaps, "Hey! What are you doing out here?"

CHAPTER 11

Cassandra

I'm caught. I'm seriously screwed. In a panic, I make a break for it, sprinting.

And then a voice rushes through my body like tingling heat. "Cassandra?"

Looking over your shoulder while running on sand isn't a great idea. I trip and fly face-first to the ground.

"Cassandra!" Lawrence calls, rushing to my side. He helps me up, brushing the sand from my shoulders with a look of concern. "Are you all right?"

"Um, I'll live." My gaze shifts to the other man. He's terrifyingly huge. Tall, with a big belly and jet-black hair. All the blood in me runs cold.

"You know this girl?" the big man asks, coming over to us.

Lawrence retracts his hands suddenly, as if not wanting to be seen touching me. "Sure," he says with a forced tone. "She was at the party the other night."

He holds his hand out politely to help me stand. "Cassandra, this is my Uncle Ned."

The famous Uncle Ned. He looks way more intimidating than how Lawrence described him. Both he and Lawrence are dressed in expensive-looking suits, as if they are headed to church or something.

"This is Cassandra," Lawrence says to Ned, moving subtly away from me as he speaks. "Cassandra… Can't remember your last name," he adds with a laugh.

"It's—" I start to answer, but Lawrence noticeably jumps to speak over me.

"She lives up past the point. The summer crowd." He turns to me and there's a flash of seriousness in his eyes. "Do you have that card, Cassandra?"

My mind scrambles for a second, but I figure it's best to play along. "Yeah. I mean, yes."

Lawrence nods. "Ned and I are about to leave, but I told him you needed me to deliver your condolences."

"Ex-exactly," I stammer, hoping against hope that he doesn't expect me to know what he's talking about. "Thanks again, Lawrence."

Ned's eyes stay on me. I swallow hard. At least I'm wearing a dress, not jean shorts and a tank top. Even still, I can't help feeling that Lawrence's uncle knows I'm out of place. As if my very presence screams, "Not from 1925!" But he couldn't possibly know. Could he?

"I'll see Cassandra down the beach," Lawrence says casually. "Won't be long."

"Of course," Ned says. "But don't dawdle, Lon. We don't want to be late."

"Yes, sir."

Ned hesitates, glancing back at me, but then heads toward the house. His house, I guess. As it was in 1925.

As soon as he leaves, I release the breath I've been holding. Lawrence says, "I'm sorry about that. I think we gave you quite a scare."

"Um, you could say that."

"Ned can be a little gruff, but he's a swell guy. Don't worry about him."

But I am worried. It can't be good that he saw me. Even if he bought Lawrence's story, it seems dangerous that I was seen by someone from his time.

"Are you going to explain what you were talking about?"

In an instant, the brightness on Lawrence's face vanishes. He sighs. "We're headed to a wake. Billy Howard died yesterday." He shakes his head. "Sorry, I forget you wouldn't know him. He was a friend of mine. We weren't close, but were both going to start at Harvard in the fall."

I set my hand on Lawrence's arm. "I'm so sorry."

"It was a motor-car accident. He…well, Billy liked a good party. I guess he was a little drunk, and he didn't see the road turn ahead…"

I shudder. "That's awful."

Lawrence turns his eyes to the sea. "I should have been there."

"Don't blame yourself, Lawrence. It's not your—"

"No, I mean it. I was supposed to go with him, but I came to meet you instead."

My stomach drops. "Oh gosh."

Lawrence goes on as if he hadn't heard me. "I told him I would go along. If I had, Billy wouldn't have been driving that car. I would have. And I would have made that turn, and—"

"You can't think like that. It'll make you crazy."

"I know… I just…" Suddenly, Lawrence throws his arms around me. He holds me tightly. I'd be thrilled at our first embrace if my heart didn't ache for him.

"I can't stop picturing it," he whispers.

I hug him back, setting my head on his shoulder. "It's not your fault. Sometimes bad things just happen."

"I know. You're right, but I still feel responsible." He breaks his grip. "Forgive me. I've felt low all morning."

"I wish there were something I could do."

"Meet me here later?"

"Are you sure you'll be up for hanging out?"

"I'd like the distraction. Perhaps not tonight, as we'll be comforting Billy's family. But tomorrow night?" A sad half smile tugs at his lips. "I still need to give you your surprise."

"Oh gosh, you don't need to worry about that."

"I want to." He looks back down the path. "I should probably go now. Ned's waiting. But I really do want to see you tomorrow, if you're willing."

"Of course."

Lawrence nods. "Until then."

I sit on the beach after he leaves. I can't shake the feeling of foreboding hanging over me. I'm probably overthinking things, as always. Death makes me squeamish. Aside from Nana dying when I was six, the closest I've come to losing someone I love was when Sarah McKay died of cancer in tenth grade. I didn't know her that well, but we were in choir together so her mom asked a small group of us to sing at her funeral. I cried through the entire thing. Not really sure why it affected me so much.

The uneasy mood hangs over me all day. There's something about what Lawrence told me. Something that's not right, although I can't put my finger on what.

After dinner, I try to concentrate on reading when I hear the doorbell ring. Mom answers. Her voice takes on that cheerful "cool mom" tone, and I know the door's for me. Frowning, I set down my book and investigate.

Brandon Marks stands in the entryway, chatting Mom up with a good-son grin. As I come in, he gives me a wink.

A wink. Okay…

"Here she is," Mom says, smiling. "I'll let you two chat."

"Thanks, Amber."

Um, since when are he and my mom on a first-name basis?

"Well, hello there," Brandon says when she's gone.

I raise an eyebrow. "Hi."

"You're not answering your phone. Did you lose it or something?"

I wrack my brain to remember the last time I used it. When your best friend is cavorting around Europe and your only potential romantic interest lives eighty years before cell phones, you don't use yours much.

"What are you doing here?" I ask, glancing behind him. No one else is waiting in the driveway. It's just him.

Brandon leans against the door frame. "I told you. I couldn't get hold of you. I was in the neighborhood, so I figured I'd swing by."

"For...?"

"Well, I wanted to ask you on a date."

"A date," I repeat.

Brandon gives a "Why on Earth wouldn't I be asking you out?" kind of smile. "I can get us into Mancuso's," he adds, cocking his head triumphantly.

I glance past him again, looking to see if someone else is in the car. "Oh, is this a double with Travis?"

Brandon frowns. "Travis?"

"Well, if anyone can get us into Mancuso's, it's him."

"What are you talking about?"

I hold up my hands defensively. "Hey, don't be offended. It's no mark of superior character that his dad is better connected. I'm merely making an observation."

But Brandon is still confused. If anything, he looks more puzzled. "Who are you talking about?"

I roll my eyes. "Um, Travis? You know, your best friend."

"I have no idea who you're talking about."

"Ha-ha," I say deadpan. "You're killing me, Brandon. Stop. I might die from laughing."

Brandon seems exasperated. "I'm not joking! Who's Travis? Does he live in Crest Harbor?"

"No, he's actually from Outer Mongolia. That's why he likes to come here for summer vacations. All that yurt living can be hard on the spine."

Brandon just stares. I fold my arms across my chest.

"Where is Travis? Did he put you up to this? I bet your phone is on right now, and he's listening to every word, isn't he? Hi, Travis. Nice attempt, but try again."

Now Brandon seems concerned. "Are you okay, Cass?"

"Excuse me?" I scoff.

He pulls his phone out of his pocket and holds it up to show me. It's off.

"I'm not joking," he says slowly. "I don't have any clue who you're talking about. I'm racking my brain, but the only Travis I know is my eight-year-old nephew, and I don't think you mean him."

He seems completely sincere. I never took Brandon for much of an actor. He's either improved a thousand percent or he has short-term amnesia.

I stare hard at him. "You're telling me that you don't know Travis Howard?"

The moment I say his full name, a light snaps on in my brain. *That's it!* That's what was bothering me about my conversation with Lawrence this morning. His friend who died…his last name was Howard.

The air in the room suddenly feels thin. There's a faint ringing in my ears.

"Travis Howard," I say.

He shakes his head. “Never heard of him.”

I take a staggering step backward. My lungs suddenly seem incapable of drawing in a breath. Then a thought comes to me, and the only thing that matters is getting to my phone. I make a beeline for the stairs.

“Cass?” Brandon runs after me. “What are you doing?”

I don’t respond. My mind is racing so fast that I can’t grasp on to a single thought. My cell phone sits on my desk. I grab it and turn it on. Brandon comes to my doorway, his brow furrowed.

“Are you okay? Cass, talk to me.”

I swipe a hand at him to make him shut up. “I have a picture of Travis. From the night we jumped the Andersons’ fence.”

“That was just me and you, Cass.”

“No,” I say firmly. “Travis was there. We took a picture. I’ll prove it to you.”

Fingers trembling, I slide through my photos. A few pictures of Eddie. Some shots of me looking bored that I sent to Jade. A picture of the house exterior from when we first came here. And then…I’m back in Ohio, waving to Jade at the airport. Frowning, I scan through the pictures. It was there. It was right there. The selfie we took in front of the fence. Travis put his arm around me. We made ironic thumbs-up gestures.

It’s gone.

“It was here,” I say, my voice weak. “I had…I had a picture of him.”

Brandon comes cautiously into my room. “Cass. I don’t know what you’re talking about. That night, it was just you and me.

I've never even heard of a Travis Howard. I think you might be confusing him with someone you knew in Ohio."

I shake my head. "No. *No.*" I scan through the pictures again. Nothing. No texts. His name is missing from my contacts. With a trembling hand, I pull up Facebook. The only Travis Howards are people I've never met. He's gone. There's no trace of him.

I look up and back away from Brandon. "This can't be happening."

He stares at me, concerned and weirded out. "What's going on, Cass? You're super pale all the sudden."

The floor feels unsteady beneath me. Dinner suddenly rises in my stomach.

"I want you to leave," I say, backing up.

"Cass—"

"Now...please."

He puts up his hands in surrender. "Fine. I'll take off, let you sort this out. Can I call you later?"

I don't respond. He nods and turns to go.

What am I supposed to do? What am I supposed to think? I need to calm down. I'm probably overreacting. I'm sure there is a perfectly good explanation for all of this.

Glancing at my phone again, I run downstairs. Mom's in the library, sitting at the computer with her reading glasses on. When I burst in, she looks up with motherly concern.

"Cass?"

"Travis Howard," I blurt out.

"What?"

"I can't find a picture of Travis that I took on my phone. Did you…delete it or something?"

Mom frowns. "No, I haven't touched your phone."

"But you know who Travis is, right?"

Her lips twist to the side in thought. "Is he from around here or back in Ohio?"

The floor feels unsteady. "Mom, Travis. Brandon's best friend? Tall, blue eyes? Only child of the Howards?"

Mom shakes her head. "And I know them?"

"They came to your party! Don't you remember? They brought you that über-expensive bottle of wine that you and Frank were gushing over."

"Well…" She's trying really hard.

"You can't honestly not know who I'm talking about," I say. There's a tremor in my voice. "You've met him at least five times this summer. He's come to the house."

Her silence says everything I need to know. I drop into one of the deep maroon armchairs to keep from falling over. This can't be happening. It's impossible.

But Lawrence's voice echoes in my ears. Billy Howard died yesterday. It can't be. It can't.

"What's wrong, Cass?" Mom's voice sounds fuzzy. It's like I'm listening to her with my head underwater. I rise to my feet and stagger out of the room.

The butterfly effect.

Three hours of frantic research on the Internet, and this is the answer I have come up with. The idea that a small event can cause big ripples over time. Lawrence choosing to meet me instead of his friend led to Billy Howard's car accident and death, which in turn eliminated the entire genealogical line he would have created, which means that as of yesterday, Travis Howard ceased to exist. He's not dead. He never lived in the first place. Either way, he's gone.

And it's my fault. Lawrence should have been with Billy. Billy should have lived, married, and had kids who had kids, who gave birth to Travis Howard.

I should have thought of this before. I've seen enough sci-fi movies to know there are ramifications when you mess with time. The time-space continuum is a fragile thing. There are consequences to even the smallest unplanned shift.

I lie on my bed, but sleep won't come. It's not possible with the chaos in my brain. I even snuck one of my mom's Xanax because I was afraid I was having a nervous breakdown. But the medicine has only slowed my pulse, not my mind.

Turning over, I stare at the red numbers of my alarm clock, glowing in the darkness like eyes—2:48. I roll to my back again. The ceiling is less stressful to look at. I try to clear my head and relax. But my thoughts are impossible to hide from. They march through my brain, an unrelenting army.

The tears return. It's been like that on and off all night. Tears of mourning for Travis. I never got to know him all that well, but I liked him. And to me, it's like he's dead. Which isn't far from reality. In a lot of ways, Travis was sitting in that car with Billy Howard as it careened off the cliff.

I smudge the tears away with my pajama sleeve, sniffling. It's not all for Travis. I'm also crying for myself. Because this turn of events has surfaced a fear that I've tried to bury thus far.

It's not safe to know Lawrence. It's not normal. It's not natural. As this case proves, interacting with him can have serious, even deadly repercussions.

And I ugly cry, because I know that tomorrow night I have to say good-bye to Lawrence Foster forever.

CHAPTER 12

Cassandra

I thought I had prepared myself, steeled my mind and heart for saying good-bye, but as Lawrence appears on the glistening white beach, I realize how desperately wrong I am. I'm not prepared. Not prepared at all.

He comes up to me with a smile that kicks me right in the chest. "I was hoping you'd be here already," he says. "Have you been waiting long?"

I shake my head. Words aren't possible yet. All I can do it stare at him.

"I brought your surprise," he says, patting his jacket pocket. "I wrote you a poem. Nothing Byron-esque, mind you. Just a few words on paper. But I thought you might like it."

Longing twists my throat. He wrote me a poem. In a moment of supreme foolishness, I'm pretty sure that I'm in love with him. It's pathetic, I know. But I'm about to lose it all. Might as well drag myself as low as possible.

I squeeze my eyes shut. *No, you have to do this.* If I'm going to follow through with what I know is right, I can't delay a minute longer. Time to rip off the Band-Aid.

"Come sit by me," Lawrence says. "I'll read it to you."

I grab his arm to stop him from sitting. "Wait."

His deep brown eyes search mine, and they're so beautiful that I almost cave again. "We need to talk."

"All right," he says hesitantly, still searching my face. "Is everything okay? You look a little pale."

"I'm not okay." The tightness in my throat winds into a knot.

"What's wrong? Did something happen?"

"It's more something that didn't happen."

"Not sure I understand."

"It's Billy Howard."

Lawrence frowns. "What about him?"

"He wasn't supposed to die."

"What?"

"I knew someone related to him. In my time. And yesterday, he just…ceased to exist."

He studies me, thoughts flickering behind his eyes. "What do you mean?"

"I know it sounds crazy, but you have to believe me. One minute I knew him. Everyone around me knew him. I had pictures of him on my phone. And then after yesterday, it's like he never was. Not even his best friend knew who I was talking about when I mentioned his name. The pictures are gone. He's gone."

"I don't understand."

"Billy Howard wasn't supposed to die. You were supposed to be with him, but you weren't because of me. And as a result, Travis Howard is essentially dead as well. Don't you get it? You and I have messed with time. We've changed things that weren't supposed to be changed, just by knowing each other."

Lawrence shakes his head. "But how could that be possible? You haven't come into my time nor I into yours. How could we have changed a thing?"

"Because you're in the past. You're not supposed to even know I exist. Look, I think we can both agree that the simple fact we can see each other is a freak of nature. Right?"

"Yes. But what does that matter?"

"This proves why it matters! Because people are vanishing, Lawrence. Because of us. Because we're playing with something you just don't mess with. I mean, for all we know, this conversation could be altering history as we speak. I could walk back into my house and find out that Hitler the Fifth has just been reelected Global Chancellor!"

Lawrence sets a hand on my shoulder. His brow is furrowed with concern. "Cassandra, you're very worked up."

I back away from his touch. "Don't tell me I'm crazy. You need to accept it."

"Accept what? I'm still not sure I understand what's going on. What are you suggesting we do about this?"

Now we come to it. I turn my face away from him, focusing instead on the shimmering curl of waves.

"We have to say good-bye."

Lawrence's silence cuts into me, but I push forward with what must be said. "You have to forget that you ever met me. And I will forget that I met you. We have to leave this beach and never come back again."

"You can't mean that," he says.

"I wish it didn't have to be this way."

"How are you so sure it does?"

"Lawrence—"

"This whole business with Billy Howard could be a coincidence. A misunderstanding—"

I smash my fingers to my temples. "People don't just disappear, Lawrence! We can't fight it. We have to move forward with our lives as if none of this ever happened."

"You think I can do that? Can you?"

"I can, and I will."

His eyes intense, he pulls the folded sheet of paper from his coat pocket and presses it in my hand. "Read this first."

"No."

"Please, Cassandra."

"You're making this more difficult than it has to be." I pull away from him, my heart pounding. "Look, it's been really amazing getting to know you. But this is where it ends, okay?"

He shakes his head. As I hand him back the poem, you'd think I was slapping him across the face. "I wish it could work, Lawrence. I mean that."

"I'll wait for you," he says, his voice tight. "I'll come out every day and night and wait on this beach."

"Please don't."

"I will."

"I have to go." *Band-Aid, Cass. The faster the better.* I turn away. "Good-bye, Lawrence."

And then, all at once, he catches me in his arms. For an electric moment, he holds me, staring into my eyes with a power that could light up half the Eastern Seaboard. Then he presses his lips to my cheek.

"I will wait for you," he whispers into my ear, sending a shiver over my entire body.

Grasping for composure, I back away. I can feel my pulse beating from my scalp all the way down to my toes. This is when I was supposed to say my poignant, preplanned words of farewell. Instead, I turn away in a daze and run off without another word.

CHAPTER 13

Cassandra

"There's, like, a monthlong waiting list to get into this place. Lucky my dad knows the maître d'."

Brandon's smile is probably supposed to come across as casually smug, though his eagerness to impress me seeps through. I suppress the urge to roll my eyes. It's incomprehensibly lame that I'm here. On a date with Brandon. I was perfectly happy sitting on the couch wrapped in my bedspread, eating a tube of processed cookie dough, and binge-watching Netflix. So, of course, Mom had to ruin everything and make me go out. She thinks she's fixing the problem.

"Can't see why there's such a big wait," I say, perusing the menu.

It's so strange to be around Brandon without Travis. Even stranger to wrap my head around the fact that I am literally living in an alternate reality right now, one where Brandon is top dog in Crest Harbor, not just Travis's wingman. Because Travis has never existed. The difference is tangible, and unfortunately I liked Wingman Brandon much better. There was something almost endearing about his nervous, trying-too-hard-to-please manner. Confident, triumphant Brandon makes me want to punch something.

"So," Top Dog Brandon says, glancing down at his menu. "What have you been doing this past week, Cass? I feel like you disappeared."

Because I did. Because I met someone infinitely more interesting and charming than you. I'd be with him now, if not for...

I close my eyes and draw in a quick breath. I need to get ahold of myself. I'm supposed to be forgetting about Lawrence. That's the only reason I came on this date. Anything to keep from thinking about that beach.

"Oh, you know," I say, shrugging. "Just the typical stuff. Joined a street gang. Sold some crack. Killed my first man in a switchblade fight."

Brandon raises an eyebrow. "Sounds interesting."

"That's Crest Harbor for you—Little America."

"You know, after seeing you break into your neighbor's backyard, I'm not totally sure you're joking right now."

I wink at him. "A lady never tells."

He offers a strained smile, and I realize I should probably lay off the sarcasm a little. Jade's always telling me I scare guys off with it.

But Lawrence liked my sense of humor.

I clench my jaw. *Stop it.*

"So," I say, trying for a light, cheerful tone. "How about you? Do anything cool lately?"

Brandon grins. Talking about himself proves second nature for him.

"Getting ready for the lacrosse championships. We practice a ton, but it's paying off. The Crest Harbor league is killer strong this summer."

Taking his pause as a cue, I smile and nod. "Awesome."

"Yeah, it's pretty sweet," he says. "We all meet up at Hector's after the games, have some drinks, swim—you know, hang out." His left eyebrow rises suggestively. "You should come sometime."

In a blink, I can picture what it would be like to date Brandon. Hangouts at Hector's. Stupid drinking games. Lots of talk about lacrosse and other sports. A few make-out sessions in his car. Perhaps one or two in the Jacuzzi, while his new, alternate-reality guy friends drink beer from red Solo cups and high-five each other for their epic displays of manliness.

It would be a perfectly adequate, entertaining summer fling. And don't I have every right to that? I'm seventeen. It's not like I'm searching for my soul mate or something.

Soul mate… The words send tremors through my stomach. I clench my teeth. Get a grip, Cass. Seriously.

"We have a game Friday night actually," Brandon says, interrupting my thoughts. "You can sit with Sara, Jake's girlfriend. You met her the other night, didn't you?"

"I think so." I really have no idea.

"Sweet. It's a date." He smiles in triumph, as if simply acknowledging that I know someone is agreeing to go out with him.

Another date. Just what I'm in the mood for. I take another long drink of my water, wishing it were something stronger.

Brandon goes on. "We could hang out at my place after the game, but my mom killed that idea. She's totally freaking out about her lame party."

"Another party, huh?"

"Yeah, she does it every year. Her Great Gatsby party."

I choke a little on my water but swallow before I make too much of a spectacle. "Great Gatsby?"

"Yeah, it's kind of a nineteen-twenties thing. Nineteen-twenties costumes, nineteen-twenties music."

This is unbelievable. In spite of my greatest efforts, I can't escape Lawrence. First, there was the movie on TV about the two time travelers who make a mess of things. Then, yesterday, when I talked with Jade, she kept going on and on about the surrealists living in Paris in the twenties. And now this.

I am supposed to be forgetting Lawrence, but thus far, I'm failing quite spectacularly.

"Sounds like a swell time," I say, my heart aching at the phrase.

Brandon keeps talking, but my mind races away from this conversation. Away from the clanking silverware and stuffy food smells and buzz of a hundred conversations in this restaurant. And I let myself go to the beach, with the gentle crash of the ocean and the soft wind and the clean sea smell. And Lawrence standing beside me, his eyes dark and thoughtful. In careful detail, I replay how he took me in his arms, how his lips pressed to my cheek. I savor the memory, each moment of it.

Poor Brandon doesn't stand a chance. I've just checked out of this date entirely.

Later, after he's dropped me off, I lie on my bed and stare at the moon, which is framed perfectly in my window. I wonder if Lawrence is looking at it as well. Is he really waiting on the beach, like he said he would? The urge to find out pulls at me. I envision myself tiptoeing down the stairs, across the lawn, and through those bushes. It would be so simple. One quick peek.

I puff out a breath. *No, Cass. Think about Travis.* I can't risk that happening again.

It really is over. There's just no other way. The thought unreasonably depresses me. I roll to my side, pulling my blanket over my shoulders. I think I'll sleep the rest of the summer. Or at least lie here in bed feeling sorry for myself.

I wish I'd at least taken that poem. I could have had something to remember him by. I sigh deeply.

And then a thought occurs to me: What if there is another way? Lawrence is from the past. There has to be information about him somewhere. Surely it won't mess with any time-space continuum to look him up. I sit up in bed, the idea lighting within me like a sudden flame.

I don't know why I never thought of it before. But there's got to be some form of information out there. Maybe a class photo from his graduating year of high school. A family picture. Something. Anything. I feel light and tingly at the possibility. Seeing him again, even in a grainy black-and-white photo, would be a dream. It's going to require all of my research-nerd skills. No Internet search will do. This is a job for an archives sweep. First thing in the morning, I'm heading straight to the Crest Harbor library.

I flop back on my bed, my heart light. Tomorrow. Tomorrow, I'll see Lawrence again.

❧

The Crest Harbor Library rests in a bed of trees, tucked in the center of the old downtown. Cozy little coffee shops and crafty boutiques surround it. Finding a parking spot proves frustratingly difficult, which puts me in a cranky mood.

I find the closest librarian. She gives me a surprised look when I ask where I can find microfilm from the 1920s, but sends me to the basement.

I pour the next few hours into scanning every newspaper and document from the twenties I can get my hands on. If only I could have applied myself like this in history class. I'm absolutely diligent. You never know where there might be a mention of him.

I can't really say why I'm so tense. It's almost as if I know there's something I'm supposed to find. Some piece of the puzzle that will help this whole crazy situation make sense.

And then I find it.

A few lines on an inner page. Dated August 9, 1925. A few lines that strike me like a bullet in the throat.

11544 Seaside Estates to enter foreclosure. Owner, local banker Edward Foster, seeks short sale, following the tragic murder of his

nephew, Lawrence Foster, on the property's private beach. The death has stumped local authorities, who are still investigating possible suspects.

The crime was committed August 5. That's only two weeks away.

CHAPTER 14

Lawrence

The streets of Manhattan are like bathtub gin: fast, cheap, and intoxicating. It's the perfect place to escape to forget Cassandra. Ned invited me to come along with him on a business trip for a few days. I agreed. Anything would beat sitting alone on the beach, waiting for a girl who never comes, a girl who very possibly was just a dream.

So Manhattan it is. The lights and noise engulf me. Meeting Ned's business associates has turned into one party after another, congregating at basement joints that serve bootlegged hooch. I'm not sure why he bothers to do business with those types, but I suppose that for a banker, money is money. I'm surrounded by sights and sounds, but even still, my mind dwells on Cassandra.

Ned and I sit in a dim, crowded speakeasy, watching the fellas get edged up while the flappers dance the Charleston, their short skirts whirling around in glittering streaks of silver and gold. Ned laughs like old friends with a raven-haired man in his twenties. He slaps the man on the arm and orders him to get his associates a few more drinks.

"Swell joint, eh, kid?" Ned says, turning back to me.

"Sure."

It's not an enthusiastic response, and Ned gives his nose a tap. "Ah, I know why you're not having much fun. Missing a certain gal?"

I tense a little. "I..."

Ned laughs. "I think I can brighten your night, m'boy."

His friend arrives with two drinks in hand, and Ned points at me. "Carlo. Take Lonnie here back to the billiards room. Let's show him our little surprise."

Carlo winks. "Sure thing."

I'd really rather stay here and wait out the party, but I can see I have little choice. Ned's in one of those moods. Reluctantly, I follow Carlo across the dance floor, weaving past exuberant dancers who either laugh or drunkenly scold us for getting in the way. We move down a dark, narrow hall where a few couples have stolen away to smooch.

Finally, Carlo opens a dingy, painted door.

"Right in here," he says, his voice tinged with a faint accent.

I hesitate. In a joint like this, who knows what could be waiting on the other side. Grinning, Carlo opens the door, grabs my arm, and shoves me in.

The room is dimly lit and filled with the stench of cigarette smoke and alcohol. Three billiard tables stand in the center, with smaller poker tables and chairs around the sides. There's no one in the room, though the buzz of music from the main dance hall vibrates the walls. I have no idea what Ned expects me to find in here.

Then a pair of hands cover my eyes. Soft hands. The scent of flowered perfume teases my nose. And a breathy voice tickles my neck.

"Guess who."

I grab the slender wrists. Pulling the hands from my eyes, I spin around.

Fay gives me her triumphant little smirk. "Why, hello. Fancy meeting you here."

"What are you doing in New York?" I ask, shocked by the sight of her.

"Neddy sent for me. Said you were being a real flat tire. Thought you needed some cheering up."

As I try to process this, Fay slides close to me. Her lips press to mine, sweet with traces of champagne. I'm still too surprised by her presence to stop her. She kisses me for a moment and then steps back. Swaying her hips slightly, she saunters over to a billiards table and perches herself on it.

"Well? Aren't you glad to see me?"

"Yes. It's just that I didn't expect—"

"I'm not so sure I'm glad to see you, Lon. You've been avoiding me awfully."

"No, I—"

"Maybe I ought to get myself another beau," she says, examining her nails. "One who pays me proper attention."

I come toward her. "Fay."

"If you really cared, you'd take me out of this awful place and carry me off somewhere nice."

"I'd like to—"

"Dandy." She hops off the table. "What are we waiting for?"

Taking my hand, she leads me back into the dank little hallway and across the crowded dance floor. On the street, bustling with glittering nightlife, she calls for a taxicab with an ease I find surprising for an upper-crust North Shore gal.

A questionable-looking jalopy chugs up and Fay pulls me inside.

"Where should we go?" I ask, still trying to decide how I feel about her unexpected arrival and her increasingly forward behavior.

"How about the Ritz?" she asks slyly.

"That's where Ned and I are staying."

"I know that, silly," she says, laughing. "Where do you think Neddy put me up?"

"Oh."

Fay leans forward and taps the back of the driver's seat. "To the Ritz. Make it fast."

We lurch off, and Fay leans over to face me. The feel of her smooth lips on my face is familiar and exciting. She pulls my hand onto her thigh, tantalizingly close to the lacy band of her stockings. Her actions stir desire in me but also resistance. What's gotten into her? She's always made her interest in me clear, but never quite this forcefully.

Besides, while I care about Fay, I feel a strange loyalty to Cassandra. Something passed between us on that beach. Even if I never see her again, she left an indelible mark on me. And being with Fay like this but thinking of Cassandra is a betrayal of both women.

By the time we arrive at the Ritz, I'm starting to panic. The way Fay glances back at me as she leads me to her room only makes it worse. I can't pretend to not understand what she's hoping for. I need to stop her. Save her the humiliation.

"Let's go down to the pavilion," I say, pulling at her hand. "Grab a bite to eat."

She laughs. "Don't be silly, Lon." She saunters ahead and pulls out the key to her room. "We'll just order some room service."

With a smile, she pushes open the door. I start to follow but freeze in the doorway. Fay sits on the red settee nearby, stretching out her legs in a relaxed but seductive pose.

"Aren't you coming in? I'm getting a draft from that open door."

I grip the door frame. "I don't think I ought to, Fay."

Her brow lowers. "Ought to what?"

"It's best if we call it a night."

She sits up, her face bright with anger. "Excuse me?"

"I'll call on you in the morning."

I don't dare meet her eyes as I turn away. It does pain me to hurt her like this. She deserves a man who'll worship her like she desires. That man, however, can't be me.

She calls my name, sharply, but I close the door, wincing. I stride down the hall, praying she doesn't follow me. She doesn't. I think she's too shocked at the blatant rejection. With a heavy heart, I go up the six floors to the suite Ned and I share.

As I approach, I notice a strip of light gleaming beneath

the door. Ned's back. I guess he's had enough bad hooch and jazz.

Raised voices drift out into the hall. I pause, my hand on the doorknob.

"We had a deal. You can't back out now."

It's difficult to make out the words, and I can't tell if it's Ned speaking or another man.

"I need more time," a different, indistinguishable voice says.

"You've had your time."

The voices lower to an indecipherable level. I put my ear to the door and then suddenly feel ashamed of standing here eavesdropping. With a frown, I turn to go. Perhaps I'll take a stroll around the hotel lobby, give Ned some time to finish up his meeting. I've only made it halfway down the length of the hallway, however, when I hear the door open behind me. I turn toward the nearest door, pretending to be just leaving a room. A short, broad man passes without so much as a glance. He's well dressed and older, but there's a hardness in his eyes. I have no idea what business he has with Ned, but something about it troubles me.

When I open the door to our suite, Ned is sitting on the plush sofa, smoking a cigarette, and staring at a stack of papers. His whole body tenses as I enter.

"Lonnie?" His surprise quickly becomes a scowl. "What are you doing back?"

My mind is still buzzing with everything that's happened in the past hour. When I don't immediately respond, Ned stamps out his cigarette in the little glass tray.

"Dammit, Lon. Why aren't you with Fay?" His anger throws me off completely.

"Where is she?" he demands. "I was told you'd taken her back to the Ritz."

"I did. She's in her room."

"And you didn't stay?"

"I..."

"You what?"

"I just felt like coming back, that's all."

"What's wrong with you, boy?" Ned growls.

I've never seen him lose his temper like this. I'm not sure if the meeting I overheard put him in a foul mood, or something else.

"Is Fay not good enough for you?" he demands.

"N-no. That's not it at all."

"Then what is it, pray tell?"

His tone rankles me. "What's it to you, whether or not I go with Fay?"

He scoffs and scrapes a thick hand through his hair. "I don't think you quite understand what's expected of you, Lon."

"You're right. I don't. What is expected of me?"

"You and Fay will be married. It's all been discussed."

I stare at him for a moment, not sure if he's kidding around or crazy. "Discussed? With whom?"

"Your father approves of the match. As do Fay's parents."

"I haven't heard a word from my father this whole summer."

"That's because he trusts my damn judgment," Ned says, slamming his fist on the coffee table.

A charged silence fills the room. But before I can grasp what I might say, Ned releases a shaky breath and rubs his face. He stands. His expression calms.

"You've had a long night. Both of us have."

I nod, still trying to understand what's gotten into him, but I'm too tired pursue it. "I'll turn in."

Ned calls my name as I reach the door to my room. I pause in the doorway.

"You must use your head about these things," he says. "You're a smart lad. A lot of people expect great things from you." His brow furrows. "You will marry Fay Cartwright. By the end of the summer. Set your mind on that fact."

CHAPTER 15

Cassandra

I should have seen this coming. The ultimate test of my resolve. After all my big talk about preserving the time-space continuum, now I find myself sitting on the back porch in the early morning, staring at the pathway to the beach.

I know I shouldn't do it. I should stand my ground. Telling Lawrence what I know might set off the butterfly effect. And who knows what could happen next? What if the next person to vanish from existence is Mom or Frank or Eddie?

It's nearly dawn. Above me, the clouds are a swirl of silver, steely blue, and watered pink with the early light. Closing my eyes, I picture the way the beach would look right now, the water all soft and metallic, the sand pristine and cool. Unbidden, the image of Lawrence appears near the shore. He's waiting for me. Once again, I can see him taking me into his arms and pressing his lips to my cheek.

I push my hands to my eyes, bending over into my lap. This is torture. I've spend the last forty-eight hours going back and forth about what to do. And no matter how many times I come to the proper, logical conclusion, my emotions always take over.

How can I not go to see him again? Am I really supposed to know what I know and simply carry on as usual? Can't I see him once more, just to say good-bye?

Those questions always lead to the one overwhelming dilemma.

How can I not tell Lawrence that he's going to be killed?

Honestly, how am I supposed to keep this information to myself? The guy has less than two weeks to live. He ought to know. Maybe if he knows, he can avoid it. *Murdered.* The word sends a churning sensation through my stomach. I grip two fistfuls of my hair and try to breathe.

I envision the beach again, all watery blue in the dawn light, and this time imagine a bloodstain spreading across the sand.

And in that moment, my body makes the decision for me. I'm on my feet. I'm walking across the cold, wet grass. I'm going to the beach, and all the reason in the world can't stop me.

As I pass through the bushes, the air takes the heavy, surreal quality of a dream. A nightmare. Calm down, Cass. He's probably not even going to be there. If he is, you have no idea what you're going to say, what you're going to do. You're insane to keep walking, but you knew that already. He's not going to be there. He's…

Not there.

The beach is empty. Like it always is. Rocks. Water. That's it.

My feet drag out a few steps. I close my eyes. I can't be surprised about this. I told him I'd never come back to the beach.

Despite what he said, he obviously gave up hope that I would change my mind. Coming out here today was futile.

I flop onto the ground, trying hard not to cry. But I'm sitting in the spot where we first met. My fingers trace a line in the cold, gray sand, every part of me aching.

Then I notice the wide indent. It's a footprint. Men's shoes.

Frank hasn't come out here since we moved in. And no one else would be walking around in men's shoes.

It was him! He was here. Swallowing hard, I hover over the print, touching it lightly with my hand. It's old. Probably made yesterday.

I look to the bushy path. Wind pulls strands of hair across my face, but no one's there. I missed him. One day late, and I missed him.

I could scream. Falling back on my knees, I swipe my hand over the shoe print, sending the sand flying to the wind. Curse me and my stupid hesitation.

"Ughhhhhhhhhhh," I say loudly, smashing my fists to my forehead. "You suck, Cass."

I sit for a long time, partly out of despair, partly out of a crazy hope that he'll come. The waves break against the sand: curling, crashing, rushing up the shore in white, lacey foam, and then pulling back to the sea. I watch the pattern repeat itself until I've lost count. I wait, hating myself more each minute for missing my chance. My chance to say good-bye. A chance to help him.

But Lawrence doesn't come. I finally have to accept the reality that he's gone for good. My legs feel heavy as I pull myself up. I don't bother to brush the sand from my knees. I'll carry it back to the house—my last memento of this place. Because one thing's for sure, I'm never coming back.

The sound of footsteps rustling through the bushes bursts through my somber silence like a firecracker. I spin around.

It's Lawrence. The sight of his warm brown eyes and tall, lean frame shatters me. He's dressed in a light khaki shirt and dark slacks, his sandy hair tousled. He's even more beautiful than I remembered. His eyes light up with surprise, and then a heartbreakingly joyful smile spreads across his face.

"You came back!"

I rush to him, unable to speak. Lawrence runs faster, closing the gap between us. All I can feel is the thud of my heart. All I can see is the faintly blurred print from the Crest Harbor Sentinel: "Following the tragic murder of his nephew, Lawrence Foster, on the property's private beach."

"I can't believe it," he says, beaming. "I came every day, hoping against hope that you'd change your mind."

Tears sting my eyes. *Keep it together, Cass. Keep. It. Together.*

Lawrence grips my arms. "Is it really you? Or are you some beautiful vision coming to torment me?"

This makes me smile in spite of the agony inside. "It's almost like you're happy to see me, Lawrence."

"Happy is an understatement," he says, beaming.

I should go. I've seen him now, and every second that I stand here in front of him, I feel the weight of the information I know. I should walk away while I still can.

"What made you change your mind?" he asks.

"It's a long story."

"I know what you mean." Suddenly his expression shifts to seriousness. "I thought about you every day, Cassandra. You have no idea how glad I am that you came back."

I'm not sure how much of this I can take. I'm going to break. Any second, I'm going to break.

"Cassandra."

"Yes?" My voice breaks.

"Will you walk with me for a bit?"

Once again, logic is shattered by the hammer of emotion. "Sure."

Lawrence holds out his forearm for me. I've seen enough old movies to know why. I lace my arm in his. He tucks it close. A rush of pleasure zips through my stomach. Being around him again, touching him, smelling the faint tinge of his vintage cologne, fills me with a dangerous amount of happiness.

It's still a beautiful morning. Perhaps a bit cooler than it should be at the end of July. Two gulls cry at each other as they swoop overhead. I wonder which world they come from, Lawrence's or mine. Or are they also separated by a century of time? For some reason, thinking about it depresses me.

Lawrence leads us toward the far point, where the waves are most tumultuous.

"I don't think a week has ever felt so long," he says as we walk slowly.

"I know what you mean."

He smiles, but this only twists the blade deeper in my gut.

He doesn't deserve to die. Not in a homicide. It can't be true. Why does it have to be true?

We come to a rocky ledge at the base of the point. Lawrence climbs up, then holds out his hand to help me up. I wobble a little on my climb, nearly slipping. He grabs for my other hand. As he helps me to the higher ledge, we're face-to-face for a moment. Separated by little more than a breath. My eyes fall to his lips, but I force myself to step away.

"You're pretty quiet," Lawrence says as we head to the end of the point. "Is something wrong?"

Yes, Lawrence. Yes. The worst possible thing. The words scream in my head: "following the tragic murder of his nephew, Lawrence Foster, on the property's private beach."

"I'm fine," I say weakly.

His eyes sweep over my face. He can see I'm holding something back. I force a little smile and lead on, inwardly kicking myself. I can't be weak. I've been through this in my mind, assessing every possible path. You can't cheat death. It's a fact. And you can't mess with fate. Telling Lawrence that he's going to die less than two weeks could set into motion the very events that will bring it to pass.

I close my eyes and try to breathe. I will be strong. I'm not going to tell him. I'm just going to spend a little bit longer with him, say good-bye, and move on with my life.

Waves slam against the craggy rocks at the tip of the point. With each thundering crash, a faint mist of water tingles on my skin. Wind bites at me, but the view of the shore, stretching for miles in either direction, makes the elements worth braving.

Lawrence finds a somewhat smooth patch of rock near the edge and sits. I hesitate but ultimately can't resist sitting down next to him. He scoots closer, smiling, and I have to fight the impulse to nuzzle my face into his shoulder. The desire to feel his arms around me rages through my heart. I stare out at the horizon to keep from bursting.

"I'm facing a crossroads," Lawrence says, also looking out over the water. "A decision has been pushed on me, and I don't know what to do."

"A decision about your career?"

"And other things..." He sighs. "My choices are to accept my family's plan for me or I'm kicked to the street."

"It's wrong," I say, shaking my head. "They should let you decide how you want to spend your life."

He smiles ruefully. "I wish I lived in your time. I can't imagine having that freedom."

"I wish you had it. You deserve better."

He scrapes a hand through his hair. "I'm not sure I do. That's part of the problem. I'm willing to accept the responsibilities that come with my life of privilege. Without my father's money, I'm nothing. I should be grateful that practicing law is even an option for me, rather than, say, digging coal out of the ground a mile under, or breaking my back behind a plow. Is it wrong to live the life people expect of you? To please the people who helped make you who you are?"

I shake my head. “But you’re still entitled to your dreams. Being rich doesn’t exclude you from that.”

“My old man thinks dreams are a waste of time. Work is the only thing that matters.”

“You don’t believe that, do you?”

He sighs. “I guess not. Otherwise I wouldn’t fill notebooks with my writing when he thinks I’m asleep.”

“You deserve to follow your dreams, Lawrence.” My eyes sting with tears as I speak the words, knowing he’ll never get the chance. He sets his hand beneath my chin, turning my face to him. His intensity melts me.

“In my mind, you have come to embody those dreams,” he says softly. “A girl from another time. Who only exists on one windswept beach. You’re a poem, Cassandra. You’re my poem.”

He takes my hand and presses it to his chest. My heart is pounding so hard that I can barely breathe.

“I feel like, if this is real, then my dreams can be real. If these feelings I have for you are truth, then the truth of my words is worth fighting for, and it doesn’t matter what people expect of me.”

Lawrence sets his hands on my face. His fingertips slide gently into my hair. My ears are ringing. I shouldn’t let this happen. But everything in me longs for it.

Lawrence’s gaze brushes over my face, tender and hungry at once. And then he presses his lips to mine.

For a moment, there’s only the crash of surf, the clean smell of cologne, and the burning heat of this kiss.

We part. Then, like magnets, our lips come together again. I turn fully to him, hooking my arms around his neck. He grips my back. Our breathing rises and joins in unison. I want more. I want to lose myself.

But then the inevitability of Lawrence's death seizes me.

He keeps kissing me, but I freeze. These lips, this hair, those eyes—they'll be gone forever in a matter of days. Less than two weeks.

I pull away. Lawrence looks dazed. His cheeks are flushed. I push to my feet. The truth bears down on me, oppressive and overwhelming. I can't breathe.

I have to tell him. He deserves to know. I would want someone to have the courage to tell me if they knew I was about to die. I have to do the hard thing and tell him or break under the weight of this secret.

Lawrence stands, his brow furrowed. "Cassandra? What's wrong?"

"I can't..." Tears burn in my eyes. I can't meet his gaze or I'll lose it. I shake my head, trying to find a breath, let alone the words to tell him he's going to die.

Lawrence cups my face in his hands. His expression is so earnest, so caring. "What's wrong?" he asks. "Is it the kiss? I shouldn't have done it, should I? It was taking advantage of you."

"No. It's not that."

He pulls me into his arms, and I don't resist. I can't. I lay my face against his shoulder. His body feels firm and warm against mine. Can't we just stay here together? Why does he have to die? Why?

"What is it, then? Tell me, Cassandra. Please."

"I know something. Something that's going to happen… to you."

He's quiet. I push through the wall of resistance in my heart. I have to do this. "I came across a newspaper from your time. At the library."

I reach for the words. They're there, but they refuse to pass my lips.

"You look like you've seen a ghost," Lawrence says softly.

The perfectly horrible, perfectly correct words to say. *I am looking at a ghost, Lawrence.*

"Tell me," he says again.

Drawing in a sharp breath, I press my face to his shoulder. The horrible words come out in a trembling whisper. "It says… that you will…die. There. On our beach."

I've done it. I've broken the one rule I know I shouldn't break. And yet I don't feel regret as much as a horrible emptiness.

Lawrence pulls me back a little to look into my eyes. "You must be mistaken," he says, but he doesn't sound very convinced. My oracle-like words seem to have rattled him.

I shake my head. "You have no idea how much I wish I *were* mistaken. But I cross-referenced with a few other newspapers to confirm. It happened. It…will happen. In ten days."

Lawrence stares out at the ocean. "Good God."

Nothing could hurt me more than the look on his face. Fresh tears sting my eyes.

"I'm so sorry, Lawrence. I had to tell you. I know it goes

against everything I said before. I know we shouldn't mess with time, but we can't let it happen."

A dazed, distant look glazes over his eyes. The color drains from his cheeks. "I don't..." His voice fades into the wind. He looks back toward the house, voice trembling. "I have to go."

"Lawrence, wait!"

But he doesn't turn back. As he staggers back toward the beach, I realize I'll probably never see him again.

CHAPTER 16

Cassandra

My cell phone rings just after noon. I'm still in bed. Not asleep. I'm lying under the covers with my eyes closed because they're sore from crying. It's been a day and a half since I last saw Lawrence. Not even two days since I told him, and yet it feels like two years.

So when the ringtone blasts into the silence of my room, I spring out of bed, hoping it's him. Then I remember that it couldn't possibly be him and my heart sinks. It's Jade. I consider letting the call go to voice mail, but at the last second I answer.

"Hi, Jade."

"Hey there," she says. "You haven't sent me ten texts a day lately. So I figure you're either finally having a good time or you've died in some tragic accident."

Funny she should mention tragic deaths…

"Please tell me you found yourself some New England hottie to pass the time."

"Ha," I say bitterly.

"Come on, Cass. You're telling me you can't find one acceptable member of the male species out there?"

"I'm not telling you that."

"So you found a guy then?"

I flop back on my bed, staring at the ceiling.

Jade interprets my silence. "Oh my gosh," she gasps. "You did, didn't you? You totally got yourself a boyfriend!"

"I wouldn't call him a boyfriend exactly."

"Cass! This is fabulous!" She sighs. "Summer love. *C'est magnifique!*"

Her joy only twists the knife in my gut.

"Tell me everything," Jade says. "I want every minute detail."

I wish I could tell her. But there's no point in trying to explain how I'm falling for a guy from 1925. Still, I ache to share this grief with someone.

"He's amazing," I say.

Jade gives a happy little squeal. I close my eyes and picture Lawrence. "Trust me when I say you've never met anyone like him. He's smart, deep…different."

"And hot? Is he hot?"

"Very."

"I'm stunned. Seriously. I'm so happy for you, Cass."

"Well, don't be. It's all over now."

"What?"

I turn over on the bed. Through the closed curtains of my window, I can see a single line of sunlight. The same sun shining on the beach. The same sun shining on 1925 and Lawrence.

"We broke up."

"Why?"

"Because. It's complicated. Trust me."

Jade sounds outraged. "You have to tell me. What guy in his right mind would break up with you?"

"He didn't. Not really. It wasn't like that."

"Well, what was it like?"

I search for the words to most closely convey the situation. "He's…leaving in nine days. And I'll never be able to see him again. Or talk to him."

"Why? Is he going to Mars or something? Good grief, Cass, I'm sure he'll have a cell phone."

"He just won't, okay? It's not his fault. That's just the way it is. We decided we might as well cut it off now. Before anyone gets hurt."

Jade is quiet for a moment. Then I hear her scoff in the angry way she does when faced with social injustices.

"That's ridiculous, Cass. And you know it."

I flop my face on the pillow. It's pointless to try to explain this to her.

"If you guys care about each other, you fight for it," she says. "I don't know what these insurmountable reasons are for you never being able to see each other again, but A, it's not for nine days, so why aren't you enjoying every last second together? And B, since when are you the type to give up?"

"There are some things you just can't fight, okay?"

Jade scoffs. "The Cass I know wouldn't let anything stop her if she'd found real love."

Her words needle right into my heart. I squeeze back the tears. "I have to go. My mom's calling me."

There's a silence. Knowing Jade, she's probably forming some final, poignant line that will cut into my soul, and I just can't handle that right now.

"I'll call you later," I say, and I press the button to hang up.

But the screen doesn't go blank. Frowning, I look down. Another call has come through right as I ended with Jade, and I've answered it. I put the phone up to my ear.

"Hello?"

"Hey, Cass."

It's Brandon. How perfect.

"Oh…hi, Brandon."

"Just calling to remind you about the lacrosse game. The other night at dinner, you said you'd come. I didn't hear anything from you this week, so I wanted to make you sure you remembered."

"Right. Um…about that—"

"It's gonna be really awesome. My friend Sara's going to save you a seat right up front. Then we're grabbing dinner at Reed's after."

"It sounds great, but—"

"Then you're coming?"

"Well…"

"I talked to your mom earlier. She's cool with it. She said

you'd mentioned it and wanted to go. I'll pick you up at six, okay?"

I smack my hand on my forehead and drag it wearily down my face. This day just keeps getting better. Now Mom's involved. She'll carry me out to the car herself if I show any resistance.

"Okay," I say, trying not to show my irritation. "Guess I'll see you then."

"Sweet."

"Supersweet."

Setting my jaw, I hang up the phone. Memo to me: Kill Mom when this date is over.

The lacrosse game ends up being just as dull and uncomfortable as I imagined. Sara's a reasonably nice person, but we have nothing in common, so we sit through the entire game with nothing but the most basic, necessary words exchanged between us.

Dinner at Reed's offers the first ray of sunshine in the form of a delightful cheeseburger and strawberry milk shake. My enjoyment is tainted, however, by two things. First, the entire conversation at dinner revolves around a heroic and detailed play-by-play of the game I just sat through. Needless to say, I have little to offer. The second problem is Brandon's uncomfortable closeness. He's practically glued to my side. I chalk it up to the tiny booths in the diner but fear that after we part ways with Jake and Sara, the behavior will only get worse.

Further proof of this comes when Brandon drives me back the "long way." It's a dark coastal road, barren of civilization. I'm onto his scheme.

"I should get back," I say, checking my cell phone for the time.

"It's only eleven," Brandon says. "Besides, I want to show you this really pretty spot. It's just up the road."

After winding around a few more curves, we arrive at a sprawling pullout overlooking the ocean. The dotted lights of mansions sprinkle across an otherwise black landscape. To the right is the shimmer of the ocean. Fragments of the moon lie across the water like broken glass. Brandon puts his car in park.

I turn to him, one eyebrow raised. "Really?"

"What?" he asks, a twinge of nervousness in his voice.

"Taking me to Make-Out Point, huh?"

"No! It's a great view, that's all."

I roll my eyes.

"I swear!" he insists.

"Okay, well, if you took me here to enjoy the view, let's get out of the car. You can see better outside anyway."

Brandon hesitates, but when I angrily fold my arms across my chest, he throws up his hands in surrender. "Fine. We'll get out of the car."

Slamming the door behind me, I march over to the stone wall. The sight of the ocean in the distance fills me with a flash of sharp joy, followed by familiar despair. I bet it's a beautiful night on the beach. What would Lawrence and I do tonight if we were together? A walk out to the point? A swim? Maybe a kiss? Even if we just sat together talking, it would be perfection.

My eyes slide closed. I think of Lawrence's lips on mine. Why? Why does it have to be this way? Why can't Lawrence be the one taking me up to the Make-Out Point?

"Nice night." Brandon's voice interrupts my sad thoughts. He comes up beside me, leaning against the wall.

"Yep."

He taps his finger on the rough stone. "Are you pissed at me, Cass?"

It's a flicker of the insecure, nervous Brandon from the Travis reality. I soften. "No," I say. "I'm not. I've just had a crappy couple of days."

"Is everything all right? You look…really sad."

He doesn't know the half of it. I shrug. "I'll be okay."

"What's wrong?"

"It's complicated."

"Is it about your stepdad and your mom? It was really hard for me when my parents got divorced. I know how it goes."

I nod. He might as well think that's my problem, since I can't very well say I'm mourning the loss of a boy I met from the 1920s who's destined to die in a week.

Brandon puts his arm around my shoulders. "I'm here for you if you need anything."

"Thanks."

He doesn't move his arm. I give him a sidelong look. It seems rude to tell him to keep his paws off me when he's being really nice. Besides, as lonely and down as I've been feeling the last few days, it's kind of nice to be hugged.

Noticing my lack of resistance, Brandon goes in for a bit more. He brings his other arm around me and pulls me to him. The strong, sharp smell of his cologne reminds me of Lawrence, and a tendril of guilt tugs at me. I shouldn't even be here with Brandon, let alone allow him to hold me.

But what difference does it make? I'm never going to see Lawrence again. No one will in a week. Am I never supposed to have another boyfriend out of loyalty to some guy I knew for a month in the summer?

Brandon's hand slides up my back, cupping my neck. His lips brush against my forehead. My heart aches. Lawrence isn't just some guy I know. He's special. I can't betray that. What I could have with Brandon would be easy, but it would never be real. What I have with Lawrence is real.

Jade's words ring in my ears. The Cass I know wouldn't let anything stop her if she'd found real love.

The realization settles upon me all at once. What Lawrence and I have…it's real. It's love. And Jade is right. That's worth fighting for.

This doesn't have to be the end. I don't know why I didn't see it this way all along. Just because the newspaper said he was murdered doesn't mean I have to accept that. Lawrence is here now. He's clearly not dead yet. We can fight this. We can make sure he lives.

With a start, I pull away from Brandon.

"Is everything okay?"

"I need to go home, Brandon."

"Um..."

He looks hurt. I have to think fast. "I feel really queasy. Like...I think I'm going to puke."

That backs him up quickly enough. "Oh. Sorry, I didn't—"

"It's okay. I started to feel it in the restaurant, but I didn't want to ruin things. It was really nice of you to take me out." I head for the car. "You'd better get me home though."

It's possible that Brandon doesn't buy my story completely, but either way, he gets into his car. I lie back in the seat and close my eyes to sell the sick routine.

We spend the drive back to my house in relative silence. As I play sick, my head spins with thoughts. Can Lawrence really fight this? Can I help? Can the two of us actually change the past? I'm itching to get to the beach and discuss the idea with him.

In the driveway, Brandon jams his car into park. I'm already out of my seat belt and opening the door. It takes everything in me not to run straight for the beach. I bend down to the open car window.

"Thanks for dinner," I say to Brandon.

He gives me a strained smile, as if he's pissed that the night got cut short, but he knows he can't actually be mad at me for being sick. "Talk to you later?"

"Sure," I say, already turning toward my house. "Bye!"

As I head in, I feel a twinge of guilt for lying and possibly hurting his feelings. But the fact is there are bigger things at stake.

Mom's sitting with Frank on the couch. They're both reading. When I come in, Mom looks up with a big smile.

"Hey, there! Did you have a good time?"

"Um, awesome," I say with a forced smile. "Really great."

Frank pats a place on the couch beside them. "Well, come on in and tell us about it, Cassie Pie."

"Actually, I was thinking I'd go out for a little run."

Mom cocks her head. "At this hour?"

"Yeah. I just need to clear my head. I would have gone earlier, but you seemed so excited for me to go on that date with Brandon."

"I don't feel good about it, Cass. It's too dark and—"

"I'll stay on our property," I say, perhaps too enthusiastically. "That was what I was thinking anyway. I'll run on the beach."

Mom gives Frank a hesitant frown but then sighs in surrender. "Fine. On the property. Nowhere else."

"Absolutely."

To keep from being a complete liar, I run all the way to the beach. I probably would have run anyway, but there you have it. As I burst through the bushes, my heart feels crushed with the weight of a dozen conflicting emotions. I long to see Lawrence again, but I'm afraid of how he might react to me now, knowing what he knows. I'm filled with hope at the thought of fighting his fate, but I'm also filled with pulsing, radiating fear. This isn't a small thing we're going up against, fighting the course of history.

The sight of Lawrence will calm me. That's what I need.

But the beach is empty.

I walk out to the water's edge with a heavy heart. Part of me knew he wouldn't be here. If I learned that I was going to be murdered on this beach, I'd stay far away from it for sure. I pick up a rock and toss it into the white-tipped waves. If I knew I was going to die, I think it would change a lot of the things I did. I can't expect Lawrence to be any different.

Despair pushes against me, though I try to fight it off. Maybe I shouldn't fight it. Maybe it's smart to acknowledge that I might never see Lawrence again.

I turn back for the house after a while. In my mind, I can almost see the faint figure of Lawrence passing through the narrow path. My resolve strengthens. Seeing him again would be worth any amount of pain. I vow right then to return to the beach every day and night until I see him again. Fighting for Lawrence means not giving up on him. Not now, not ever.

CHAPTER 17

Cassandra

I return to the beach the next morning. It's a hot day, with brilliant, white sunshine. I run all the way to the shore. And this time he's there. Waiting for me.

At first, I think it must be a hallucination. He's sitting on the sand in a white linen shirt. His hair looks messier than normal, but in a way so endearing and sexy that I want to bite my fist. When he turns, I know he's real. He looks pale. Dark circles ring his eyes. This is someone who has come face-to-face with his own death. The sight of him, so vulnerable and alone, breaks down any semblance of control I had over the situation.

I run to him and he jumps to his feet to meet me halfway. We collide in a fierce embrace. For a long while, we do nothing but hold each other. Then, he takes my face in his hands and kisses me. The feel of his lips pressing against mine fills me with trembling heat. I hook my arms around his neck, squeezing my eyes shut and trying to ignore the pain that still sits on my heart. The only thing that matters right now is this kiss.

Lawrence breaks away, winded and flushed. His eyes scan

my face, taking in every detail, and then he presses his forehead to mine.

"I was hoping you'd come," he says breathlessly.

My voice trembles. "I didn't know if you'd be here."

He holds me to him. "I've been waiting since before dawn."

"You have?"

"I didn't want to miss the chance to see you again."

I exhale, pressing my face into his chest and wanting to crush my very being into his.

"I've decided something," he says as he kisses my hair. "If I have to die, I'd be crazy not to spend as much time as possible with you."

My heart beats strong and fast. Being close to him like this, everything feels so perfect, so right. "I've decided something too," I say. "You're not going to die."

He steps back to meet my gaze.

"We're going to fight this, Lawrence. There's no reason we can't fight it."

His brows come together. "Fight it?"

"Yes," I say firmly.

He sighs. "And how will we do that? I'm going to die, Cassandra. You read the newspaper."

"But there's time."

"Yes, but if there were any way to stop it, you'd never have read about it in the first place. The fact that you saw that article means it will. There's nothing we can do."

I grip his shoulders. "I refuse to accept that."

"Refuse all you like. That won't change anything."

I want to shake him. "Don't be this way! We can beat it, Lawrence. You're still here. Alive. Talking to me. It's not over until it's over."

I grab his hands and lead him to our favorite spot on the beach. We sit side by side. He squeezes my fingers so tightly it almost hurts. He's afraid. How can he not be? "Does it say?" he asks, not meeting my eyes.

"Does it say what?"

"Does the newspaper say how I die?"

The question punches me right in the gut. It's almost as bad as telling him the first time. "Don't make me..."

"I want to know."

"I can't."

"Please, Cassandra. I have a right to know."

It's true. But even still, the words stick in my throat like drying cement. "Murder," I whisper. "It said murder."

The frightened look on his face crushes me.

"It doesn't matter what it says."

He gives a bitter, mirthless laugh. "How can it not matter?"

"Because it's not going to happen," I insist. "You're not destined to die this young. I refuse to believe that. I've given this a lot of thought. Maybe what's destined is that I was meant to meet you on this beach. I was meant to find that article. Maybe that's why I can see you. Because I'm supposed to save you."

He processes the thought wordlessly.

"See? Then everything makes sense," I say. "This summer, before I met you, I was lost. I knew something was missing in my life, but I had no idea what. Now I know. I came to this awful house so that I could meet you and save your life."

"I suppose it's possible," Lawrence says carefully.

"It's the only explanation that fits! But even if it wasn't true... even if fate had nothing to do with it, I'm here now and I can save you."

He sets a hand on my cheek, his eyes intense. "You really think so?"

I press my hand over his. "I do." I sound more confident than I feel, but I want to give Lawrence hope. We both need that.

He's silent.

"You don't have to believe me just yet," I say softly. "But will you at least let me try?'

"I suppose I can't stop you."

"Not really, no."

The corner of his mouth turns up in a half smile. "I think you might be a little crazy, Cassandra."

"A little?"

He laughs. "Okay, a lot."

"That's more like it."

CHAPTER 18

Lawrence

It's Saturday morning. I'm supposed to die on the fifth. I have seven days to live.

The thought strikes me the moment I open my eyes. What a way to wake up! Though frankly, I'm amazed I slept at all. I'd given up lying in bed at around one in the morning to sit out on my balcony, listening to the waves.

I've already run through the gamut of emotions—fear, sorrow, rage, disbelief, despair, punctuated with fierce stabs of hope. I have to trust that Cassandra can do what she thinks she can. This "Internet" they have in her time can give her vital information. And in this case, information is everything. We have the advantage of her being able to find out exactly what will happen to me before it occurs. That fact alone makes me think I might just have a chance. A chance to beat this. I dress quickly, eager to see Cassandra.

Ned is having breakfast on the deck with Aunt Eloise, who came to check in on her poor, lonely bachelor brother. It's warm and brilliantly bright outside. The wind carries the scent of sea and grass. I breathe it in, and it takes everything in me not to run out there right now. But Cassandra and I have agreed to be extra cautious to keep from arousing any suspicion.

Ned glances up from his paper as I sit. We've been on frosty terms ever since New York, though I can see he's trying his best to gloss over it. Eloise daintily pecks at her grapefruit, gabbing about what she'll wear to the party that Ned's throwing here next Saturday night. My attention jolts at her words. One week. That's the night I'm supposed to die.

"Oh!" Aunt Eloise says. "Morning, Lonnie, you dear boy."

"Good morning." I smile, quickly nodding to her. "Lovely to see you, Aunt. Now, what's this I hear about a party?"

Eloise beams. "Hasn't Ned told you? It's a big gala for your uncle's business. Some big mortgage, right, Ned?"

"A merger," Ned says with a chuckle. "You remember me telling you about it, Lon. We've finally sorted things out with Cooper Enterprises."

"Swell," I say, my mind spinning over this news. A party on Saturday night. I'm certain that's where it will happen. Someone at the party means to kill me. Unfortunately this opens up the list of possible suspects dramatically.

"Any fun plans today, Lonnie?" Eloise asks, sipping her tea. "Meeting up with your friend Charles? Or maybe our dear Fay?"

Ned's gaze flickers up, but when I meet it, he looks back at his paper.

"I'm not sure," I say, pouring myself some coffee.

"You should. She's been missing you, you know." Eloise smiles. "A charming girl, that Fay. And after all, Lonnie, it's not every day you get to meet a real New Yorker."

Ned shuts his newspaper abruptly, and I set the coffeepot down with a clink.

"What are you talking about, Eloise?" Ned says. "Fay's the Cartwrights' only daughter. Her family is from here in Crest Harbor."

Aunt Eloise munches her jam-covered toast, shaking her head. "No, I don't think so. Gladys Harper's sister's husband works with Jeffery Duncan, and he says that Fay is staying with his family for the summer. Up from New York for the summer. Says he thought everyone knew that. He says Fay was born and raised on the Lower East Side. A real New York girl from a New York family."

Ned scoffs loudly. "Well, I think Gladys Harper's sister's husband is full of bushwa."

"Why, Ned!" Eloise says, appalled.

He frowns. "My apologies, Eloise." He then folds his paper and stands. "It seems I have a rather low tolerance for idle gossip this morning."

He starts inside but then turns me a look. "Lon. Can I have a moment?"

I'm still so baffled by this allegation about Fay that I follow him without protest. Is Aunt Eloise simply spouting tall tales of the society hags? Or is this girl I'm supposed to marry even more of a stranger to me than I'd realized?

Ned leads me into his office and sits at his desk with a deep frown.

"It's rubbish, Lon. If I can teach you one lesson, it's to never listen to old gossips. They spin so many stories that they lose track of what's true and what's a lie."

I fold my arms across my chest. "Fay did seem pretty comfortable when she visited me in Manhattan."

"She's a comfortable kind of girl," Ned says.

I raise an eyebrow. "Well, I'm glad someone was on that trip."

Ned drums his fingers on the papers on his desk. He seems to be searching for the right words. "Listen, Lon. I've been meaning to apologize about the way I acted that night. I'm not your father, though I love you like a son."

This admission warms me a little.

"I'd just had a rough time, you see," he continues. "Bad business trip."

I immediately think about the argument I overheard in his hotel room. Not to mention the headlights I saw in front of the house at two in the morning. Then I hear Cassandra's voice: "murder." My pulse jumps. This could be my chance to get the vital information I need.

"Any trouble, Uncle Ned?"

He rubs his forehead but then forces a smile. "No, son. Nothing you need to worry about."

"You can tell me," I say. "It might be important. More important than you know."

Ned frowns a little at my cryptic statement. I lean forward

across the desk. "Is there someone in New York who might want to hurt you?"

"What's all this about?" Ned says, his face going red. "You've been watching too many talkies, Lon."

He's not going to give me anything. Maybe he wants to keep me out of it. Maybe he thinks he's protecting me. How wrong he is. I'm about to press harder when I notice the papers on his desk. They're stamped with past-due notices in angry red ink. Ned spots my gaze and flips a file folder shut, covering the papers. He stuffs the stack in his desk drawer, and I catch a glimpse of the name at the top of the file: Cooper Enterprises.

"At any rate," Ned says, trying to act casual. "I suppose I should be off. Have a few things to finalize for that merger."

"The merger with Cooper Enterprises," I say, trying to meet his eye.

He won't look at me. "That's the one, Lonnie." He stands, brushing off his suit coat. "You know, I'm having drinks tonight with Jerome Smith, the big cheese over at Cooper. You ought to join us. It'll be a good learning experience for you to see how business works."

I think of Cassandra anxiously waiting for me on the beach. "I'm not sure I'll be able to, Ned."

"Oh nonsense. What plans could you have? You're not going down to that beach again, are you?"

Tension snaps me like a whip. "I..."

But Ned seems to have made the comment glibly. He pats me

on the shoulder as he breezes out of the office. "We'll be in the library just after supper. I'll expect you to be there."

"You need to go." Cassandra is calmly resolute. It's rather endearing to see the change that's come over her since she decided to fight my fate. She reminds me of a lady detective in one of the dime novels I used to devour as a kid. No stone can be left unturned, no clue deemed trivial.

"I want to be with you tonight," I tell her, brushing my fingers through her soft hair.

"Later," she says. "This is more important."

"More important than spending my final week with you?"

"We've spent all day together. Besides, you'll have a lot more than a week if we take this seriously." She presses her lips to mine in a swift but wine-sweet kiss. "You do some digging tonight. Get me information I can use, and I'll be here on the beach, waiting for you."

I don't argue. The girl has me completely besotted. I head back inside to freshen up in my room. Looking in the little, round mirror on my wall as I comb my hair, I think about her, about the softness of her skin, fragrant as a rose petal. Like music, the first lines of a poem drift into my mind. My gaze falls to the blank sheets of paper on my desk. They're serving dinner downstairs, but a few lines can't hurt. I need to get this down.

I'm just scratching off the final lines of the poem when a knock raps at my door. I sit up with a start. The dim light from my window betrays a later hour. Who knows how long I've been writing? Ned's certainly wondering where I am.

"Coming," I call out as I jump up from my desk and straighten my tie.

Walking down to the library, I rebuke myself. Ned's bound to become suspicious of that beach with me going there so much. I have to be more careful. The last thing we need is for him to start paying attention to what I'm up to. And what if he really investigated those suspicions? It could be a disaster. At the polished wooden doors to the library, I resolve to be my usual, chipper self tonight. But when I step into the room, the sight I'm greeted with throws me for a loop.

I expected Ned and this Jerome Smith character, but the library is nearly full. At least a dozen men stand scattered about, sipping brandy and smoking Ned's best Cuban cigars. I don't know these men. They aren't Ned's usual crowd. These aren't upper-crust Crest Harbor men. They do seem to have money. Their sharp, tailored suits proclaim that much. But something about them makes me think they know their way around the rougher streets.

"Here he is!" Ned's voice booms across the room. "Lonnie, come on over here."

I force a polite smile as I head over to him, but my eyes dart from one face to another. In the corners of the room, I notice four men who have the unmistakable air of bodyguards. They're big and stone-faced and watching every move I make. My throat tightens.

Am I being paranoid? Has knowing that I will be murdered in a week made my brain turn everyone into a murderer?

Ned passes me a brandy, which I happily tip back. The warm, spicy drink sizzles through me, calming my nerves a bit.

"Lon, I want you to meet Kip Hawkins." Ned slaps his hand on the shoulder of the slight man beside him and gives me an overly jovial smile. "Jerome Smith couldn't make it. Had some business. You know how it goes."

I nod, though I can't help but feel the significance of this apparent slight, and it puts me all the more on edge.

Kip Hawkins extends his hand with an oily smile. "Pleased to make your acquaintance."

"Lon here is the one I was telling you about," Ned says, beaming. "Has quite the promising career ahead. Top of his class at prep school. And star of the basketball team too!"

"My uncle likes to exaggerate," I say, forcing a smile.

Ned laughs. "Nonsense! Bright kid, our Lon. With a bright future. College and law school, and once he's done with that, it's straight to the top firm in New York. Business law. Just like his old man."

Kip Hawkins nods and smiles. "Excellent. Maybe you can teach your uncle a thing or two."

Ned laughs loudly—too loudly—at the comment. "Ain't that the truth? Yes, sir, this kid's a champ. And a real catch with the ladies. Good thing too, because, boy, did he get himself a prize gal. Isn't that right, Fay?"

I frown, but follow Ned's outstretched hand. At his gesture, a crowd of three men near the fireplace glance over at us and then part. Fay is perched on one of the big, burgundy armchairs, talking quite closely with a big, muscular fellow in his twenties with black hair and olive skin. Italian, I think. When the men around them move, her eyes snap to me.

Fay always looks beautiful, but tonight she's dressed to kill in a tight, red gown that cuts low on the top and rides high up her slender legs. She takes a casual puff from a long, slim cigarette holder. The smoke curls like a white snake from her scarlet-red lips. With a little smile, she hands the cigarette holder to the muscular fellow she was speaking with. He doesn't take his eyes off her.

"Why, hello, Lonnie," she says, her voice more sultry than usual.

Ned laughs again and slaps Kip Hawkins on the back. "What did I tell you? Have you ever seen such a sweet little honey as that one?"

Fay rises fluidly from her chair. Without moving her gaze from mine, she glides across the room toward us. Every man here watches her. And how could they not? She positively oozes allure.

"Your nephew really is a cad," she says to Ned, coming to his side and linking arms with him. "He's been so busy studying lately. What's a lonely girl like me to do?"

My face feels hot. Suddenly I wonder if this wasn't Ned's plan in inviting me here: to throw me in Fay's arms again.

"Aw, Lon's not studying," Ned barks. "He's been spending all his free time at that ugly, old beach. You'd think this one were training to be an Olympic champion backstroker or something."

Fay's eyebrow lifts slightly. "Interesting. He's never mentioned a penchant for swimming before."

I scramble for a reply, but Ned talks over me. "You ought to take her out there, Lon. Yes, that's a swell idea. Go show Fay your beach."

Taking Fay to the beach is, of course, out of the question. Not with Cassandra waiting there for me. I try my best to appear as relaxed as possible. "I don't think so."

"Aw, take her," Ned says, his voice overly loud. He gives me a suggestive nudge in the ribs. "A little moonlight swim doesn't sound too bad, eh, Lonnie?"

Fay smiles. "Of course, I couldn't ruin my new dress, so I guess that means…"

Ned roars with laughter, and I decide I loathe him when he's drunk. The other men laugh too, and Fay smiles, enjoying every ounce of their attention.

"I shouldn't," I say, taking a step away from Ned. "It would be rude to leave the guests."

"Oh nonsense. We're just a bunch of old men talking about drab things."

I give him a pointed look. "I thought you said this would be a good learning experience for me."

Ned's smile fades somewhat, and a glint of severity comes into his eyes. "I've changed my mind."

Fay reaches out for my hand. "Do take me, Lon. I fancy a walk on the beach anyhow. All this cigar smoke is making me positively ill."

"There now," Ned says, the sharpness still in his face. "You take Fay out to get some fresh air."

A tremor of panic crawls through me. How would I explain Cassandra, waiting on the beach for me in her strange, future clothes? And worse, how would I explain Fay to Cassandra?

Fay grabs my hand. "Oh, come on, Lawrence. Don't be such a chump."

Ned's eyes narrow ever so slightly. He has the same look on his face that he did that night in New York. "Go on, son."

Fay pulls me out the glass double doors and I go along. I have enough to worry about right now, and angering Ned seems imprudent. Besides, surely I can stall Fay before we get to the beach.

"It's been ever so long since we were alone together," Fay says, her grip tight on my hand. "One would almost think you'd stopped caring for me."

I sigh. "Fay…"

She stops abruptly. Spinning around to face me, she puts her finger to my lips. "Don't speak, darling. Let's just enjoy the moment."

Her arms latch around my neck. There's something in her eyes I haven't seen before. Almost as if she can tell that I noticed, the strangeness vanishes, and she gives me one of her sly smiles.

"Kiss me, you cad."

Her lips come to mine, hot and urgent, and she presses her body against me. Fay's always been a forward girl, but there's definitely something different about her tonight. A force to her kiss. Almost like anger.

I grip her upper arms and peel her off me. "Stop."

She's breathing hard. "What is it?" I catch a steely glint in her eyes. "We need some privacy, don't we?"

She grabs my hand and pulls me toward the path and the beach. Alarm flares inside my chest like a light. It would wound Cassandra deeply to see me like this. And with the way she's acting tonight, Fay's sure to make some kind of scene.

I forcefully halt, jerking Fay's slender body toward mine with the inertia. She falls into my arms with a giggle.

"That's more like it." She kisses me again. Her tongue slides along the inside of my mouth. A flicker of raw desire heats in me, but I put it out. I don't love Fay.

As she grabs for my belt, I take her by the arms. "I won't do this, Fay."

"Why not? Why have you been turning me away? Is there someone else?"

"It's not that," I say. It would do no good to tell her about Cassandra, even if I did leave out the little detail that she's from a hundred years in the future.

Fay's eyes narrow. "I know you want me, Lawrence. You've wanted me all summer. Stop playing noble."

I pull my hand away. She laughs, but there's no mirth in her voice or on her face.

"You're pathetic. You're not man enough to take me."

I shake my head. "I respect you too much."

"You're a bad liar," she snarls.

She tries to kiss me again, but I pull her off. Then she starts to fight, trying to kick me and punch me with all her strength.

I struggle to make her look at me. "What's gotten into you, Fay? Why are you acting like this?"

"Let go!"

Her eyes flash toward the house. They're focused on something. Her lips form words, but when she notices me following her gaze, she cries out.

"No!"

I see him. The muscular Italian fellow from the library. The one who was speaking so intently with Fay. He's standing on the stone veranda. Watching us. I have the feeling he's been watching us the entire time.

And Fay knew he was there.

The stranger darts into the bushes, but it's too late. I stare at Fay. "Who is that?"

"You think I know?"

My grip on her upper arms tightens. "You were talking with him in the library."

"He's nobody. Just some rube."

"Why was he watching us?"

She smirks. "Maybe he thought he'd get a good show."

"You told him to watch us, didn't you? Why? Did you think I was going to hurt you? Did you think you weren't safe?"

"That would have been ridiculous, seeing as how you won't lay a finger on me."

She pulls herself free from my grip. She's struggling to look like she doesn't care.

"Fay. Talk to me. Tell me why you're being this way. Is it… lady troubles?"

Her eyes narrow. "You're a bastard, Lawrence."

With that, she dashes back toward the house. I stand there for a moment, still trying to wrap my brain around her actions. When I get back in the house, however, no one seems ruffled. Thank goodness she didn't make a scene. I search the room for the fellow who had been watching us. But he's long gone.

Gritting my teeth, I move deeper into the library. In spite of the upsetting events with Fay, I can't forget my real objective in attending this party. I need information about Cooper Enterprises for Cassandra. I won't leave the party without it. My suspicions remain, however, as I look around the room full of strange faces. Who can be trusted? No one, it seems.

My gaze falls on a man sitting nearby. He's dressed in a too-large business suit and is flipping aimlessly through the large atlas on the coffee table. He's drunk. Perfect.

I bend down and give his arm a friendly pat, putting on an easy smile. "Hey there, chum. Looks like your drink's almost gone. Want a refresher?"

He smiles. "Why sure, son. Thanks."

I refill his brandy quickly, scanning the room as I go. Ned's still talking with Kip Hawkins, and most of the other men seem distracted with their various conversations.

"You're a real pal," the drunk man says as I hand him a fresh glass.

"No trouble at all." I motion to the chair on the other side of the coffee table. "Mind if I sit down?"

"Be my guest," he slurs.

"Thanks."

He holds out a hand. "Name's Hank."

"Lawrence," I say. I take a casual sip of my drink. "So, you from Cooper Enterprises?"

Hank tips his glass in the air. "That's the one."

"High-up fellow? Or middle man?" I grin. "You'll pardon my nosy questions. I'm going to law school, see, and I'm real curious about the way these big businesses run."

Hank chuckles. "Sure, sure. No problemo." He takes a drink. "I suppose I'm high up, in a manner of speaking. I, uh, help oversee the under-the-table stuff, if you know what I mean."

The hairs on the back of my neck stand on end. Bingo. I try to appear nonchalant. "Under-the-table stuff, huh? Like what?"

"Oh you know." He swipes his hand through the air. "Stuff."

I manage a tight smile. "Dangerous stuff?"

He laughs. "Nah. Not dangerous for me. I run a tight ship over there at Cape Row."

"Cape Row?"

"The warehouse. Smith keeps us there in the shadows, by the docks so's the coppers think there's nobody there."

I take mental note of the information. Cape Row. Warehouse.

Hank stands abruptly. "Listen, I gotta get some fresh air. Suddenly not feeling so swell, you know?"

I jump to my feet. "Can I ask you another quick question?" He blinks blearily at me, which I take as a yes. "Who's that young guy? The one with the dark hair? Bigger fellow. Tall and thick?"

Hank shrugs. "How should I know? All them Cartelli brothers is hard to tell apart. Anyways, thanks again for the drink, kid."

He shuffles off, and I watch him go. Cartelli. I make a mental note to ask Ned about the family later. I don't know how the brother I saw fits into the picture, but it seems significant. And I suspect this won't be the last time I hear that name.

CHAPTER 19

Cassandra

Good librarians are always there when you need them. Or at least that's what I'm counting on as I march into the library for my first day of research. But as I burst through the front doors, my visions of an army of helpful researchers are dashed.

The library is packed to the gills with people. Some kind of party? There are vases of fresh flowers. A string quartet. And a huge banner reading "L. James Winthrop: Crest Harbor's Greatest Treasure."

It's the last thing I need right now. Every librarian is surrounded by people holding little plastic plates of hors d'oeuvres and chatting in polite mumbles. Don't they realize that I need help? Gritting my teeth, I spot a woman with an official-looking name tag and a bright-red scarf, and shoulder my way over to her. "Excuse me," I say, trying to convey in my tone that I'm not here to chitchat.

She turns from her conversation with an older man and smiles at me. I get right to the point while I have her attention.

"I need to find all the information I can about Crest Harbor in the nineteen twenties."

"You might want to start in the nineteen thirties," she says. "You're researching James Winthrop, I assume?"

I try very hard not to roll my eyes. What is it with people around here worshipping their petty local celebrities?

"Never heard of him," I say deadpan. It's a lie. Just to ruffle her feathers. I'm pretty sure we read one of his poems in English.

She looks satisfyingly offended. "I see."

"I'm looking for something else. A project for…school."

She points vaguely to her left. "Microfilm is your best place to start. On the basement level. East wing."

I nod and march off with a grimace. Thanks for telling me what I already knew. I guess I'm on my own with this one.

I set up camp in the microfilm section. There's no time to mess around. I have six days to find a murderer.

Six days.

Thanks to Lawrence, I have a few leads to research. Cooper Enterprises. Cape Row. And the names Jerome Smith and Cartelli. I can do this. I'm going to do this.

As the hours pass, however, it becomes clear that I'm trying to find a few needles in a haystack. Reel after reel of microfilm and endless articles filled with names and places that mean nothing to me. It takes me three hours to find even a mention of Cooper Enterprises, and it ends up being a fairly dull account of the company renovating an old textile mill.

My eyes start to blur. My mind wanders. More than once, I find myself staring into space, lost in visions of Lawrence. I'd give anything to hang out with him all day, talking on the beach and feeling his arms around me, his lips on mine. His lips trailing down my neck. His hands squeezing my waist. His tongue…

Focus, Cass. I have to focus. If I can find leads that will help, it's worth being here and not with Lawrence. By four in the afternoon, I'm not so sure anymore. A whole day spent researching with nothing to show for it. My eyes are dry as paper and crossing from information overload. I know staggeringly little for how much reading I've done. I'm not going to make any progress with my brain this fried.

Despair grips me. A wasted day. A day I could have spent with Lawrence, gone forever. I can't get those hours back. The thought makes me want to cry. I flop my head on the table.

"Can I help you with anything, miss?"

I sit up with a start. It's the librarian from before, the one I was kind of rude to. She doesn't seem to remember. Her smile is warm and genuine.

"I don't think so," I say. "I'm just having trouble finding what I'm looking for."

She nods knowingly. "It's difficult. Like trying to find a needle in a haystack?"

"Took the words right out of my mouth."

She glances at the stacks of microfilm boxes piled around me and then lifts one. "All nineteen twenty-five. Are you looking for something in particular that happened in that year?"

“Well, more something I think might have happened.”

“Have you considered checking a year behind or ahead?”

Maybe I’m delirious from hours of eye-crossing tedium, but I could swear I see a lightbulb snap on over her head. I must be wearing my emotions on my face because the librarian gives me a smile. “Good luck.”

I make a beeline to the drawers of microfilm. Drawing in a breath, I close my eyes, make a circle, and point to a drawer. March 1, 1927–May 1, 1927.

The first box yields nothing. Despair threatens again, but I swallow it down. The second one is also useless. But then, finally, in the third box, I have a breakthrough.

It’s a newspaper article discussing the arrest of several key executives at none other than Cooper Enterprises. My pulse quickens as I skim the text. This is significant. It has to be. Granted, it says nothing about murdering an innocent teenage boy, but they’re obviously a corrupt company, and this proves it. Who knows what they’re capable of?

I sit back in my chair, suddenly overwhelmed. The day has taken a toll on me. I feel exhausted but also deeply relieved. I need to talk to Lawrence, to tell him to look into Cooper Enterprises too. I gather up my makeshift campsite around the microfilm projector with shaking hands. My heart soars. Thank you, librarian lady.

I speed all the way home. As I pull up to the house, however, I notice a red car in the driveway.

Brandon. I push my forehead against the steering wheel. “Just perfect.”

Any hope of sneaking in unnoticed vanishes when I open the door. Mom and Brandon stand in the kitchen, directly in my line of sight. Mid-laugh, they both notice me.

"There she is," Brandon says with what I'm sure was intended to be a suave smile. "Feeling better?"

Mom's expression cools. "Where on earth have you been?"

"The library," I say, dropping my bags in a pile on the floor. "Like I said this morning."

"The library and…?"

"That's it," I say. "I went straight there and came straight back."

Mom folds her arms and raises an eyebrow. "You expect me to believe you've been at the library for eight hours?"

I sigh. Maybe I could make a run for the beach. I'll hide with Lawrence until my family decides I must have drowned and go back to Ohio.

"Maybe I don't want to know," Mom says. "I can't imagine what could possibly compel a teenager to spend all day in a library during summer break."

"Ask the librarian if you don't believe me."

Mom reprimands me by narrowing her eyes. "Well, lucky for you, Brandon here has convinced me to let you two hang out, instead of grounding you immediately."

This night keeps getting better and better.

"I brought that movie I was telling you about," Brandon says, holding up a DVD case.

This entire conversation is the last thing I need. My brain is fried and my nerves are frayed. There's no way I'll miss seeing Lawrence tonight. He's probably waiting for me as we speak. Brandon and his stupid movie are not going to keep me from that beach.

"Great," I say, forcing a smile. "I'm looking forward to it. Should we start in about an hour? You can go and...get Slurpees or something."

"Cass," Mom says, disapproval thick in her voice.

"There's some stuff I need to take care of. It's really important."

Brandon purses his lips. "I could go. I mean, if that's what you really—"

"That would be great."

"I don't think so," Mom says. She steps out of Brandon's line of sight and gives me a stern, why-are-you-being-so-rude look. "Brandon's been waiting almost an hour for you. Whatever you have to do can wait until tomorrow."

"It actually can't."

"It can and it will." Now I'm getting the behave-or-you're-grounded look.

I weigh the risks of defying her. Being grounded at this point would be pretty bad. Maybe I can rush Brandon out the door. Feign sickness again halfway through the movie. Lawrence will probably wait a while for me. Hopefully. I swallow a heavy sigh.

"Great," I say. "Let's watch then."

Mom nods. "I'll make you two some smoothies. How about that?"

"Sounds ginger peachy," I mutter.

Mom breezes off to the kitchen, and Brandon gives me a sheepish smile. "Hi, there."

"Hi."

"I was worried about you the other night."

I avoid his gaze. "Oh yeah?"

"You got so sick so fast."

"Yeah," I say. "It was kind of crazy."

"I've been trying to call you all day."

"I've been busy."

"Studying at the library?" Brandon asks, raising a sly eyebrow.

"Yes."

"And what are you researching?"

"What, are you Barbara Walters now?"

He laughs. "How about we start the movie?"

"Good idea."

He stands there awkwardly for a minute before I realize this is my house, and I should probably take him to the entertainment room.

I tilt my head to the side. "This way."

As we pass a back window, I can just make out the bushes near the beach. A fierce longing to run and meet Lawrence grips me. There's so little time. I should be spending every second trying to save him.

"Great TV," Brandon says, breaking my train of thought as he flops on one of the leather couches.

"Yeah," I manage, trying to sift as much of the irritation out of my voice as possible. "So…I'm pretty tired. Maybe we can just watch some of the movie?"

"Whatever you feel like," Brandon says with a grin.

Oh boy. I hope he doesn't think that was a veiled request to make out.

I put on the movie, despite my brain screaming with resistance. Stalling as long as possible, I stand by the TV, fumbling with the volume, the color, the sound quality.

"Hey, you in the front row," Brandon says. "You're blocking the movie."

I offer a token laugh, and he pats a place next to him on the couch. "Come on. You don't want to miss the beginning. There's a killer car chase."

"Sounds…awesome."

I sit as far to the side of the couch as possible, but Brandon slides next to me. He smiles, as if we're going to snuggle up. Where does he get the idea that something's going to happen between us? I assume I can ascribe it to this new, sans–Travis Howard alternate reality we're living in now.

As the movie plays on the screen, I fold my arms tightly across my chest to discourage any hand-holding action. Ten minutes in, Brandon's arm goes around the back of the couch. Two minutes later, as a gas truck explodes on the screen in a burst of orange flame, he slides it around my shoulders.

I give him a pointed look, but he just smiles. "Sweet movie, huh?"

I sigh and glance at the clock. I'll give this twenty more minutes before I claim exhaustion. Mom ought to be appeased by twenty minutes.

"You look really pretty tonight," Brandon whispers, his breath tickling my ear.

All at once, it hits me. I'm doing it again. Relapsing into the same way of thinking that held me in a prison of angst all summer. I've tried to be whatever everyone else wants me to be, convincing myself that it's what I want. But I know what I really want now. And I'm not going to pretend anymore.

I take a deep breath, sitting up. "Look, Brandon. We need to talk..."

He stiffens. "Okay."

"I think you're a really great guy—"

"Who wants smoothies?" Mom glides into the room, holding a tray with two big glasses filled with pink Strawberry-Banana Delight. *Excellent timing, Mom. As always.*

"Looks delicious," Brandon says, flashing a grin.

"It's my own special recipe. I won't tell you the secret ingredient. Let's see if you can guess."

I get to my feet, and Mom's smile fades.

"Cass? What's wrong?"

"I can't do this," I say. "I...have to go to bed."

Without waiting for a response, I run upstairs. I push my bedroom door shut and lean against it. I sit there for a long time. The stress is starting to grate on me.

Across my room, the sheer white curtain on my window rustles, caught in a gust of evening wind. I can smell the ocean. The beach. My jaw sets.

Snapping into action, I lock my door and scramble to turn on some soft music on my radio. The old row-of-pillows-under-the-blanket-that's-supposed-to-look-like-my-body trick seems a bit middle school, but I'm not above that. I tug a black sweater over my shirt and slide into black pants. Apparently I'm not above looking like a pathetic ninja either.

The great thing about living in a huge house is that it's fairly easy to sneak around. There's only one close call as I slide past the study, where Frank is on a late video conference with Beijing. I don't know where Brandon went, and I don't care. Mom's probably going to yell at me. Also don't care. As I break through the bushes to the beach, it's all worth it.

Lawrence waits in our usual spot. He turns, but instead of rushing toward me, he just studies me. I tug at my shirt, self-conscious.

"I look dumb, I know, but I had to sneak out."

"You're a vision, Cassandra."

Now, he comes toward me. The feel of his kiss is even better than in my daydreams. We spend the first half hour or so reminding each other of that fact. Every second in that library, every tense word with Mom was worth it if it buys me more moments like this.

The thought of the library reminds me: we have important things to discuss.

"We need to talk about Cooper Enterprises," I say as Lawrence moves his lips down the line of my throat.

"Do we have to?" he asks between kisses.

My eyelids flutter with pleasure. "Mm-hmm." I sit back a little. "I mean, yes. We have to talk. No more kissing."

"Well, that's no fun."

"We can have fun later. Right now, we need to discuss what I researched today."

"Or..." Lawrence pulls me close again. "We could kiss now and talk later."

I resist his embrace. "This is serious, Lawrence."

He sighs. "You're right. So, did you find out something about Cooper Enterprises?"

"Yes. They're trouble," I begin. "This article I found is from nineteen twenty-seven. It talks about how almost all the top guys at Cooper are arrested."

"For?"

"Crime. Mostly business related, I think, but the article didn't really go into much detail."

Lawrence frowns, deep in thought. "I could have guessed this. I thought I smelled a rat."

"It seems really serious."

He nods. "I'll do a little digging tomorrow."

I grab his arm. "Be careful. Don't go seeking out trouble just to impress me. I'll make out with you regardless."

Lawrence nods. "Very good to know." Then his smile fades. "But maybe I'm bringing trouble just by knowing this information."

"Don't talk like that," I say, cringing.

"I'm sorry. I don't mean to be morbid."

"This is useful information," I say. "And if we're cautious and thorough, it could be what saves your life."

He presses his hand over mine. "I want to believe that."

"I won't give up on you, Lawrence. I really believe this is my destiny. And maybe..."

My voice drops off, and he frowns a little. "Maybe what?"

"I don't know," I say hesitantly, looking down at my feet.

"No, tell me."

"It's just... I can't help but think..." The right words seem lost to me. "If fate is preventing us from seeing each other anywhere but on this beach, then maybe after I save you, we can see each other beyond this beach."

I almost don't dare look up at him. When I do, he watches me as if trying to understand. "You mean, you think we'd be able to travel into each other's times?"

My face warms. "It's a stupid thought."

Lawrence's voice is gentle. "No, it isn't."

"It is. Time travel is impossible."

"And yet, here we are, a hundred years apart and in each other's arms."

A thrill of energy passes through me, and our eyes meet.

"What if you're right?" he says. "Do you know what it would mean?"

"It means that you and I could be..."

"Together," he says softly, lifting my hand to interlock it with his own. "Truly together. With nothing keeping us apart."

CHAPTER 20

Lawrence

If I could, I'd spend every one of my five days left—every spare minute—on that beach with Cassandra. She's like a tonic to me, healing all of my fears. I want to sit with her, basking in her warmth and beauty. But life, unfortunately, moves on. And I have to present the appearance of normalcy to the people around me, one of them being Charles.

I agreed forever ago to meet him at the club today. I'd back out if not for the sobering thought that this might be the last time I see him. So, somewhat grudgingly, I dress for the day and head out to the sunny acres of Crest Harbor's most exclusive country club.

Charles is waiting for me at the bar when I arrive. Naturally. Sharp in a white linen suit, he sips a Bloody Mary and eyes a nearby table of well-heeled club girls. They peer up from under the brims of their cloche hats and giggle to each other.

"Too pretty for you," I say to Charles as I grab the bar stool next to him.

"Quiet," he mutters. "I think I almost have them fooled."

But just then, the girls rise conspicuously from their table and glide out to the veranda. A moment before they go, the tall, dark-eyed girl, the beauty of the group, glances over her shoulder with a challenging look directed at me, raising her eyebrow with a smirk. Then they breeze out.

Charles punches me in the arm. "What's the big idea, Lon? Isn't one dame enough for you?"

"Don't blame me, Charlie boy. My mama gave me these good looks. I didn't ask for them."

He harrumphs and then taps the bar. "Another of these," he says to the bartender. "And make it a double."

"A little early to get bent, wouldn't you say?"

"I'm carpe-ing the diem."

I put my arm around his shoulder and pull him away from the bar. "Sounds good, only I need you to help me carpe it in another way."

"Whad'ya have in mind?"

"How does a little Grade A spying sound to you?"

A grin pricks at Charles's mouth. "Why, Lonnie, you old rascal. What are you up to?"

"You'll see."

We drive along the coast, Charles gabbing my ear off about the latest girl he's going to woo. I try my best to be myself, but my hands are clammy on the steering wheel. I can see my act isn't working well. And as I pull into the grummier part of town, Charles's suspicions seem fully stoked.

"Say, where are we?"

I try to appear casual. "Cape Row."

Charles turns a sharp look to me. "Cape Row? What do you have in mind, Lon? Getting us killed for sport?"

"I already told you what I have in mind," I say. "A little spying."

"Spying on whom?"

"No one you know. Just some fella who works with my uncle."

Charles frowns. "Sounds dull. Don't tell me we're on some business errand for Ned."

"Not exactly."

I almost drive past the old warehouse, but then I recognize the strange design on the rusted side wall and slam on the brakes. It's the same design I saw on those red-stamped letters from Cooper Enterprises. My insides are flipping around like a fish out of water.

"This is it." Hands shaking, I pull my car behind a large pile of weathered crates and park. Charles eyes me quietly for a moment and then folds his arms across his chest with a grimace.

"All right. You gotta tell me what's going. For cryin' out loud, Lon, you look like you've seen the Grim Reaper."

He has no idea how accurate he is. "You could say that."

His expression is serious. "Tell me."

I take a slow breath. I know I can't tell him everything, but I suppose it would be nice to share this burden with at least one other person.

"It's hard to explain. I think my uncle might be mixing with the wrong sort of people. And I think it could cause trouble. Serious trouble. Danger, even."

Charles scratches the back of his neck. "Jeepers."

I nod grimly. "Come on. I want to investigate this place."

"You sure it's safe?" Charles asks, eyeing the ominous-looking warehouse.

"I don't know."

"Well, that's reassuring, Lon. Thanks."

I climb out of the car and he follows, sticking close behind me.

The warehouse to Cooper Enterprises isn't empty. At the far end of the building, workers are unloading a flatbed truck stacked with wide barrels. The foreman leans against the wall, smoking a cigar as he watches his men work. I grab Charles's sleeve, and we duck behind the warehouse.

"What are you thinking you'll find here?" Charles asks as we creep along in the shadows.

"I don't know. I guess I just want to get a feel for the place."

"I think we can safely write it off as dodgy."

We reach the back of the warehouse. With my stomach pressed to the wall, I peer around the corner. As shoddy as the front of the building looked, the back is worse. Piles of junk sit festering all over the crumbled asphalt. A large puddle of stagnant water reflects the silver clouds above, shivering slightly in the wind. And an old jalopy rots in a crown of yellow weeds.

Wait...

That jalopy. I recognize it. It was the one parked outside

Uncle Ned's house in the middle of the night. The realization grabs my throat, pinching off any breath.

"What is it?" Charles asks.

I press my finger to my lips to shush him. Only now do I see that I've brought him into a very dangerous situation.

"We have to split," I whisper. "Right now."

The sharp tones of men's voices cut through the air, freezing Charles and me in place. Someone steps outside. A jolt of nerves rushes through me. It's the man I spoke with in the library. The drunk one who told me about Cape Row in the first place. What was his name?

Hank.

He looks so different now. It's more than the crisp, white suit or slicked hair. It's the way he carries himself—it's clear he's ruthless and in charge. Was his drunkard persona all an act? An act to deceive Ned and me?

A muffled cry heralds the arrival of others. Two big, burly types step out dragging a third man between them. This one's hands are bound behind his back. A burlap bag has been tied around his neck, covering his head. Charles and I exchange a look. Charles's face is ghost white.

The burly men throw their captive to the ground in front of them. His head hits the puddle of stagnant water with a dull splash. He groans and rolls onto his back.

"Lon," Charles whispers, his voice trembling. "This is bad."

I shush him and turn back to the sight before us. A cold, deep sense of dread settles over me. But I can't look away.

The man with the bag over his head is sobbing, saying something, but I can't make out the words. Hank smooths his slicked hair and gives a muffled order to the two bigger men. One of them pulls something from his coat. Before I can even see for certain what it is, there's a fierce bang, and the man on the ground goes limp.

"Holy Toledo," Charles whispers.

I can't take my eyes off the man on the ground. A circle of red expands from the bag over his head. So is this what Hank meant by "under-the-table stuff." Cassandra was right. Cooper Enterprises is dangerous. More so than I ever imagined.

"Holy Toledo," Charles repeats, his eyes the size of saucers.

My whole body feels like lead, but I know we need to get out of here, and we need to go fast.

"Holy—"

I grab Charles by the arm. "Run," I say.

We dash back to the car. But what if those thugs saw my car? Other men could be waiting for us. Waiting to see who's spying on them. Or someone could be watching from inside the warehouse. The foreman with the cigar.

I grab for Charles again. "Wait!"

He's panting. "We gotta get out of here, Lon!"

"We have to make sure it's safe first."

We creep to a pile of crates near the edge of the building. Trembling, I lift my face just over the top of the stack.

The car sits where I parked it. Movement in the corner of my eye catches my attention. Hank strolls out of the warehouse, wiping his hands with a handkerchief. The two thugs follow close behind. If they walk another twenty feet, my car will be in their line of sight.

We have a minute. Maybe less.

"Now, Charles!" I say. "Run!"

I leap out from behind the pile of crates with such force that I nearly tumble headfirst into the asphalt. But then my feet hit the ground and I lurch ahead. Just behind me Charles is panting.

Shouts fly like bullets through the air. The men have spotted us. And if Hank has his wits about him, he'll know exactly who I am.

CHAPTER 21

Cassandra

I thought the first day at the library was bad. Today is torture. Maybe it's because I know what Lawrence is up to today. He wouldn't tell me any specifics, but I can guess. It has something to do with Cooper Enterprises, and right now, he should be staying as far away from them as humanly possible.

He promised me he'd be careful. And I promised him I wouldn't worry. I'm trying with every fiber of my frayed, somewhat damaged sanity to do so, but this is a difficult oath to keep.

Maybe impossible.

I just need to see him. I want to feel his warm pulse. I want to lie against his chest as it expands and contracts with air. I need to keep him alive. A prickly, chilling thought pushes into the back of my mind. What if we've already messed with the time-space continuum? Has Lawrence being aware of me and of his own potential death changed his actions, which have, in turn, changed the course of the future?

I waited for him for a solid hour at the beach this morning. Only the gulls and the gray waves broke the cloudy stillness. And I know, I know, he has to do what he has to do. But couldn't he at least come say a quick hello?

The ever-present knot in my stomach tightens. I'm not sure how much more anxiety I can take. All I can do is dive deeper into my research and pray for another breakthrough.

I'm lost in the glowing projection of microfilm when the scrape of a chair pulling out startles me to attention. Mom sits down at the desk next to mine.

"Well, well," she says. "You really are at the library."

I stare at her, incredulous. "Did you seriously come all the way down here to see if I was lying?"

"Oh, come on, Cass. You didn't expect me to buy your story wholesale. It seems a little hard to believe that you're spending your gorgeous summer days in the library."

"Well, I am. As you can clearly see. I suppose you can give me a little credit now."

She shrugs. "I guess I have to. What are you doing here anyway?" She examines an empty microfilm box labeled "December 1, 1928–February 1, 1929."

My hands tense on the edge of the table. It takes all my restraint not to snatch the box away from her. Must appear calm. Must not arouse suspicion.

"Oh nothing, really."

Mom's eyebrow raises, and I know I won't get away with that answer. My mind races. *Think, Cass.* There has to be something plausible I can tell her. In desperation, I scan the secluded lower level of the library for ideas. Think. *Think!*

All at once, it comes to me.

"It's something for Jade," I say with a shrug. "She's studying the surrealists in the nineteen twenties. I guess she thinks we could collaborate on a senior project for AP Art History when she gets back."

Mom frowns slightly, looking back at the box. I hold my breath.

"Well...it seems pretty unfair of her to ask you to spend your summer holed up in the library while she flits around Paris."

I swallow a sigh of relief. "It's fine. She's doing research in Paris. Granted, it's more entertaining, but *c'est la vie*."

Mom looks into my eyes. It's that "I'm trusting you to be honest with me" gaze that has leveled me many times before. And sure enough, guilt surges through me. I hate lying to her. I avoid it at all costs. But this is different. I could never explain this to her. At best, she'd think I was crazy and worry even more. At worst, she'd ban me from the beach. So I give her a smile and pat her arm.

"I'll be fine, Mom. You can go knowing you've done your motherly duties and checked up on me."

Her eyes narrow. "Okay, but I want you home for dinner. Five thirty. Not one minute late, you understand? And we're spending time together as a family after that. It seems like between this research business and your newfound love of running, I barely see you."

I bite my lip. Dinner is doable. Spending a night with the

family is out of the question. But I'll cross that bridge when I come to it.

"Sure, Mom. I'll be there."

She gives me a kiss on the top of my head. "Don't you study too hard, okay? School is great, but during the summer, you need to be out enjoying the world."

"Okay, Mom."

When dinnertime rolls around, I'm not ready to leave the library. But time keeps moving, no matter how much you want it to wait. I'd never before realized how precious a minute could be. An hour. A day. They pass by so fast, and you can't do anything to stop them.

I trudge up the steps into the main wing of the library. As I reach the top step, my eyes fall on a painting hung across the way. Light from the sunroom above has illuminated the painting despite the nearly hidden obscurity of its placement.

I can't say why, but I find myself walking toward it. It's a painting of a beach—not exactly our beach, but similar. Above the indigo water, a full moon glows. The light from the moon paints over the ocean and the shore in a thick band. Something about that moon pricks at my brain.

Wasn't it a full moon when I met Lawrence? In my mind, I picture it. I remember a pulse of light that seemed to flash across the waves, but I'm not sure if that really happened or if it was a dream. That whole first meeting feels like a movie that I watched happen to someone else.

I stare at the painting for a moment before leaving, a strange, disconcerted feeling coiling around me. As I walk through the automatic doors of the library's main exit, I toss another glance back at the painting. The pale circle of the moon in the painting stands out across endless shelves and stacks of books between.

Walking to my car, I pull out my phone and type "next full moon" into my Google app. A little moon icon pops up, along with the information.

The next full moon is August 6.

I draw in a sharp breath. August 6. The day after Lawrence is supposed to be killed. I stop in my tracks. What does it mean?

I need to go home and get some food in my system. I'm seriously starting to crack.

As I drive away, however, I can't help but feel that this is all somehow significant.

CHAPTER 22

Cassandra

Dinner has never lasted so long. Don't get me wrong. I love my family. Frank's up to his usual corny humor, and Eddie is his always adorable self. But all I can think about is Lawrence. The anxiety has been building all day. I have to see him soon or I'm going to go genuinely insane.

I'm almost done helping Mom clean up from dinner when Frank marches in, holding Candyland like a waiter presenting a gourmet dish.

"Who's up for an epic journey through a land of sweets and lollies and wonder?" he trumpets.

Eddie cheers. "Me! Me! Me!"

I ruffle his hair. "I'm afraid I'm going to pass. That Molasses Swamp really freaks me out."

"Nice try, Cass," Mom says, wiping her hands dry on a kitchen towel. "We agreed on some family time tonight."

"And we just had a nice dinner together."

"You're playing a round of Candyland," she says, calm and unyielding. "Not another word about it."

Eddie bounces in his seat. “Sit by me, Cassie!”

My gaze darts to the back door. I envision Lawrence waiting for me. Resistance boils inside me. But I can’t afford any more of Mom’s suspicion. I spread a tight smile across my face.

“Candyland it is.”

After three rounds, all of which Eddie magically wins (because Frank cheats), they finally release me to “go to bed.” Following last night’s procedure, I wait until I hear the click of Mom and Frank’s bedroom door before sneaking down the stairs and out the back.

I sprint toward the beach, certain that gravity will stop working at any second and I’ll take off like a rocket. Ahead, I catch sight of the path. A sight I’ve come to love. But tonight, I feel dread. An inexplicable urgency crackles through me. Too much time has passed without seeing Lawrence. Anything could have happened in the last twenty-four hours.

My lungs burning in my chest, I slam through the scratchy branches. The pound of surf and salty taste of ocean rushes over me.

Lawrence is lying on the wet sand by the shore break. Black waves tipped in foam wash over his motionless body.

My heart stops. The ground seems to fall out beneath my feet. I’m propelled forward in shock.

I’m too late. He’s gone.

But then he sits up. His eyes connect with mine, and he smiles easily. “There you are.”

I skid to a stop. “You’re…not dead.”

He laughs a little. "Not for five days, remember?" Then he stands. "Are you all right?"

"You scared the crap out of me. Do you have any idea how worried I've been today?"

With a concerned frown, he takes me in his arms. "I'm sorry. But I'm all right. See?" He hugs me tightly. "Flesh and blood. Alive as can be."

I press my face into his neck. The shock of thinking Lawrence was dead sends shivers through me. But I won't talk about it. I can only imagine what's going on in his head lately. No need to add any dark thoughts to the mix.

"Never mind," I say, hugging him. Only then do I notice he's wet. I pull back. "Were you swimming? In your clothes?"

He shrugs, grinning sheepishly. "I got bored waiting for you."

"I have never met someone so enamored with the ocean."

"Like I said, it's good for the soul." He takes my hands. "Come on. I'll show you."

His skin feels cold. Like dead flesh. A chill runs through me.

"Lawrence—"

"I'll hold on to you the whole time," he promises, pulling me toward the water. "And we won't go deep."

"We can't."

"Aw, don't be a scared Susan. The water's cold but bearable."

"No," I say, pulling out of his grip. He stops at the sharpness in my tone. I close my eyes, my pulse still racing. "It's not that I don't want to. But I just don't think I can have a good time until I know you're going to be okay."

Lawrence exhales. "Cassandra..."

"No," I say. "We have to work. Now, tell me what happened today."

A shadow crosses Lawrence's face.

"What is it?"

"You're not going to like it," he says.

His ominous tone makes my stomach twist. "Tell me."

Lawrence smooths his wet hair back. "Charles and I did a little digging around a Cooper Enterprises warehouse. We saw...things."

"What things?" I demand, grabbing him.

"I don't want you to worry any more than you already are."

"Are you crazy? This is important. Tell me now, Lawrence."

He scratches the back of his neck. "We saw...a man being executed. Shot in the head behind the warehouse."

Ice spreads through my chest. "Are you serious?"

He nods grimly. "We barely escaped."

My fingers dig into his arm. "You mean you were noticed?"

"It's not as bad as it sounds—"

"What are you talking about? Of course it's bad! These people are dangerous, and you being seen by them..."

My voice drops away, lost in the heaviness of the implication. Could Lawrence have just created his own fate? Or sealed it?

Judging by look on his face, I'd say Lawrence has already trudged down this dark road. I pull him into a hug. Seeing him this way makes my heart burst with a mix of sorrow and determination.

"It doesn't matter," I say firmly. "It's pretty clear that someone at Cooper Enterprises is responsible for..." I can't say the words. I pull away, heading for the house. "Jerome Smith. That was his name, right? I'll go look him up right now."

Lawrence grabs my hand. "Don't."

When I turn, his gaunt fear brings tears to my eyes.

"Don't leave me yet," he says, his voice soft, almost as if he's ashamed of the request. My heart breaks.

I fall into his arms and he closes me in a tight embrace. He holds me as if I'm his lifeline, as if I'm the lone railing that will keep him from pitching over the edge of a cliff. I hold him, overwhelmed by the heaviness of my task. Can I save him? Is there really a chance, or are we just kidding ourselves?

Lawrence releases a trembling breath into my neck. "Would you think less of me if I told you I was afraid?"

"How could you not be? I'm afraid too, Lawrence. So afraid."

His grip tightens. He's nearly squeezing the breath out of me. "I don't want to die."

Then suddenly he releases me. His expression is desolate as he stares out over the black, rolling waves.

"Forgive me, Cassandra. I don't mean to burden you with these thoughts. I should bear this alone. Like a man."

I grab his shoulders, forcing him to look at me. "You listen to me. We're in this together. Understand? I'm not giving up on you. And you shouldn't give up either. I was sent here to save you. I'm going to figure out who wants to kill you so we can save your life, and then we can be together."

I listen to myself and a dry laugh escapes. "Trust me, I would never be this cheesy if I didn't truly believe what I'm saying."

He pulls away. "Maybe you shouldn't believe," he says quietly.

I'm stung by his words. "What?"

"It's a fairy tale, Cassandra."

"Oh, is it? And what about this?" I motion to him and me and the beach. I take his hand and press it to my cheek. "What about this?"

He stares into my eyes, as if grasping for the thin strands of hope I'm offering. He sets his other hand on my cheek. I press my hands over his.

"If we can see each other," I say. "If we can touch each other with almost a hundred years separating us, how can you think it's a fairy tale that I'm meant to save you? It's fate, Lawrence. It's destiny. We're meant to be together. You need to believe that."

"I want to believe."

"You have to believe it. It's the only chance we have."

He exhales shakily. "Cassandra."

His lips press mine, firmly, hungrily, desperately. I meet his with equal force.

We stay there, locked in an embrace. Our kisses are a prayer of hope and longing. A desperate prayer to whatever force has brought us to this beach. A prayer to match the beauty and certainty of the waves that crash against our feet.

CHAPTER 23

Lawrence

Another sleepless night. Perhaps plain old exhaustion is what will kill me in four days.

But honestly, how am I supposed to lay my head on that pillow and drift away as if I know nothing? I'm staring death in the face. Sleep isn't really an option.

Last night, however, it wasn't despair and fear that kept me awake. It was visions of Cassandra. In the black hours of predawn, I walked the empty halls of my uncle's house, wondering how I deserved such an angel in my life. My delivering angel.

She can save me. I feel it in my very core, hope twisting and thrumming and alive in my heart. Why else is all this happening? I've never been one to think much about fate or divine plans, but Cassandra's theory is starting to seem more and more plausible.

And so early morning finds me awake and dressed with no place to go. Cassandra insisted she spend the day researching Cooper Enterprises. I still can't picture this "Internet" and "microfilm" she talks about. Sounds like a bunch of horsefeathers, if you ask me. But she seems to think it can help. I suppose I have no other choice but to trust her.

After grabbing a quick breakfast, I hop in my car and go for a long drive. It's supposed to clear my head, but it doesn't. All I can think about is Cassandra, about what would happen if we cheat death. Is it really possible that she could travel into my world, or I into hers? Such thoughts seem almost ridiculous to entertain.

But what if?

As I whir past the rocky cliffs and ocean, I picture a future with Cassandra. With her by my side, I'd keep writing. I'd tell my old man that I don't want to be a lawyer. I'd break free from the carefully sculpted life that's already been built for me and seek some brilliant, gleaming, unknown horizon. With Cassandra, I could do it.

I find myself on the overlook where Charles likes to take his latest squeeze late at night. The thought makes me grin. Parking my car, I step out to survey the view. It's much more spectacular in the daylight, but I suppose that's not really the point.

Leaning against the craggy stone wall, I conjure up visions of Cassandra. What would it be like to take her by the hand and lead her off the beach? See what she looks like eating breakfast in the sunny kitchen, her hair mussed from sleep? I want to take her to the opera and hold her hand as the lovers sing their final duet. I want to lie beside her in my bed and take her in my arms as we fall asleep to the serenade of crickets.

My breath trembles at these yearnings I cannot quell. I watch a pair of white gulls soaring high on the salty wind. They weave together in the radiant sky, crying out to the eternities. How is it that these birds can be together, but Cassandra and I can't?

A determination, stronger than anything I've ever felt, overcomes me. I won't live without her. By the time I get back to Ned's house, my dreams have filled me with a wild, pure energy. It channels into a single thought: the future.

Ned calls for me as I come inside, but I'm on a mission. I go straight for my room and burst through the door. I drop to my knees by my bureau. Hidden in folds of trousers in the bottom drawer, I find it. A small wooden box. And inside that, my mother's ring.

In the late-afternoon sunlight, the sapphire looks like a small star pinched between my fingers. A dozen tiny rainbows dance on the carefully cut lines, casting light around the room. It's perfect. Holding the ring, I feel a pang of sorrow. I wish Mother could have met Cassandra. She would have loved her sharp wit and carefree energy. The two are alike in many ways.

This was the first piece of jewelry my father gave my mother. They were too young to marry but still deeply in love. When Father went away to Europe on holiday, he gave it to Mother as a token of his undying affection in spite of the hundreds of miles between them. Mother always cherished it. Sometimes I think she loved it even more than the large diamond engagement ring that came a few years later.

A shadow falls over me, muting the ring's shine. "Why, Lawrence. For me?"

There's no mirth in Fay's tone. When I glance over my

shoulder, her eyes are as dark as storm clouds. Her legs are planted defiantly. She's completely lost her carefully perpetuated persona of sensuality. I stand to face her.

"Do you have anything to say to me?" she asks, venom simmering in her voice.

What can I possibly say? She'd reject the truth even more than any weak excuse I could provide. I should have anticipated that this moment might come. Sooner or later, I am going to have to address Ned's crazy idea that Fay and I are engaged. But now I'm at a loss for words.

Her lip curls with distaste. "Nothing, huh? You seem to have plenty to say when I'm not around."

I frown. "What do you mean?"

She stomps to my desk and yanks open the drawer. "I did some reading while I was waiting for you." She grabs a handful of my writings. The pages crinkle in her clenched fist. "Care to explain this?"

I grab her wrist. "Let go of those."

"You let go," she says. She struggles out of my grip, bringing her freed hand across my cheek with a hard slap.

I tense my jaw against the smarting pain. "I suppose I deserved that."

"I'll say you did," she snaps, her eyes welling with angry tears. "You've been giving me the runaround for weeks. And now I know why."

"I'm truly sorry if I hurt your feelings. However, you had no right to read my personal papers."

"I'm your fiancée!"

"You're not. No matter what agreement you and my uncle have come to."

"Who is she?" she shouts. "Who is this girl you've been seeing behind my back? Who is this Cassandra?"

I've never seen her like this. Fay's always so cool and in control. Always seductive and smiling. Always seeming to have the upper hand. She's beside herself now. And I can't help but feel that it's not just about me jilting her.

I touch her arm. "Fay—"

"Take your hands off me, you cad!"

"You need to calm down."

"I won't!" She pulls away, panting with rage. For a moment, she looks like she might strike me again, but instead she storms for the door.

I step in front of her, blocking her way. "Why are you so upset?"

"Why do you think, you idiot? I just found out my beau has been running around with some floozy."

"Don't lie to yourself. This isn't about me. You don't want to marry me, Fay. You never have."

"Proves what you know," she snaps, but her eyes won't meet mine. Her discomfort with even the slightest questioning of her motives sharpens my suspicion.

"I don't know anything about you," I say, narrowing my eyes. "I've never known anything concrete." She tries to shove past me, but I don't let her pass. "I had an interesting conversation with my aunt the other day. She seemed pretty convinced that you're a born-and-raised New Yorker, Lower East Side."

Fay's stare meets mine. She's speechless for a moment before she retorts, "Your aunt is nutty as a fruitcake."

"She knows someone who knows you."

Fay sniffs. "Is that right?"

"Jeffery Duncan. He says you're staying at his house for the summer."

"Never heard of him," she says, trying to get past me.

I block her again. "I always did find it strange that I'd never heard of any Cartwrights in Crest Harbor. That I never met your loving parents. Was never invited to brunch or supper or even tea. The fiancé of their only child, and I never so much as bumped into them at a party."

"You're ridiculous," Fay says. "You've cracked."

"And speaking of parties," I say, talking over her. "What about the other night at Ned's party? Who was the man? Why did you tell him to watch us?"

"I don't know who he is."

"You're lying. Is he your lover, Fay? You two were standing awfully close in the library," I say.

She shakes her head, looking bitterly amused. "You're unbelievable, Lawrence. He's my brother. He's been away on family business. He came to visit me."

I'm speechless. Fay thinks she's proven me wrong. Little does she know. All I can think of is what Hank told me before he stumbled away drunk. All them Cartelli brothers look the same.

"Your brother," I say carefully.

"Yes," she affirms with a toss of her head.

Somehow, I don't think she's lying about this. Looking back, I can see the resemblance.

"Your brother," I repeat.

"Like I said," Fay snaps. "Some of us are faithful. Some of us wouldn't dream of running around with anybody else."

"If he's your brother, then why is his last name Cartelli? Is that your real name? Fay Cartelli?"

The color drains from Fay's cheeks. Her eyes widen. Her lips part, but for a moment, no words come out. Then, with a firm shake of her head, Fay's rage returns.

"Ridiculous!"

"Is it?"

"Don't you dare try and change the subject, Lawrence. We're not talking about me. We were talking about you and your no-good philandering."

"How can I be faithful to you when I don't even know you?" It's a low blow perhaps, but not untrue. In the couple of weeks that I've known Cassandra, I feel like I understand her better than I ever have Fay.

"I've given you everything!" she shouts.

"Only your kiss. Never your heart. You keep me at a distance. It's like you don't want me to know who you really are. Maybe because you're really Fay Cartelli from New York. Why, Fay? Why are you pretending to be someone else?"

She pushes me with all her strength. "Let me past, you big brute."

"Please. I want to talk about this."

"No!"

"I'm begging you."

She shakes her head, but tears roll down her cheeks. "Leave me alone!"

I've never seen her cry. Not even so much as a glassy eye. The sight shocks me. Fay lowers her face, her shoulders shaking with sobs. Stunned by this show of emotion, I fold her into an embrace. She allows it, though I can feel the tension in her body.

When she calms, I ease her back and gently lift her chin so that her tear-filled eyes are level with mine. She looks conflicted, scared. I brush my fingers along her cheek, wiping away the streaks of kohl. She's undeniably beautiful. It's not that we didn't have some good times this summer. I feel like somewhat of a cad for hurting her. I don't want things to end like this. I take her hand.

"Tell me one true thing, Fay. Just one thing."

She searches my gaze, as if analyzing what to say. And then, all at once, her face hardens.

"I'll tell you one true thing," she says, her voice low. "You'll be sorry for the way you treated me, Lawrence Foster. Mark my words."

Glaring, she pushes past me, and this time I let her go.

CHAPTER 24

Cassandra

After another long day of research at the library, the thought of coming home to dodge suspicion at dinner makes me linger in my car long after I've parked it. You'd think Mom would be happy I was staying away from drugs or binge-drinking parties or whatever else most parents worry their teenagers will get into. But no. My mother is on full watch because her daughter spends too much time at the library. Who's the abnormal one here? Her or me?

When I finally drag myself into the house, however, only Frank and my little brother are there. Frank's making pancakes for dinner and letting Eddie sit on the counter to help pour the batter on the griddle. For a three-year-old, it's basically the coolest thing ever. When Eddie looks up at me, his big, blue eyes sparkle with delight.

"We're cookin', Cassie!"

I come over and ruffle his hair. "I can see that. You're doing pretty awesome, kiddo."

Frank flips a mostly burnt pancake high in the air and tries to catch it with the spatula. It flops back on the griddle, crumpled in a gloopy blob. Eddie giggles loudly.

"Nice one, Frank," I say.

He grins sheepishly. "What can I say? I'm no cook, Cassarino."

"Clearly. Where's Mom?"

"Having dinner with some friends."

"Some stuck-up society ladies, you mean?"

Frank just shrugs. "Hey, if that's her jam." He flips another pancake. This one tears in half. "How about you? Have a hot date?"

I sneak a glance toward the back door. "Actually, I think I might go for a little swim or something."

Frank smiles. "You've been spending a lot of time out there, haven't you?"

I go on alert. "Um, well, I guess. I-I really like swimming."

"I think it's fantástico," Frank says, swirling his spatula with a flourish. "It's nice that someone is getting use out of the beach. I always found it too rocky for swimming, but hey…"

"If that's my jam," I finish.

He winks and taps his nose. "Exactly."

"Well, enjoy your pancakes," I say, giving Eddie a quick kiss on the top of his head.

"Enjoy your swim," Frank says.

"I will."

In my room, I toss my bag on the bed and am about to head out, but passing the mirror makes me stop cold. Could I look any more disheveled? I guess a day of intense research doesn't exactly lend itself to glamour. Who knew?

I instinctively reach for a T-shirt and jean shorts, but another outfit inside the closet catches my eye. Hanging near the back is a pale pink sundress. I had written it off as too prissy, but tonight, it strikes me as romantic and feminine. I pull it on. Examining myself in the mirror, I find myself pulling my hair out of its messy bun. Loose waves fall over my bare shoulders. Grabbing my research, I run back downstairs toward the beach.

Halfway down the path, music wafts past my ears. I pause, listening, uncertain of the source. I find it when I reach the beach.

Lawrence has been busy. A deep red blanket is spread across the sand, held down by big, brass lanterns on each corner. Plates of food rest all across the top. And a gorgeous, vintage record player, the kind with the big, dark horn curling out the side, sits in the center. Scratchy old jazz music lifts over the soft sound of the surf.

Lawrence reclines on the blanket, reading a worn book and eating some funny-looking candies. When he notices me, he sits up. Then he pauses, seeming to take in every inch of me. The look in his eyes releases a swarm of butterflies in my stomach. I give the dress a self-conscious tug.

"I don't know why I—"

"It's lovely, Cassandra," Lawrence says, a smile spreading over his face. "You're lovely. Truly."

I blush and sit by him on the blanket. "So, what's all this? A picnic? Looks like mostly junk food."

"My favorite foods. Minus Starsparkles, of course, given that I'm supposed to forget they exist."

"You mean Starbursts," I say, laughing. "But I'm glad you've remembered your solemn oath."

He gives me a salute and then pops a grape in his mouth.

"You're listening now to my favorite music," he says, motioning to the record player.

I point to the book he'd been reading when I arrived. "Your favorite poetry?"

He nods, and then his smile fades. I touch his hand.

"I want to enjoy them all," he says. "In case…it's my last chance to do so."

I squeeze his hand. "It won't be. Don't even let yourself think it." I hold up the papers I brought. "Look. I did tons of research into Cooper Enterprises today. There's some really incriminating stuff. We've got our culprit. Here, look at this."

"Cassandra…"

"Just one second. Let me find this article…"

As I shuffle through the pages, Lawrence sets his hand over mine. He pulls the pages away gently and sets them aside.

"Not tonight," he says.

"We have to discuss this, Lawrence. There isn't any other time to do it."

"I know."

"It's not that I don't want to take a break, but we're down to the wire here. We have three days. Less than three days. We have to figure this out now."

A soft, thumping sound draws Lawrence's attention. It's the record player, reaching the end of the song. He lifts the needle gently. For a moment, he studies the four records resting against the player before choosing one. A women's soft, melancholy voice drifts out of the horn. Lawrence stands and holds out a hand. "Dance with me?"

"Lawrence…"

"Please, Cassandra. Just one dance."

We need to discuss my research. It's the key to keeping Lawrence safe. And yet I find myself standing. He slides an arm around my waist and takes my hand in his. Gently, he pulls me close, and we start to sway to the music. Lawrence moves with confidence and ease. He doesn't take his eyes from mine. He's different tonight. So much more intense than normal, and it's making me all fluttery. I can't stay with the beat, and I keep stumbling over the blanket.

Lawrence presses a single kiss on my cheek. "You're a pretty lousy dancer. You know that?"

"Hey! Do you want me to step on your foot?"

"More than you have already?"

"Careful. I have access to futuristic weapons that will blow your nineteen-twenties mind."

He laughs. "You're right. I don't know who I'm dealing with."

"No. No, you don't."

He twirls me out for a spin, which I only barely complete.

"I propose we be done with dancing now," I say, sitting down.

Lawrence comes beside me. "On one condition."

"Okay…"

"No more of this," he says, pressing a hand over my printouts.

"But, Lawrence—"

"Please," he says. "I know it's important, but it's not the way I want to spend one of my last nights."

"Don't say that."

"I have to say it, Cassandra. We both have to accept the fact that, no matter how hard we try or what we know, I will probably die on Saturday."

The cold truth of his words stares me down, unavoidable. Lawrence holds my hands firmly. "Tonight, I want to live. I want to be with you. I want to show you the things I love and I want you to show me the things you love. Give me one night, Cassandra, and then tomorrow we'll go back to dodging fate.

"Can you give me tonight?" he whispers.

I nod. He presses a kiss to my lips. My heart sings, wanting more. I meet his lips with passion. He pulls back, an amused smile tugging at his mouth.

"Easy, dollface. I'll be here all night."

"Oh please! You're the one who brought a blanket, not to mention your puppy-dog-eyed request to enjoy your favorite things one last time. Don't try to tell me this isn't an elaborate scheme to get in my pants."

Lawrence laughs, seemingly shocked and delighted by my talk. He puts a hand over his heart.

"I had no intention of defiling you, I swear it. Unless, of course, you want to be…"

I go to elbow him, but he pulls me against his chest. The momentum makes us topple to the ground, and I land on top of him.

"Why, Cassandra!" Lawrence says with feigned shock.

I punch his shoulder and then kiss him hard.

When we sit up, Lawrence unbuttons his shirt collar. "I think you and I need something to cool off."

"Don't tell me you want to go swimming."

He searches the food on the blanket and then grabs two glass bottles. He holds them up.

"How about a Coca-Cola instead?"

"Nice!" He tosses me a bottle and I examine it. "Vintage Coke. They've stopped putting cocaine in it by the twenties, right?"

Lawrence shrugs and lifts his Coke. "So what should we toast to?"

"To tonight," I say, clinking my bottle to his.

"Here's to not getting a wink of sleep."

I raise my eyebrows as we sip our drinks. He totally wants me.

But for the next few hours, things stay completely tame. After a quick trip back to the house to make Mom think I'm in bed, I sneak back out, and we eat every single piece of candy and cookie on the picnic blanket. Then Lawrence tries to teach me to Charleston, an endeavor that doesn't end well. We listen to every one of his records, dancing like fools. Well, I look like a fool. Lawrence may be from the twenties, but the boy has swagger. It's incredibly sexy.

After the records, we drink more Coke and then walk along the shore break, laughing and running as the waves splash against our legs. Lawrence recites poetry. I draw a portrait of him in the wet sand. We talk endlessly about everything.

It's perfection.

We finally settle on the blanket. I lay tucked in Lawrence's arms, gazing up at the stars. The rhythm of the waves lulls us into a drowsy silence.

"Cassandra," Lawrence finally says.

"Mmm?"

He turns on his side to look at me. He brushes a lock of windblown hair from my face. "I don't know what will happen in three days..."

"You shouldn't—"

He sets his fingers against my lips. "I don't know what will happen on Saturday, but I've decided it doesn't matter. No matter what, I'm lucky to have met you. And if I have to die, if fate insists on having me, then I'll leave this life happy. Because I met you. Because I was able to know you and love you. Even if just for a few weeks."

A lump lodges in my throat. But it's too late. I have no control over my emotions at two in the morning.

"You love me?" I ask, my voice choked.

He nods, stroking the back of his fingers down my cheek. "I do. I'm in love with you, Cassandra."

I can barely process his words without crying.

"I'm going to save you," I whisper.

"But don't you see? You already have. My soul is full just knowing you."

My eyes tingle with the threat of tears. "I'm in love with you too. I can't lose you. I need to know that all of this wasn't for nothing."

He sets his hand to my cheek. "You have me tonight. That's all we can know for certain."

I hold his gaze, yearning to feel the calm that he possesses. And then I understand. Either one of us could die in the next three days. We could die tomorrow. All we have is right now. A fire burns through every inch of me. I kiss his hand.

"Then let's make tonight count," I whisper.

He kisses me, his lips soft and achingly sweet. Lawrence pulls me on top of him, and every nerve end tingles with sensation. I'll worry about tomorrow later. For this one breathtaking, beautiful moment, we have forever.

CHAPTER 25

Cassandra

Dawn on the beach is surprisingly cold. Lawrence and I are wrapped in each other's arms and the blanket, but it's still chilly enough to wake me. In a way, it's a good thing. I need to sneak back inside before Mom wakes up. I turn a little, searching for my phone amid the tangle of blanket.

Lawrence releases a sigh in his sleep, drawing my attention. He looks so sweet that I impulsively want to kiss his eyelids. Thinking about last night, a rush of heat crackles over my cheeks and neck. I'm instantly self-conscious. Does my breath stink? Do I look like death warmed over?

Not that Lawrence would say anything if I did. I lie back on the blanket and watch him for a minute. This whole situation still feels like a weird dream. I'd be lying if I didn't say that a tiny part of me wonders if he's a ghost. An even bigger part of me wonders if there's really any chance to save him.

I touch Lawrence's hand lightly, feeling the smoothness of his skin. I've been so focused on trying to figure out who's going to hurt him that I've barely entertained the question of what comes next. Each moment I've spent with Lawrence has been with the urgency that it could be our last. What will happen when we can be together without limits? And more importantly, where will we be together? We can't stay on the beach forever. So whose world do we settle in? Mine? His? Can I really leave my life behind to be with him? Can I ask him to do the same?

The questions pile on, and I pull my hand from Lawrence's. Unease seeps into what should be a perfect morning. I close my eyes, wanting to unthink these thoughts.

Lawrence shifts beside me. He opens his eyes, blinking slowly. A smile spreads across his face.

"It wasn't a dream then."

This makes me smile as well. "Nope."

He stretches with a happy sigh. "Divine." I laugh a little, and he traces a line along my jaw. "You're perfection, Cassandra."

"Mental note: Lawrence is particularly complimentary in the mornings."

He smiles. "You should take advantage of that more often in the future."

"I'll try." But his mention of the future calls back the unsettled feeling. I check the time on my phone. Six a.m.

"What's that?" Lawrence asks, resting his chin on my shoulder. His messy morning hair is outrageously cute. I tuck my phone beneath me, giving him a quick kiss.

"Futuristic stuff. You're not allowed to see it yet."

"If you insist." But he darts a hand to my pocket to try to grab it.

"Hey!" I successfully pull away my phone, and he grabs my key ring instead.

"Aha!" He says. "I've got your…" He holds up my keys, examining them with a furrowed brow. "What on earth is this thing?"

I laugh. I carry a lot of junk on my key ring. It must look like a pretty crazy contraption to him.

He holds up my house key. "This is some kind of key, but what are these other things?"

I grab the little stuffed elephant. "Meet Charles Xavier. I got him in junior high. Long story, that one."

"And this?" he asks, touching my mini flashlight.

"Push that little button there, and see for yourself."

He does, and the flashlight glows white and then flashes red. Lawrence startles and stares with amazement. It's pretty adorable.

"Do I even want to know what this one does?" he asks, pointing to the pepper spray.

"Actually, no. You don't. All I'll say is that it's a weapon of sorts. Meant to protect me from bad guys."

He turns an awed look at me. "Fascinating."

"Trust me, there are way cooler things in the future than this piddly little key ring."

"What kinds of things?" he asks. "Describe them to me."

I waggle a finger at him. "No more future talk. We're in a precarious situation as it is. Let's not push our luck." I sit up and pull my fingers through my hair, which must look like a mangled sloth perched on my head. "Speaking of which, I think we should plan our next three days."

Lawrence sighs. "Back to business."

"Um, yes. We don't know how things are going to play out on Saturday. So today and tomorrow is our last, safe, forty-eight-hour period. We have to make it count."

"Make it count?" Lawrence repeats, looking at me with a hopeful smile.

I shove him. "You know what I mean."

"Killjoy," he says glumly.

I start gathering the papers from last night. "Is everything still going as planned with the party Saturday? Nothing out of the ordinary?"

He starts to shake his head but stops. His brow furrows. He's quiet, as if he's wrestling with an idea.

"Lawrence?" I touch his arm. "What is it?"

"Well…something happened."

Fear unfolds in me. "What?"

"It didn't have anything to do with Cooper Enterprises."

"Okay. So tell me."

Lawrence shakes his head. "It seems like madness to even suggest."

"Spit it out, Lawrence. You're scaring me here."

"See if you can learn anything about the Cartelli family from New York. Lower East Side."

What's with the sudden shifty eyes? "Okay…"

He releases a slow sigh. "See if the name Fay Cartelli comes up."

"Fay Cartelli. Got it." He doesn't look at me. I draw a little swirl in the sand, trying not to feel suspicious. "So, who is she?"

His cheeks flush with color. "Have I never mentioned her?"

"You haven't."

"She's a...friend of mine."

My heart drops. "A friend."

He seems uncomfortable. "Essentially... Perhaps a bit more."

I want him to be joking, but I can tell he's not. I try desperately to keep calm. "Oh."

"Cassandra, it's not like it sounds."

"So, she's not your girlfriend?"

"No...not exactly."

"What does that mean? 'Not exactly.'"

He rubs the bridge of his nose. This time, his silence tells me everything I need to know. I push to my feet. Lawrence jumps up after me.

"I meant every word I said last night. I love you, Cassandra."

I shake my head but don't dare speak.

"Fay means nothing to me," he says. "She never did. And once I met you, she meant even less."

"But that didn't stop you from dating her?"

"Don't be this way. Please, Cassandra. I never gave myself to her. You have to believe me."

I can't even look at him. "I need some time."

He sighs. "Time is the one thing we don't have."

Bitterness rises in my throat. "You think I don't know that?" It's taking every ounce of my strength not to cry. "I have to go. My mom will be up soon."

"Cassandra, please." He sounds miserable. "Will you come back?"

I turn back to the house without responding.

"I'll wait here," he says. "All day if I have to."

Back in my room, I crawl into bed and curl up in a ball beneath the blanket, body and spirit spent. I lie there for at least an hour, eyes shut, heart aching with each beat. But sleep won't come. It's probably just as well.

Eventually, the clanking sounds of breakfast being cooked drift up into my room. I have no intention of going downstairs, but the longer I lie here, the more I realize that I can't risk getting on Mom's bad side. I slink down to the kitchen and sit zombielike through breakfast with Mom, Eddie, and Frank. They're discussing a sailing trip up the coast for the weekend. I feel like my insides are being ripped apart. I want to be furious with Lawrence, but I may only have two days left with him. Do I really want to waste them being angry? Last night was very special. Some people never get the chance to have that kind of romance. I know that. I can't let my insecurities taint that. But to think of Lawrence being with another girl… It makes me physically exhausted.

After breakfast, I drag myself upstairs and collapse on my bed. I get under my blanket again. Part of me wants to stay here the rest of the day and feel sorry for myself. But thankfully, the rest of me knows I can't do that. It's already nearly eleven. The day is slipping away. Every minute I waste in this bed is a minute I could be spending with Lawrence.

Rolling onto my back, I press my hands over my eyes, wishing I could push the knowledge of this Fay girl out of my head.

But I can't. So it's time to grow up and deal instead of sulking about it. Lawrence is all that matters now.

I grab my laptop and flop it on my stomach. I enter "Fay Cartelli" into the search engine. It's a long shot, I know.

Sure enough, I find the website for a graphic designer in Dallas and some random girl's Facebook page. Pursing my lips to the side, I try "Fay Cartelli 1925."

After sifting through five pages of search results, I find nothing. I try at least ten more variations of her name, adding different words with no success.

And then I search: "Cartelli Lower East Side New York 1925." On the second page, I notice a site dedicated to New York during Prohibition. It's right there.

The Cartellis. A prominent crime family from the Lower East Side.

The hair on the back of my neck prickles. I stare at the screen. It can't be possible. There are probably dozens of Cartellis on the Lower East Side. The likelihood of one of them being related to this Fay chick is astronomically small.

But then...what if? We're dealing with a murder here. Last time I checked, murder is kind of the mob's specialty. Of course, you have to wonder why they would bother killing a seventeen-year-old living in ritzy Massachusetts.

Unless, of course, he was cheating on their daughter. The thought slams me right in the chest.

Am I the reason Lawrence is killed?

CHAPTER 26

Cassandra

"You can't think of it that way, Cassandra. You'll drive yourself crazy."

It's ironic that Lawrence is the one with less than forty-eight hours to live, but he's trying to calm my panic attack.

"I knew we shouldn't have messed with time," I say, unable to draw a good breath. "I said it from the very beginning. You mess with the past, and you screw up the future. Once we realized what was going on, we should have left each other alone."

He grips my hands. "We have no way of knowing if Fay's family is even responsible for my death. You could be panicking for nothing."

"They're mob, Lawrence. An Italian mob family. Have you ever seen *The Godfather*? Do you not understand how these people operate? They kill at the drop of a hat. You said Fay was mad when you guys parted?"

He scratches the back of his neck reluctantly. "Yes."

"And why was she mad? Because you told her about me?"

"Well no, but she did find out about you…in a way. I can't imagine her actually trying to have me killed for it."

"Not her. But what about her big, mean, mobster daddy? Her creepy brother who was watching you?"

I massage my temples while Lawrence ponders the idea. As if things weren't scary enough, pressing him for details only makes me freak out more. I feel like I'm spinning out of control.

"I should warn Ned," Lawrence says. "All this time he's thought Fay was a Crest Harbor girl. Rich, clean-cut, one of us. He has no idea who she really is. If he knew, he'd never have thought to…" The color in his face drains away.

"What's wrong?"

The words fall slowly from his lips. "We were supposed to be married, Fay and I. Ned had it all arranged."

I sit back, reeling from the revelation. "Wow."

He grabs my hand. "Please don't be hurt, Cassandra. It was never official. And it wasn't ever my idea. I didn't even realize it was Ned's plan until a week or two ago."

"You don't want to marry her?"

"No. I told you, I never loved Fay. My uncle's been pushing the relationship since the beginning."

"Well, I'd say your uncle has some pretty crappy judgment."

"But that's just it. He doesn't realize who Fay really is. When he finds out, he's bound to break off the agreement. Maybe the mob goes after Ned."

I put the pieces of the theory in place. "And you get caught in the crossfire."

Lawrence exhales, scratching a hand through his hair. "We don't know anything for sure."

"Yes, we do," I say. Each word burns in my throat. "We know that if you hadn't met me, you'd be safe. I'm the reason you're killed. It's my fault. I never should have come back to the beach. I knew what happened to Travis, but I just didn't care—"

"It's not your fault."

"Of course it is!" I shout. Then, breathing hard, I stagger back. "All this talk about fate and destiny? It's crap. I just convinced myself of it because I wanted to feel justified in coming to see you. I wanted a reason to ignore the warnings that were clearly laid out for me. I've been selfish, and now look what's happened."

Lawrence takes my face in his hands. "Don't talk like this. I won't hear it."

I shake my head, breaking from his grip, and he takes me in his arms.

"Look at me."

"No."

"Cassandra."

I feel heavy with the burden of everything that's happening. I just want to run away. Cry. Scream.

"I would never take back a moment of our time together, Cassandra. Not a single breath. Not a single word. Meeting you has been the greatest thing to ever happen to me."

Tears burn behind my eyes. Squeezing them away, I press my lips to his. He hooks his arms around me. Our kiss pulses with longing and fear and hope. When we break apart, I press my forehead to his.

"I'm scared," I whisper.

He strokes the hair from my face. "So am I. But now is the time for courage. We know so much more than when we started."

"But we still don't know how to keep you safe."

"We know about Cooper Enterprises. And Fay's family. That's big. You better believe I'm going to have my eyes wide open on Saturday night."

My stomach twists at the mere mention of it. "You're planning on going to your uncle's party?

"Am I supposed to stay in my room all day?"

"No! You're supposed to get in your car and drive as far away from here as possible."

"That might save me on Saturday, but what about the next day? The next week? Don't you think they'll come looking for me? The only way to stop my death from happening is to face the murderers, whoever they are, head on."

He's completely serious. A surge of unexpected anger rushes through me.

"Are you crazy? Do you want to be murdered, Lawrence? Do you honestly think you can go up against the mob and not end up with a bullet in your head?"

A coldness settles in his eyes. "You have no idea what it feels like to know that you may die in the morning. Do you know how much thought I've given this?"

"Of course I do! Because it's the only thing I've been able to think about, same as you."

"It's not the same," he insists.

"How can you say that?"

He shakes his head, turning from me in frustration.

"You're trying to be brave!" I shout. "But you'll just get yourself killed!"

"If I run away like a coward, it will be my uncle who dies. He has no idea about Fay or even about Cooper Enterprises. He'll throw his big, happy party and wind up dead."

His eyes are red and glassy with pain. The sight fills me with the desire to hold him and kiss his tears away. But I don't. The tension of our argument crackles between us.

"I care about you, Lawrence."

He scoffs. "Well, I happen to care about my uncle."

"I'm not saying—"

"I know exactly what you're suggesting—"

"I can't lose you. I'd never forgive myself. I'd never get over it."

"Cassandra—"

"No! I won't calm down." It feels like someone is sitting on my chest. I can't breathe. "I'm trying to save your life, Lawrence. Promise me you won't go to the party."

He sighs heavily and then pulls me against him. Feeling his arms around me is like oxygen. I press my face to his neck. I hate that we're spending our last day arguing. It's all wrong.

"I can promise you that I'll be careful," Lawrence says. "This is my life and my uncle's life on the line here."

He touches my chin and lifts my face so I'll meet his eyes.

The sound of a sharp exhale makes us both look to the bushes with a start.

Brandon stands on the beach, staring at us with a look of utter betrayal.

CHAPTER 27

Cassandra

Brandon looks like he's been slapped. For a moment we're all frozen in place. Then I step away from Lawrence.

"Brandon—"

He holds up a hand to silence me. "Don't."

"Let me explain."

"No need," Brandon snaps. Then he says bitterly, "So this is why you've been blowing me off. You know, your mom told me you'd been spending a lot of time at the beach, but she thinks you've taken a sudden interest in swimming. I guess we've both been played."

Lawrence and I exchange a swift, tense glance. He senses as well as I the potential seriousness of this turn of events. I have to diffuse the situation quickly. Too bad my words have abandoned me.

"This isn't what you think" is all I can manage.

Brandon sputters. "Spare me, Cass. It's kind of obvious what's going on. You know, you could have told me you were dating someone. It's not like I can't handle it."

"I know that."

"So why didn't you say something?"

"Look, I don't owe you every detail of my life, okay?"

"Whatever," he snorts. "You know, in some ways, I'm glad I saw you with Suspenders here. Now I know everything I need to about you."

The impulse to tell him off again burns in my throat, but I swallow it. I guess I deserve it. And besides, I need him on my side. He can't tell anyone about Lawrence. It's bad enough that he's been seen. I don't even want to think about the ripple effect this all might bring about.

"Brandon, I'm sorry, okay? I never wanted to hurt you. I actually tried to tell you, but—"

"But what?"

When I don't immediately answer, he holds up a hand. "You know what? Never mind. I know why you didn't tell me. It's because you're a drama queen. You love having secret boyfriends and leading guys on."

"That's not—"

"Don't lie to me, Drama Queen."

Lawrence takes a tense step forward. His fist is tight at his side. "I'll ask you only once to speak to Cassandra with more respect."

Brandon turns to Lawrence, his eyes suddenly bright with rage. "Is that right? And who exactly do you think you are?"

Lawrence's fierce glare stays locked with Brandon's.

"Both of you chill out," I say. I have to get Brandon away. Every second he spends here is dangerous. Every word complicates our situation.

"No, really," Brandon says. "Who is this guy? I don't recognize him."

My stomach tenses, but I force a laugh. "So you know every person in town?"

"Pretty much." Brandon gives Lawrence a scrutinizing look.

"Trust me," Lawrence says with irritation, "we don't know each other."

"My point exactly. Anyone worth knowing is on my radar."

"Or perhaps you're not as popular as you presumed," Lawrence says.

I shoot him a warning look, but he's still staring down Brandon.

Brandon's jaw sets. "You want to come a little closer and say that to my face?"

"Gladly."

Brandon and Lawrence both step toward each other, and I run in between them.

"Stop it. Both of you." I turn to Lawrence. "Maybe you should go."

"I'm not leaving you with this goon. He's fighting mad."

Brandon sneers. "Goon? What, are you from the fifties or something?"

"I can handle him," I say pointedly to Lawrence. We have no other choice.

Lawrence doesn't respond, but I can tell he's not happy with me. Finally, he nods once. "Fine. But I'll check to make sure you're safe very soon."

"Do that."

Lawrence starts back to the house. As he passes Brandon, he bumps Brandon's shoulder deliberately.

I could kill him.

Brandon's eyes flash. Lawrence continues walking, and I hold up my hand, as if I could stop the impending explosion.

"Brandon—"

But he's after Lawrence like the snap of the whip. I fly after them.

"Brandon, wait!"

In the thin alley of bushes, Brandon grabs hold of Lawrence's shirt and spins him around.

"You want to make this serious, bro?"

Lawrence pushes Brandon's arms away. "Take your paws off me."

"Stop!" I shout.

They both ignore me. Brandon gives Lawrence a fierce shove. The bushes shake where he lands, causing a bird to flutter into the sky. I've never seen Lawrence look so angry. I grab him from behind.

"Leave it," I say. I press my face to his neck and add in a sharp whisper, "Think about where we are."

Lawrence gives me a tense glance, but then we both notice Brandon coming at us, eyes blazing. He throws a punch, and Lawrence darts out of the way, pushing me to the side to protect me. Brandon swings again, and this time when Lawrence dodges, he jumps back.

Too far back. He begins to blur.

Not realizing this, Lawrence retreats further. He blurs even more.

"I'm not going to fight you," he says, but his voice is muffled.

Brandon freezes, and terror grips me.

"Lawrence!"

Only now does he realize what's happening. His eyes widen. He makes a move toward the beach, but Brandon is blocking the way. Brandon advances, and Lawrence has no choice but to back up another step, becoming even more obscured by the shadows of time.

"What the hell?" Brandon's voice is soft with confusion and shock.

I grab Brandon's arm. "We have to go back to the beach."

He shrugs out of my grip, not taking his eyes off Lawrence.

Lawrence looks to me. His expression is hard to make out, but I can tell that he's as alarmed as I am. What can we do? What can we possibly say?

Then, out of nowhere, Lawrence turns and runs, vanishing completely into 1925.

This is bad. This is beyond bad.

I grab Brandon, so that he faces me. He stares at me, waiting for me to explain what just happened. But no words come.

Brandon steps through the bushes. When he reaches the backyard, he looks around. Looking for Lawrence. But Lawrence isn't there. Brandon slowly raises a hand to his forehead. Then, after a moment, he speed walks for the house. I'm paralyzed with fear. This is exactly what I was afraid would happen. The worst-case scenario.

I run after him. "Wait! Brandon!"

He strides ahead without looking back. I run in front of him, trying to block his path.

"I can explain."

He shakes his head, backing away from me like I'm a leper. "Don't talk to me."

I follow him through the house and out the front door. As he gets in his car, I lean through the driver's side window.

"Brandon, please. It's not what you think."

He looks me in the eye for the first time. He's afraid. I can see it. I touch his hand, which grips the steering wheel, white-knuckled.

"You need to give me a chance to explain," I say.

Brandon fumbles for his keys. His hand trembles as he turns it in the ignition.

"I have to go."

The engine revs to a start.

"Brandon."

Without another word, he pulls the car into gear and roars away. I jump back to avoid getting run over.

I call Brandon twelve times over the next three hours. I even track down his home number and ask his mom if I can speak to him. She goes to get him and then comes back on the line to awkwardly fumble over some line about Brandon being asleep. At four thirty in the afternoon. Hanging up the phone, I flop back onto my bed, unsure if I want to scream or cry.

A menacing train of what-ifs roars through my brain. What if Brandon tells my mom about Lawrence and she prevents me from seeing him? What if that awful chance meeting sets off the butterfly effect again? But that's not even the worst of it. What if somehow the bargain we've made with fate was contingent on secrecy? I could save Lawrence as long as no one knew we were messing with time. But now Brandon knows. Maybe the deal is off. Maybe I'll walk back to that beach, and everything will be like it was before. And Lawrence will be on his own to face his death.

CHAPTER 28

Cassandra

I'm going to lose it. The stress of this whole situation will break my sanity. I have no doubt of this. I pace on the warm sand, waiting. It's been forty-five minutes. Lawrence still hasn't come. I refuse to accept what that might mean. My heart couldn't bear the pain.

I'm going to kill Brandon. Someone has to answer for this. I'm going to go completely rogue and extract my revenge on the entire town of Crest Harbor. One by one, I'll—

"Cassandra."

I spin around. At the sight of Lawrence, my eyes slide closed and I exhale with relief.

"I'm so sorry," he says, rushing to take me in his arms. "Ned was home and I couldn't get away."

I melt into the embrace. "It doesn't matter. I'm just so glad that you're here now."

Lawrence kisses me. I can feel the difference in his kiss. There's an urgency, a hunger to make each embrace count. I recognize it because I feel the same way.

We hold each other for a long time and then sit together in the sand.

"So," Lawrence says finally, "what do we do now?"

"I've given this a lot of thought, and I think we have to accept that Brandon could be a culprit in your murder. Or at least cause a chain of events that will lead to your murder."

Lawrence exhales slowly, ruffling his hair with frustration. "I'm a fool."

"It's not your fault. It's mine. All of this is my fault. At the start of this, Cooper Enterprises was the only plausible suspect. Now, thanks to my meddling, Brandon and this Fay girl's family have both become possibilities."

I want him to tell me I'm wrong, but even he can't muster the lie. "If I'd just followed my instincts and left things alone. If I'd left you alone."

"Don't say that."

"Why not? It's true. If I had never come back to the beach like I promised, you'd have a long, happy future to look forward to."

"Don't talk like this, Cassandra. I won't hear it." He holds the side of my face. "I don't want a future without you."

His lips come to mine. My eyes sting. I don't deserve this rush of adrenaline at the feel of the kiss. I don't deserve someone to love me so perfectly. It's an ideal summer evening—golden and warm and fragrant. Everything about tonight, possibly our last night together, should be perfect. And it would be if not for this horrible, sinking fear that I've ruined everything.

"You shouldn't take this so hard," Lawrence says softly. "Nothing may come of this Brandon business."

"Or everything might."

"There's no way to know, so we might as well not think about it."

Lawrence laces my hand in his. "I don't want to spend our time together like this."

"Neither do I."

He kisses my cheek, and the warmth of his lips runs through my entire body. But tonight every sweetness is overpowered by the bitter reminder of what Lawrence is about to face.

"I'd better go in for dinner," I say, my heart heavy. "Mom's probably wondering where I am."

Lawrence brushes a strand of hair from my face, tucking it behind my ear. "Will you sneak out when your parents go to bed?"

I nod, hoping I'll be able to shake this gloom by the time I come back. If these really are my final hours with Lawrence, I want them to be like last night, not this.

"See you later," I say.

Lawrence pulls me into a hug. "I'll be waiting."

My feet feel like stones as I head back to the house. The last thing I want to do is leave Lawrence. I should be in his arms, not moping a hundred years away. Sitting in the kitchen with Mom, Frank, and Eddie and pretending to be fine. Dodging questions from Mom. Torture. But when I step into the house, it's not Mom waiting for me. It's Brandon.

A zing of terror cuts through me. Is he back to fight with Lawrence? Is he planning to reveal my secret to my mom and Frank? It's as if all my worst what-ifs are suddenly coming true at once.

"Who let you in?" I ask.

The silence in the house rings like a heavy note in my ears. I don't think anyone's even here. Maybe they went in to pick up something for dinner and bring it back.

"Let's go for a drive," Brandon says.

For a moment, I don't move. What is he up to? Maybe he's planning to kill me.

I almost roll my eyes at my own thought. Brandon is many things, but murderer isn't one of them. Still…I don't completely trust him. But I need to get him back on my side. Maybe there's a chance I can make this right.

"A drive where?" I ask cautiously.

"Does it matter?"

"I suppose it doesn't, provided we avoid dark alleys and abandoned warehouses."

Brandon maintains his stone expression and walks away. Tossing a nervous glance at the back door, I discretely text Mom and follow him.

For the first seven minutes of the drive—I watch each one pass on the dashboard clock—neither of us speaks. Then I stare at the tailored lawns and summer trees rolling past in a green blur. The thoughts in my head seem to be passing in a similar way. What do I say to Brandon? How am I supposed to make this better? He saw what he saw. I can't feed him some line and pretend that he didn't. He needs some kind of explanation. Trouble is, when I think about it, there are very few ways I can envision this going well.

"Brandon…"

His gaze cuts to me, sharp and yet full of an unreadable emotion. Fear? Anger? I can't say.

"I want answers, Cass."

"I know."

Brandon waits. "Well, what in the hell happened back there?"

I'm tempted to gaslight him, to pretend that I didn't see anything, that he's crazy. But my instincts scream out that if I do, he'll go searching for proof of his claims. Besides, Brandon deserves the truth. All things considered, he's not a bad guy. Had this summer gone differently, he and I could have been friends. Maybe even more. It may be the biggest risk I've ever taken, but somehow, deep down, I know I need to be honest.

"Pull over," I say, setting my hand on Brandon's arm.

He hesitates but parks his car on the side of the road. The ocean glows in the early evening sun just beyond the bluff, strengthening me.

"Logic is going to resist what I'm about to tell you, Brandon. You're not going to believe it. You're not going to want to believe it. But you have to trust what you saw. Hold on to that. It was real. You're weren't imagining it."

"Enough. Tell me what I saw."

I steady my voice. "You were right. Lawrence isn't from around here. Well, he is. But not in the way you'd think. He's from a different Crest Harbor. One that existed…in nineteen twenty-five."

Brandon's eyes narrow slightly, but his gaze stays on me.

"I know this going to sound insane. Trust me, I struggled with it a lot at first. I still have to be convinced of it sometimes. But Lawrence is from nineteen twenty-five. He lives in the same house I'm living in now, only almost a hundred years in the past. And for some reason, which neither of us can figure out, I can see him on that beach."

More silence.

"The beach is the only place though. That's why he disappeared as he walked back to the house. He goes back into nineteen twenty-five. That's what you saw."

Brandon shakes his head slightly, anger flaring in his cheeks. "I'm not stupid, Cass."

"I know you're not. That's why I'm being honest with you."

"I'm not stupid!" He slams both hands on the steering wheel.

"Then believe me."

Brandon huffs. Then shaking his head again, he revs the engine to a start.

"I told you it would be hard to believe, but that doesn't mean it isn't the truth."

He jams the car into gear and spins it back onto the road, the wheels screeching in protest.

"If you give me some time, I'll tell you everything I know."

The car burns back down the street. Brandon radiates fury. I anticipated this reaction, but he's headed back to my house. Is he going to tell my mom everything I just said? I need time to get him on my side.

"Give me a chance to prove it to you, at least," I say.

White-hot silence.

"It doesn't make any sense to me either, okay? But it is what it is. I can't change the facts to make them more believable."

I can't handle his wordless rage right now. I can't handle any of it. It's all too much. I wish I were back in Nowhere, Ohio, wondering what college I'll go to and what I want to be when I grow up.

"Are you going to tell my mom I'm insane?" I ask, tears stinging my eyes. "Are you going to turn me in to the police or something?"

In response, Brandon pushes down on the accelerator.

"Do whatever you want, okay?" I snap. "At this point, I don't even care."

The sandcastle Lawrence and I have been living in is finally toppling beneath the wave of reality. We couldn't keep this secret forever. Brandon will tell Mom, who will drag me to some nice shrink, and Lawrence will die on that beach tomorrow. Brandon pulls the car up my driveway. I wipe away the tears on my face. They won't do me any good now.

He slams on the brakes and unlocks the doors but doesn't put the car in park. "Go," he says, staring out the windshield.

A flicker of hope lights in me. "You're not…going to tell my mom what I've said?"

Finally, Brandon looks me in the eye. He doesn't seem as angry as I thought. More confused.

"I don't ever want to talk about it again. And I don't ever want to talk to you again. As far as I'm concerned, this conversation, that conversation on the beach, none of it ever happened. Deal?"

I nod, blinking back surprise. "Are you sure you're not going to tell anyone?"

"Good-bye, Cass."

"I just—"

"Good-bye."

I stumble out of the car. "Okay, bye."

Before I can give him a final wave, Brandon zooms away.

Watching him speed down the driveway, I'm not sure what to feel. I guess it should be a relief, but I also can't completely relax. It's almost too good to be true…

Rubbing the shiver off my arms, I head back to the house. Mom's still gone, so I go straight for the beach. I just want some time with Lawrence.

Passing through the bushy path, however, the hairs on the back of my neck stand on end. Something's off. Something's wrong.

Another step and I see them.

Lawrence and Mom. Standing together on the beach.

They both look up at me at the same time. Lawrence's expression says it all. Though Mom's furious, thin-pressed lips do a good job as well.

At that moment, part of me gives up. Maybe destiny is involved, just not in the way I thought. Maybe Lawrence is destined to die, and the more I'm in the picture, the more certain that becomes. Everything I do to help him only seems to get us both deeper into trouble.

Mom folds her arms across her chest, letting her glare sink in. At this point, though, I'm done. I throw out my arms.

"I don't know what to say, Mom."

She looks more disappointed than mad. I've never been the sneaking out type or one to lie to her. "I think your friend needs to leave."

Lawrence and I exchange a tense glance.

"He lives on the other side of the point," I say quickly.

Lawrence gives an imperceptible nod, then bows his head to my mom.

"Again, I apologize, ma'am. I never intended any disrespect."

Mom visibly softens at his politeness, though she still tries to maintain her look of stern disapproval. "I hope to meet you again under better circumstances."

"Indeed."

Lawrence starts down the beach, casting a glance at me over his shoulder. We'll see each other later, but even so, I don't like seeing him leave. There's so much we need to plan for tomorrow. These interruptions are giving me a serious headache.

When he's far enough away, Mom turns to me, and her expression hardens.

"How long?" she asks.

I feel sick to my stomach. "It's a really complicated situation, Mom."

"This explains your behavior lately," she says with a sigh. "You know my rules about lying."

"I've never really lied."

"All that time you spent 'on the beach'? All those 'trips to the library'?"

"I really was at the library! You saw me!"

She shakes her head. "Don't make this worse."

"Mom, listen—"

She holds a silencing hand in the air. "We'll discuss this later, when I'm in a better mood. For now, you are grounded. And I mean at the house. No beach."

My whole body tenses. "No."

"In your room for the rest of the night. I will be watching the stairs," she adds. "I know you snuck out the other night."

I grab her arm with desperation. "Mom, please. I can't—"

"Enough," she says firmly. "I need some time to think about what I'm going to do with you."

"Mom!"

She points to the house, a clear command. She can't do this to me. Not today, of all days. Lawrence and I need to spend every minute crafting a plan for tomorrow. I won't abandon him. I can't.

"Move it, Cass," Mom says. "You're just making things worse for yourself."

A wild, fierce energy wells up in my chest, and I want to scream, "You can't make me!" Eddie does that all the time. Maybe I should give it a try. Or maybe I just make a break for it. Hide out until she gives up looking for me.

I think of Lawrence, of how much he needs me, and I take a slow breath to calm myself. For him, I will show control. If I play my cards right with Mom, we can work this out. And then I can get back to the beach. Lowering my gaze penitently, I head into the house.

Mom follows me all the way up into my room. I sit on my bed, trying to think of the perfect, humble thing to say.

"I expected so much more from you, Cass."

"I'm sorry."

"Sorry isn't good enough. It's going to take time to earn back my trust."

She starts to close the door but pauses. "Oh, and while we're on the subject, there's no way you're staying home tomorrow."

"What?"

"You're coming on the sailing trip. I'm going to keep a close watch on you. Whoever this boy is, he can fend for himself tomorrow."

No. *No.* This isn't happening. I jump to my feet, staring at Mom in complete horror. But she's unmoved. Without flinching, she pulls the door shut. With a harsh bang, I'm sealed in my room.

And Lawrence is on his own.

CHAPTER 29

Lawrence

How would you spend your last day on earth? It's a popular party game to ask around a circle. I can't remember now what I've said. I'd never imagined I'd spend my last hours on the beach.

Waiting.

It's been hours, but she still hasn't come back. Watching the sun set slowly on my final day, it hits me that she might not come back at all. Maybe she got into more trouble than I thought. Maybe she's sick or hurt. Maybe the strain of trying to save me became too much, and she left forever. Moved on to less bizarre, more uncomplicated relationships.

I want her back. It's more than I can bear. I'm exhausted from the desperate loneliness of waiting here, staring at the bushes, yearning for her to come.

And then, at long last, I hear the rustle of branches. My heart leaps into my throat. I spring to my feet.

But it isn't Cassandra. It's Aunt Eloise. I feel like I've been thrown against a wall and shattered into a million pieces.

"There you are, Lonnie!" she cries. "Ned's been looking everywhere for you! How long have you been out here?"

I'm so disappointed I can hardly speak. "Not long."

Eloise bustles over to me, frowning deeply. "I was hoping you'd help me get things ready for your uncle's party tomorrow." She looks me over. "Are you all right? You're quite pale."

"I'm fine," I say, but I can't even manage a forced smile to assuage her concern.

Her frown deepens. She reaches out and puts her hand to my forehead. "I believe you're ill, Lon. Come inside and rest."

"I'll be all right. I'd like to stay out here and think a little more."

Eloise stammers. "Well, you can't. It's suppertime. I have to be heading back home, you know."

"I'm sorry I missed your visit today," I say, the words falling from my lips with no conviction.

"Well, Ned has someone he wants you to meet."

I swallow my frustration with Aunt Eloise. She isn't trying to be tedious. I have no intention of eating tonight, but I can see that she's not going to leave me alone until I come inside. With a sigh, I head back to the house. Eloise struggles to keep up with my pace.

"Better go in and freshen up, Lon," she says. "He's a very important guest for your uncle. Businessman. A bigwig, Ned says."

I stop in my tracks and Eloise nearly crashes into me. "Jerome Smith?"

Eloise blinks, startled. "What?"

"Ned's guest," I say, speaking carefully so she'll understand the gravity of the question. "Is he a bigwig from Cooper Enterprises?"

"I believe so. You know I don't follow those kinds of things, Lonnie. I can barely keep up with Ned's dinner conversations."

She motions me back inside. The house looms ahead, glowing through the darkness of night. It's inviting and lovely. And yet my feet plant in the grass. My knees are locked, and a persistent ringing sound is growing louder in my ears. A chill I can't shake rushes over my entire body.

So it begins.

We enter the house. I walk Aunt Eloise to the door, perhaps to stall the inevitable. But once she's on her way home, I have no choice. I have to face whatever this night will bring. Each step feels like something out of a strange, shadowy dream. I can hear Ned and his guest talking. Their voices sound cordial enough, but my stomach crawls. I move stiffly into the dining room.

I expect to see the heartless assassin from the warehouse, but Jerome Smith looks quite normal. He's older, with a thick, white mustache and an expensive suit. He appears rich and snobbish, not evil. And yet as I enter the room and he looks up, I catch the distinct glint of hardness in his eyes. This is a man capable of murder.

"Ah, there he is!" Ned bellows. I can see his tense mood in the beading sweat on his brow, in his cheerless, tight smile. I can hear it in his overly loud voice. "Lonnie, my boy, we've been waiting for you."

I can barely mumble a weak apology as I take a seat at the

long table. My eyes are fixed on Ned. Why is he so on edge? Does he know the truth about Cooper Enterprises?

"This is Jerome Smith," Ned says, motioning to the mustached man. Then he motions back to me. "My nephew, Lawrence. He's the one I was telling you about. Has quite the promising career ahead. He'll be in a top firm in New York. Very soon!"

"Once I finish college and law school," I explain.

Jerome Smith clips a look to Ned, and he nods. "Of course! Of course that's right."

I've never seen my uncle so nervous. He must know the kind of danger he's in.

I picture the whole scenario. A dinner-table confrontation. Shouts. A gun is pulled. Aimed for Ned. I jump in the way. A bullet pierces through my chest, lodging somewhere near my heart.

But Cassandra's article said I die on the beach tomorrow. So, maybe I crawl out there with my dying strength, in hope of saying good-bye.

Nausea sweeps over me like a cold wave. Such dark, terrible thoughts. I look at Ned and Jerome Smith, and realize that the conversation has gone on. I can see their mouths move, but the only sound is this darn ringing in my ears.

I push my fingertips into my eyes. All this picturing of how I die is enough to drive me completely mad.

A hand comes down on my arm, startling me to consciousness. It's Jerome Smith. His brow is furrowed.

"I say, son. Are you quite all right?"

His hand is like a red-hot brand on my skin. I jump to my feet. The dizziness nearly overtakes me.

"I'm not well." I pull the words from somewhere in my rapidly constricting throat. And then I turn and run. I run until I reach my room and slam and lock the door. Breathing hard, I press my back to it and slide to the floor.

I stay there for a solid hour. But even as I sit still and breathe, my pulse doesn't slow. Air still feels heavy and scarce in my lungs. My hands tremble.

Each tick of the second hand circling the clock pricks me like a pin. Each stab of pain makes me hate myself more and more. I'm afraid. So afraid. But I can't be a coward. Ned is in danger. How can I abandon him like this?

My eyes press closed, and I think of Cassandra. I need her. Her strength. Her intelligence. Her fire. I'd give anything in the world to have her by my side at this moment.

But I'm on my own. I've known that from the first moment she told me about the danger. Opening my eyes, I take a slow breath. And I stand.

I let the pounding of my own heart fuel each step I take as I leave my room and head down the stairs. The light from the dining room glows on the polished marble floor of the entryway. The voices of Ned and the man from Cooper drift out into the shadowy silence.

Breathe. That's all I have to do. Keep breathing.

Ned's voice rises above the other. Sharp. There's an edge to it. An edge of alarm. Of fear. Desperation. For a brittle, stinging moment, I'm paralyzed. And then I'm running into the dining room.

The two men are still at the table, but Ned and Jerome Smith are standing, leaning forward, their hands pressed to the shiny mahogany surface. Ned's broad face is flushed, his eyes wild. They turn to me.

At first, I'm not sure what exactly to say. I want to order Jerome Smith out of the house, but I'm not a complete fool.

"I need to speak with you, Ned," I manage.

"This isn't the time, Lon," he says harshly.

"It's very important."

Smith scowls. "What's the meaning of this?"

"What are you implying?" Ned counters.

My pulse throbs in my temples. But Jerome Smith isn't reaching for a hidden gun. He just seems confused and irritated by my presence.

"I have to talk to you," I say again to Ned. "You need to trust me on this."

"What could possibly be so important?" he asks, his face getting redder.

Smith pounds a fist on the table. "What kind of game are you playing here, Foster?"

I turn to him, anger boiling over. "You're the one playing games, making out like you're operating a respectable business when really you're a bunch of crooks."

It's as if the air has been sucked out of the room.

Ned's face now turns white as the wall. Smith stares at me.

"I know what you're trying to do to my uncle," I go on, emboldened. "The threatening letters. The late-night visits in old cars. It's extortion, and we're not going to stand for it another moment."

"Lawrence." Ned's voice is hard.

"It's the truth, Ned," I insist. "You may have a faint idea of the kind of people who you're dealing with, but I've looked into them. I've learned terrible things—"

"This is all entirely amusing," Smith says without a shred of mirth in his face. "The kid here thinks we're the crooked ones."

I snap my gaze to his. "What do you mean by that?"

"Leave it, Smith," Ned says, his eyes burning.

"The boy's going into law. He ought to learn the meaning of extortion."

"Not another word," Ned growls.

Smith continues, talking over him. "In fact, I'm starting to wonder if you have more double-crossing tricks up your sleeves, Ned."

"What is he talking about?" I demand.

Smith scoffs loudly. "Your uncle never explained the terms of this lovely little merger we have going on tomorrow?"

A coldness creeps into me, snuffing out the anger. Ned is breathing hard. He avoids my gaze.

"What's going on?" I ask, my voice broken.

Smith shakes his head. "Your uncle has been so deep in debt for so long that he can't see up from down anymore.

And it's gambling debt no less. Pathetic. His coming to us is the only thing keeping him from being eaten alive by collection agencies."

My head's spinning. The ringing in my ears has returned. "Ned?"

"He's as much of a crook as I am," Smith sneers. "We're only taking him on because he's made big promises. Put some big collateral on the line. He's apparently made some patched-up, shady deal with unnamed entities. He won't even tell me who."

"A vicious lie," Ned says, tearing his hand across the table. His glass of water flies through the air, smashing against the wall with a tremendous crash.

Smith points a threatening finger at Ned. "Don't you dare try to deny it."

"I will deny it. You can't bring your lies and filth into this home any longer."

"You're a fool," Smith growls. He shoves his chair to the side. "I'm not staying here another minute. As of this moment, you can consider the merger off."

Ned's eyes widen. "Wait."

"Forget it. I'm not going to be played as a fool, Foster. I don't know what you're up to, but I sure as hell don't like it."

He storms out of the room.

Ned flies after him. "Smith! Wait!"

I'm stunned but rush after them.

The front doors are open. I can hear Ned screaming at Jenkins to start his car.

I'm alone in the center of the grand entryway. It's dark, and a cold wind from the open front doors blows in. Chills prickle all over my body. The room seems to be spinning, but I know I'm standing still. The threat on my life has never felt so real. So raw.

And then, from the grandfather clock in the study, the chimes of midnight ring out.

It's Saturday. August 5. The day I will die.

CHAPTER 30

Cassandra

It's here. Saturday. August 5.

Watching the clock on my phone turn to midnight, I feel a part of me break inside.

Maybe I believed it would never actually come. That somehow, just by loving each other and creating something beautiful in this world, we'd cheat the past. We'd cheat destiny.

But now, we'll cheat nothing.

I haven't stepped a foot out of the house since Mom grounded me yesterday. Not for lack of trying. I begged, groveled, cried, and slammed doors, but Mom stood her ground. I can't even sneak out when she's asleep, because she's tweaked the house alarm system to go off if any doors or windows are opened.

So I stay at my laptop, frantically searching the Web for any morsel of wisdom. Some hint of a message sent from some distant cosmic portal that Lawrence will be okay. As the early hours of the morning snake by, I vacillate between despair and hope, confidence and despondency.

It isn't until the sound of my opening door wakes me that I

realize I'd fallen asleep facedown on the desk, one arm flung across my keyboard. The brightness of morning assails me. I sit up with a start and gasp at the sharp cramp in my neck.

Mom's standing in the doorway. "Good grief, Cass. Were you up all night IMing with your boyfriend?" She sighs with frustration. "I should have thought to take your computer."

"First of all, no one calls it 'IMing' anymore. But anyway, no. Don't worry. He doesn't even have a computer."

Mom frowns. "Then what were you doing?"

"Does it matter? I didn't leave my room." I swallow any more snarky comments. I have to be smart. I have to play my cards perfectly right now.

"Mom," I begin, keeping my tone calm and even. "I've been doing a lot of thinking, and I'm hoping you will be willing to make a compromise with me. If you let me stay home today, I'll—"

"No way," she says, shaking her head. "You're coming sailing. That much is decided. We can discuss the terms of your grounding later, but as far as today is concerned, there's no getting out of it."

"But, Mom—"

"I'm sorry, Cassandra. You can't change my mind on this. Frank and I talked a lot about it last night, and we think some family time is exactly what you need."

"I'll have all the family time you want. Just not today. Please trust me when I say that today, of all days, it's extremely important for me to be able to stay home."

She smiles a little. "Everything feels extremely important

when you're a teenager. You trust me. It's not as earth-shattering as it may seem."

Her condescending tone makes my toes curl. "It's not fair."

"This is what happens when you lie to me."

"I never—"

"Stop." Mom gives me the I-mean-business point with her finger. "We're done talking about this." She starts to close my door, and I jump to my feet.

"Mom, please!"

She sighs. "Cassandra, will you relax? It's not like he's going to disappear if you don't see him for one day."

The cruel irony of her words takes my breath away.

"Get dressed," she says firmly. "We're leaving in ten minutes."

CHAPTER 31

Lawrence

The first hours of my final day pass like years. After walking the silent house, I finally settle again in my room. I know it's not inherently any safer in there, but where else can I go?

Words won't come to me, so I don't write. Sleep abandoned me long ago so I don't lie on my bed. All I can do is sit on the cold floor and listen. Listen for Ned to return home, for raised voices—anything. But the house remains unbearably still.

Dawn finds me on my balcony. I'm wrapped in a blanket, but even that doesn't keep out the chill. The sight of the rising sun has never looked so bleak or filled me with such untenable dread. I fall to my knees, pressing my forehead to the marble balcony, unable to stand it all.

Cassandra, I need you. I need you with me.

I stay like that, drifting in and out of restless sleep, until the sun has climbed and brushes the tops of the trees in the garden. I awake with a start. A feeling of urgency grips me. I should be doing something, anything to stop the impending doom.

But as the morning unfolds before me, I'm struck by how

normal everything seems. As if the rest of the world has failed to realize that I will die today. And why should they? I suppose I expected dark rain clouds. Ominous ravens swooping overhead, letting out mournful cries.

But today is bright and sunny and beautiful. Gulls swoop high above, and a lark sings cheerfully. The house is no different. When I finally venture cautiously into the downstairs, every corner is abuzz with anticipation of the party tonight. Servants trim the lawn and wash Ned's Rolls Royce. Caterers and decorators bustle back and forth with bright, glittering armloads of food, champagne glasses, and decor for the party.

Only one thing remains out of place. There's no sign of Ned.

I long to see Cassandra. I wish we could talk about what I should do. After not seeing her last night, I need to go wait for her now. She must be beside herself with worry. I want to comfort her. I need her to comfort me.

After watching the steady flow of party preparations for a good ten minutes and deeming it safe, I head outside. The sun beams down on me like a spotlight, illuminating me for any dangerous entity to see. My skin tingles as if I'm being watched. I have to be brave for Cassandra. Everything will be better once we are together. As I cross the lawn, however, my eyes fall on a man. He leans against a marble pillar on the back patio, watching the hustle and bustle as he smokes a cigarette. The hair on the back of my neck stands on end. I recognize him. But from where?

All at once it hits me. Hank.

I see him now as I saw him last, casually ordering the execution of a bound, unarmed man. My knees lock. And then, as if summoned by my silent terror, Hank's face slowly turns in my direction.

The instinctive need to survive takes over. I know it draws more attention to me to run, but I can't help it. In that moment, all that matters is getting back into the seclusion of my room. I race through the house, slamming my door behind me and locking it. My heart beats furiously in my chest.

That was too close. He still might have seen me. He might be on his way after me right now. I tear open the button of my shirt collar. Even so, breath comes in short, tight gasps. I press my forehead to the cool wood of the door.

Cassandra, what am I going to do?

I can't go to the beach now. I can't risk being seen. I hate myself for hiding like this, but my body refuses to let me do anything else.

The afternoon drags by with intolerable slowness. Then early evening. By seven, the first guests start arriving. Music floats from the outdoor bandstand. Laughter and the rumble of bright conversation ripple through the house.

Unable to bear the sight of my room a minute more, I slink down the stairs and into the shadows of a rarely used sitting room. I need to see if Hank is still in the crowd. I need to look for Uncle Ned. By now, the anxiety of waiting has worn my nerves raw. I hide in darkness, listening to the pulse of the party outside and feeling more painfully alone than I imagined possible.

Peeking out between the silk curtains, I watch the swirl of lights and brightly colored dresses. It's happy, carefree, oblivious chaos outside. I imagine my gaze pushing past them, traveling to the calm beauty of the beach. The sun will be setting soon, sharpening the colors, casting brilliant, golden light over the waves. I imagine Cassandra standing at the shore break, her long hair and white gown flowing behind her in soft ocean breezes. Her arms reach for me. Her lips form my name.

And then, like a flame searing past my eyes, I catch a glimpse of red in the midst of the swirling party guests. The sight brings me out of my dreams. I know that color, that dress. I know that sharp swoop of black hair.

Fay.

She moves through the crowd, searching. For me? I watch her, my heart rate rising. She happens to move closer to the window where I stand, unaware that I'm nearby. But she comes close enough for me to see her expression. Anxiety sharpens her gaze. She looks frantic, turning around any male guest near my age to get a glimpse of his face.

She is looking for me. And she's afraid.

Before I can think about what I'm doing, I'm out of the house and into the ruckus of the party. I lose sight of Fay.

The unsettling feeling that I'm being watched grips me once more. The relentless music and the roar of chatter oppress my ears. I cut a look to either side, but there's no sight of Hank. Looking for Fay, I nearly crash into a waiter carrying a tray of fluted champagne glasses. A man with a barking laugh shoulders past me, as if I'm not even there. A woman with too much kohl smudged around her eyes asks me if I've seen a little white dog in a clown collar. Dizziness fills my head like water. I spin away when a pair of dark, sultry eyes meets mine through the blur of faces.

I've never been happier to see Fay. She runs up to me, out of breath.

"Lon. Where have you been?" Her eyes still flash with unmistakable fear.

I grip her shoulders. "What's wrong, Fay? What happened?"

She catches her breath for a moment. Or is she perhaps searching for the right words?

"You were right," she begins, her voice tight with clenched-back emotion. "I've been keeping a secret from you. From the very beginning. I never should have—"

"I know," I say, pulling her into my arms. I can't bear to see the shame on her face. She's hardly to blame for the sins of her family.

But she pulls from my grip, staring into my eyes with confusion, even a little betrayal.

"How long have you known?"

"I only just found out. But I don't hold it against you, Fay. Your family may have mob ties, but that doesn't make you a criminal."

She steps back.

"I watched you from the window," I say softly. "You looked so afraid. Are they coming for me? Your family?"

She shakes her head slowly. "You don't get it, do you?" She grabs my jacket lapels. "You're in danger, Lawrence."

"I know that. Did you tell your family I jilted you, and now your father wants to defend your honor?"

"What? No! My father's not the one you need to be afraid of."

"Then who?"

Fay's eyes grow dark, even in the intense, golden light of sunset. "Your Uncle Ned. He's coming for you."

CHAPTER 32

Cassandra

The sailing trip with my parents brings me close to a mental breakdown. I move through the stages of grief multiple times.

Denial. This can't really be happening. I'm not gliding happily over the ocean while the love of my life faces death. There's just no way.

Bargaining. I'll do anything if you let me go back. I'm sick. You have to take me back. I'll break a hole in the bottom of this boat if you don't let me go back.

Anger. So much anger. This one took up most of the day.

But as I sit curled at the stern of the ship, watching the sun sink into a shimmering ocean, the depression sets in. Hard.

My forehead drops against the cold metal of the railing. I stare at the last wavering band of light, unable to catch a good breath. My eyes burn from fixating on the sun. Or maybe I'm going to cry. I've been holding back tears for most of the day.

Saturday is over now, and Lawrence is probably dead. And I did nothing, nothing, to save him.

"Cass?"

Mom kneels beside me. Her hand rests on my shoulder, and the look in her eyes is one of overwhelming love and concern.

The tears come.

Huge, shaking sobs. The stress and fear and sorrow of the past few days are unleashed all at once. My mom holds me and I cry my heart out.

"Tell me what's going on, Cassandra," she says, stroking my hair as I bawl into her shoulder. "I'm so worried. Did someone hurt you? Did this boy hurt you, Cassandra? If he did, so help me, I will rip his—"

"No, Mom. It's nothing like that."

"Then what? I've never seen you like this, Cass. Even in the middle of the divorce. I'm scared, honey. You need to talk to me."

But what can I tell her? The truth? Brandon's reaction proved there's no point in even going there.

Or is there? Maybe I could give her a version of the truth. At this point, what do I have to lose?

I draw in a trembling breath. "Lawrence. That's his name. And I'm in love with him. But he's in trouble. Not with the law or anything. It's something with his uncle's business, I think. He's in danger."

Mom frowns. "Why would he be in danger if it's the uncle's business?"

"They're just bad guys, okay? Trust me. He's in serious danger. He may…get hurt."

Mom pulls me close again in a hug. "I'm sure he's okay, sweetheart. You're scared for him because you care about him, but—"

"No," I say, pulling back. "He's going to get hurt. I know that."

"How can you—"

"I just do. You have to believe me on this. I know it doesn't make sense. It sounds crazy. But I know. For a fact. And that's why I wanted to stay home. I have to help him."

Fresh tears cut down my face. Fresh pain claws at my heart. Mom brushes the hair from my eyes. She's silent, analyzing me with her gaze. After a long pause, she looks at Frank playing with Eddie at the bow. Everyone's pretending not to watch the crazy teenage girl losing it in the corner. Mom's brow lowers.

"Greg," she says, turning to the captain. "Take us home. The fastest route possible."

My eyes widen. Mom strokes my hair and smiles. "The day's not over. I'm sure this Lawrence kid is going to be okay, but if it's that important to you to help him, well, that's a worthy thing. And I'm proud of you."

I fling my arms around her. "I love you, Mom."

"Love you too, kiddo."

The wind whips my hair behind me as the captain turns the boat. Gripping the stern rail, I stare out at the land in the distance. The first star has pierced through the gradually darkening sky. I close my eyes tightly.

I'm coming, Lawrence. Please don't let it be too late.

CHAPTER 33

Lawrence

Fay has always been mysterious and hard to read, but this is different. I put my hands over her fists, which still grip the lapels of my jacket with desperate force.

"What do you mean, Ned's coming for me? What are you talking about?"

"He's the one behind all this," she says, her eyes wild.

"Behind all what?"

"Everything! Oh, Lon. I didn't want it to come to this."

"Tell me."

"There isn't time. He's coming."

"Fay, please."

Her eyes dart around. "We have to go somewhere private. It isn't safe to discuss it here."

She weaves us through the crowd. It's as if I'm in the middle of a strange dream. We settle in a more secluded garden area, paved with brick and decorated with wild rose. Fay sits on the stone bench but then stands.

"It's hard to know where to start."

"Try."

She exhales shakily. "You know my family is part of the underground crime world. Well, so does your uncle. That's the reason I'm here. I guess he's been in some bad business deals. Really bad. He came to my family for help. He made an unorthodox deal with them. A deal involving you and me."

"What kind of deal?"

Her eyes lower.

"Speak plainly with me, Fay. If you had any idea what I've been through in the past twenty-four hours, you wouldn't mince words."

"Your uncle promised you to the Cartelli family. He told them you'd work as a lawyer for my father to help make sure his tracks are covered on the legal end."

She's speaking the words, but the idea seems too outlandish to believe. "What on earth made him think I'd ever agree to such a thing?"

"That's where I came in." Her gaze becomes distant. "'Such a pretty girl,' Papa always used to say. 'One day, you're going to help the family like Nico and Riff.'"

She touches her face, lost in thoughts. "He trained me from the time I was twelve. Taught me subtle ways to get exactly what I wanted from a man. How to carry myself. How to talk. How to dress. How to be every man's dream come true. But he always made it very clear that I'd never be able to choose my own man. I couldn't even go on dates. My only interactions with men outside my family were for training, under Papa's watchful eye."

Hearing Fay open up like this, seeing the sad, vulnerable girl inside, I'm overcome with the desire to protect her. I take her hand.

"I'm sorry."

She shrugs. "It wasn't a bad life. In fact, Papa spoiled me terribly. Any new dress I wanted. Jewelry. Shoes. Trips to the seaside with Mama and Isabella. As long as I understood that when the moment came, I could not disappoint him."

"And that moment came when Ned offered me as a lawyer," I say, putting the pieces together.

She nods. "I was the bait. I was supposed to seal the deal. Once you were in love with me, I'd see to it that you kept me happy, even if it meant working for my father."

I lower myself onto the stone bench, my head throbbing with all the new information. Was it possible? Could Ned really sink so low?

Little by little, pieces from my memory fill in the story. Ned introduced Fay to me. He arranged the first several meetings and that night in New York, when he was so insistent that I would marry her.

And then there was everything I learned last night. Jerome Smith telling me about Ned's gambling debt. His revelation that the merger with Cooper Enterprises was only possible at the promise of Ned's arrangement with "unknown entities." Like the mob.

"I can't believe it," I say softly.

Fay comes beside me. "Can you forgive me, Lon?"

I look at the girl before me. It's strange to see her in this completely new light. She's a different person in many ways. And yet, she's still the same beautiful girl I've known all summer. I tuck a strand of her jet-black hair behind her ear. "Of course I forgive you. It's not your fault. You were just doing your duty."

"It may have been duty at first," she says, choking out the words, "but I came to love you, Lon. Truly."

I take her face in my hands. "Oh, Fay."

Squeezing her eyes shut tightly, she grabs my collar and presses a kiss to my mouth. I'm filled with a tempest of conflicting emotions. Cassandra has my heart, but somehow I can't push Fay away. I don't know if I'll see tomorrow. And Fay's lips are warm and soft, like they always were. I allow myself a single kiss.

"Well, isn't this a pretty sight. And here I was worried."

At the sound of Ned's voice, Fay and I pull apart.

He's standing right in front of us, dressed in a stylish suit that almost looks comical stretched over his huge body. The sight of him sends rage through me. My fists tighten at my side.

"Easy, boy," Ned snarls, his expression suddenly becoming severe. "You've done enough damage today. Let's not make it more."

"You owe me an explanation," I say, clenching my jaw.

"I'm sure Fay here has given you her own warped version of events."

"Is it true then?" I ask, the sting of his betrayal piercing me. "Did you really lose everything to gambling debts? Did you really promise me to the mob? Did you really try to push me into a marriage so that I could solve all of your financial problems for you?"

Ned swipes a hand through the air. "I did what I had to do. You'd do no different. It's not like I was giving them your head on a platter, boy. With Roberto, you'd be rich and powerful beyond your wildest dreams. It's better than anything your stupid father could secure for you. I'm doing you a favor."

I shake my head slowly. "How could you think I'd ever become a criminal? I guess when you've sunken to that level, you think anyone will."

"You're not as noble as you fancy yourself." Ned scoffs. "You're as low and common as any man here."

Fay jumps to my defense. "Don't you dare insult him."

He whirls around. "Keep quiet." His eyes burn with rage. "You have no right to tell me what I can and can't do. You're nothing! Completely useless! If you'd done your job in the first place, we wouldn't be in this mess, you worthless slut." As he speaks the insult, he brings the back of his hand hard across Fay's jaw.

She lets out a cry of pain. Blood brightens her bottom lip. Shocked and furious, I grab Ned's arm, pulling him away.

"How dare you strike her!"

Ned shoves me. Fay's eyes glisten with angry tears. "Now you see your uncle's true colors, Lon."

"Shut up," Ned barks.

"I'm not going to shut up," Fay cries. "My father may be a

criminal, but at least he owns up to who he is. You try to pretend that you're a wealthy businessman. You throw all these parties so people will respect and admire you. But I'm going to tell everyone what a lowlife you are. I'm going to tell them all!"

Ned grabs Fay by the wrist, bending it at an unnatural angle. She cries out.

"Let go of her!" I lunge forward, grabbing him by the collar. Once again, Ned shoves me back, his sheer size giving him frightening strength. When I go for him again, he lands a punch to my jaw so hard that I crash backward into the stone bench.

Ned spins to deal with Fay, but she has one of her red shoes in hand, and with a shout, she brings the high heel down into Ned's face. He roars with shock and pain. Free from his grip, Fay runs headlong into the party, disappearing into the movement of the crowd.

Ned lets out a furious growl. Pressing a hand to the cut on his face, he tears off after her.

"Ned!" I shout, running to keep up with him. "This is between you and me! Leave her alone!"

Ned makes his way through the crush of the bodies writhing and dancing, but they engulf me. In a blink, I can't see Ned anymore. And I can't see Fay either. I call her name, but the cry is lost in the music. I turn a full circle, looking frantically for her.

Nothing.

A trio approaches me, goading me to join their game of hide-and-seek. I push past them without as much as a word. I have to find Fay. She was right. My uncle is the dangerous one.

And then, like a steam engine right into my chest, a thought strikes me. Is my uncle the one I should have been suspecting all this time? *Is my uncle the one who kills me?*

All at once, the music and laughter of the party fade. The colors and lights blend together around me. Across the lawn and into the shadows, the sight of Fay running, her red dress like a smear of blood. Ned is little more than an arm's length away.

In slow motion, Fay tosses a terrified look over her shoulder. Her eyes connect with mine. And then, she turns to the bushes. To the path.

Like two ghosts, she and Ned vanish into the dark beauty of the beach.

The beach.

A thudding heartbeat. A shallow breath. Everything else is blotted out by darkness.

But I know what I have to do. And for the first time in days, I'm not afraid. In fact, after so much turmoil, I marvel at the elegance of it all. Fate found a way to get me on that beach. And I accept it. Because I must. Because I won't let fate have anyone else. And if I don't stop Ned, Fay will die as well.

Closing my eyes, I take a deep breath and walk a final time to the sea.

CHAPTER 34

Lawrence

The odd calm I felt approaching the beach is shattered the moment I break through the bushy path.

Fay is lying on the sand. Ned's kneeling over her, smashing his fists into her with animallike fury. Fay screams and holds up her arms to try to block him, but it's no use. With his strength, he'll break her delicate body in minutes.

A roar tears from my lungs. I fly at Ned, ramming into him with all my weight. It's enough for me to make him stumble back.

"Dammit, boy," he shouts. "You stay out of this!"

He lunges forward, shoving me to the ground. I turn back to Fay, who's lying motionless on the sand, and I spring back to my feet.

"Leave her alone, Ned." I slam into him again. It's like pushing my shoulder into a stone wall. "She's done nothing!"

"She's ruined everything."

"No! I'm the one who ruined your plan. I'm the one who broke her heart and sent her away."

Ned staggers away from Fay. His face is flushed. He stares at me, breathing hard. I bend over, trying to catch my breath as well.

"I found someone else. Someone I love. I've never loved Fay. Not like that. Your plan never would have worked, Ned."

He shakes his head. "You're wrong."

"I'm telling you, I never would have married Fay, let alone worked for the mob."

Ned's gaze stays on me, unbroken. "So you would have left me to the wolves then, Lonnie? After everything I've done for you? After everything I've given you? I've treated you like a son, dammit. I've loved you."

His words reveal his desperation. A pang of regret grips me.

"I'm sorry, Ned. I want to help you. And I will. But not like this."

"Well, it's too late!" Ned voice rises in pitch and fervor. "The mob is ready to pounce. Don't you get that? Once they catch word that the Cooper deal fell through, I'm a dead man."

"Maybe if we go to the police—"

"The police? Are you mad? They're just as bad as the Cartellis. And they want blood, just the same. My blood."

I take a tentative step toward him. "There has to be another way."

"There isn't! This was the only way, Lon. The only way!" He's yelling now, his voice coarse and raw.

"I'm sorry."

His left eye twitches. "You're not sorry. Don't lie to me, boy."

"Ned..."

"No." His shoulders heave. "This is all your fault. You want to see me choke. Admit it!"

"I love you, Ned. You have to believe me."

"Liar."

Like the crack of a whip, his arm flies forward. His fist connects with my jaw in an explosion of pain. I fall to the sand. The moon overhead blurs and doubles. Then Ned's face blots it out like an eclipse.

He lifts his fist again, but I roll out of the way and scurry to my feet. He's stronger than me. I know that. But I'm faster. When Ned lunges again, I dart out of the way. He whirls around and gets the tail of my shirt in his fingers. He drags me toward him.

This time, I deliver a punch to his face. And while Ned reels, I dash away. He presses the spot where I struck him. He rushes at me, arms out like a linebacker. I try to dodge to the left, but he anticipates my movement. His fingers clamp, viselike around my throat.

Ned jerks me up. His face bent with blind rage, he smashes his fist into my cheek. Across my jaw. Over the crown of my head. Each blow blazes against my skin. I hear my own voice gasp in pain, but I feel oddly as if I'm watching him beat me from a distant, high place.

Ned pauses to catch his breath. Then, clenching his teeth together, he delivers the blow that sends me to my back.

My head hits the water with a splash. The upper half of my body crashes into the shallow wave break. The cold shocks me. Gasping, I flail up, but Ned's already on top of me. His massive hands close around my neck. In his eyes, I see nothing of the man I've known my whole life. The man I called "uncle." He's far away. Perhaps gone forever.

With a grunt, Ned pushes me beneath the black water. Instantly, darkness engulfs me. I claw at his hands with all of my strength, but I know it's no use. I'm weakened, and he's twice as strong as me. My body writhes and flails, but he's straddling my waist, pinning me beneath the waves.

My lungs burn for breath. My eyes burn with salt water. The wounds Ned's fists opened on my skin burn and bleed into the sea. My chest thrums and seems to tear apart from the inside out, yearning to breathe. Gripping Ned's hands, I struggle to make out anything in the rippling black water above me. But there's nothing. Everything fades into darkness.

It's over.

I shut my eyes. I don't want it to end this way. I'll gather my final tendril of life and pour it into thoughts of Cassandra. Perhaps, wherever she is at this moment, she'll feel it and know how much I love her. I'll leave this world thinking only of how I love her.

Good-bye, Cassandra.

CHAPTER 35

Cassandra

I've never loved any sight more than that of the backyard. Basked in pale moonlight, it's magical. I'm flying, soaring over the grass, past the gardens, toward the beach. The smell of the ocean in the distance is the substance that pulses through my veins.

I'm coming. I'm coming, Lawrence.

I push past the branches in a daze. I explode onto the beach.

And immediately shrink back a step. There are people here. Strangers. A woman sleeping on the sand and a big man down by the shore. Recognition flickers through me. I know him. I've seen him before.

Lawrence's uncle. Ned.

There's a splash. Another person. A body being held under the water. I recognize the twitching legs.

Lawrence. It's Lawrence.

"Lawrence!"

I barely recognize the anguished pitch my voice takes as I fly toward the water. Ned's dark features are twisted, unrecognizable with rage. By the time he sees me, my head is connecting with his chest.

The impact probably hurts me ten times more than it does him. But it's enough. He teeters backward, thrown off balance. His arms swirl in the air.

Lawrence bursts from the water. He gags and coughs. His limbs flail, grasping for life.

But he is alive. Blessedly, beautifully alive.

I'm still screaming. "Lawrence!"

He blindly flings himself forward and collapses on the sand. He presses his face to the ground, gasping for air with his entire body. Deliriously happy, I reach for him.

The shadow falls over him before I realize what's happening. Ned. Lunging toward me. His hands close around my shirt. He lifts me like I'm a rag doll. One shove and I'm on my back on the sand, the wind knocked out of me.

I blink in shock. But when his face comes into view again, I scramble back to my feet. Trembling like a caged rabbit. I hold up my arms, anticipating the next blow.

But Ned only stares at me. His brow lowers. "You."

I have no words. My heart thrums within me, threatening to explode out of my chest.

"You must be the one he fell in love with," Ned says slowly, the realization coming to him. "I should have known. I should have listened to my instincts that day on the beach."

"I won't let you hurt him."

Ned laughs. “This night keeps getting more and more aggravating.”

I back up slowly, my eyes darting frantically around the beach for something to fight him with. A stick, a rock—anything.

A flicker of movement catches my eye. The woman on the beach is stirring. Whose side is she on? Ned’s or Lawrence’s? Is it worth the risk to try to get her to help me?

“You’d better leave now,” Ned says. “Before I have to deal with you too.”

“I’m taking Lawrence with me.”

“You’ll leave right now and keep your damn mouth shut. That’s what you’re going to do.”

In spite of my shaking knees, I stand straight. “I won’t let you hurt him.”

“Suit yourself.”

Before I can even take a step back, he’s lunged for me. I land hard on my side. My key ring cuts into me, sending shooting pain down my leg.

“Mama taught me to never hit a girl,” Ned says, clamping his hand over my shoulder to hold me down. “But you see, she didn’t realize how often that’s necessary.”

Panic radiates through me. My body’s trembling with fear. My leg throbs where the keys dig into my flesh.

Wait.

My key ring.

In a split second, I have the swirling memory of the morning Lawrence and I spent on the beach. I see myself explaining each item on the key ring, laughing at his wonder. The elephant. The flashlight.

The pepper spray.

Bursting with adrenaline, I push onto my back, freeing up the pocket. Ned pins me down, but with my free hand, I have just enough momentum to rip my key ring from my shorts.

The keys and knickknacks jingle loudly. The flashlight glows red. Ned straightens, staring at the key ring.

"What in the—?"

His surprise gives me enough time to snatch the pepper spray. I grab for the tab and rip it free. Squeezing my eyes shut, I press down. All I hear is the hiss of the canister emptying.

Then a pained howl.

My eyes fly open again. Ned has reeled back. He's pawing at his face, shrieking. I scramble to my feet. I can't believe it worked.

Movement catches my attention again. The strange woman is bent over Lawrence, frantically trying to revive him. She's on our side. That's good. We don't have much time. Ned will only be incapacitated for a few minutes tops.

I race toward them. Not even noticing me in her panic, the woman cups Lawrence's face in her hand.

"Lon? Wake up! We have to go!"

There's something about the way she spoke his name. About the way she's holding his face.

She looks up with a start.

It's a girl my age, not a woman. She's beautiful, with a short black bob and dark, sad eyes. All at once, I know who she is.

"Fay."

She stares at me, speechless, and then she closes her eyes. "You're Cassandra."

I fall to my knees at Lawrence's other side. "Look," I say urgently. "We both love Lawrence, and right now he's in danger." I set my hand over hers. "I'm sorry, Fay. I truly am."

"Don't be." She straightens. "What should I do?"

"Run and get help. The party's still going on?"

"Yes."

"Then go get everyone you can find. Tell them Ned's snapped. Tell them he's trying to kill you. Say anything that will get a group of them here."

She nods in agreement and I watch her run back to the party, filled with a sudden rush of hope.

"What did you do to me?" Ned roars. He splashes water on his face, but the salt probably only heightens the sting.

Lawrence is completely out, but I can feel a heartbeat. He's not dead. He's not going to die. We're going to beat this.

I circle my arms around his chest, but he's heavier than I expected. Gritting my teeth, I begin to drag him to the bushes. If I can just get to the bushes…

"Girl!" Ned screams. "Where are you?"

I pull Lawrence another half inch. Why is he so heavy?

"I may not be able to see you, but that doesn't mean I can't snap your neck."

I have to stay strong. *Come on, come on. Move, Lawrence.*

Ned staggers toward me. "Where are you, you filthy little slut?"

I can't let myself entertain what will happen if Ned gets his vision back before Fay returns. Keep pulling, Cass. Pull like your life depends on it.

Lawrence's eyelids flutter. Gasping for air, he jolts his head up and looks at me.

"Cassandra!"

Ned staggers in our direction. "Run, Lawrence!" I pull at his torso. He groans with pain as he rises to his hands and knees. We're so close to the bushes.

But not close enough.

"There you are," Ned barks. "I'm going to enjoy squeezing the life from your throat."

He grabs for me. I scream, and his hand closes around my wrist.

"Ned!" Lawrence shouts, his voice strained as he reaches for us. But Ned's massive hand circles my throat.

I scratch at his fingers with my free hand, but he doesn't even flinch. His upper lip curls with rage, and his vice grip tightens, squeezing off my windpipe.

The bushes suddenly explode with people. A cluster of men bursts onto the beach, their faces bright with alarm.

"Hey!" One of them bellows, seeing Ned and me. "Let her go!"

"She wasn't kidding," another one yells. "He's snapped!"

The crowd doesn't give Ned a chance to comply. They rush him, tackling him to the ground. I fall to my knees, gasping. More people from the party come out onto the beach, craning their necks to see. Fay emerges from the bushes. Her gaze goes to Lawrence, then to me. My heart's still pounding and my breath heavy, but I nod. She nods back.

There's a commotion on the beach. The group of men drag Ned back toward the house. Others shout for the police to be called. People are talking loudly, explaining what happened to newcomers, expressing their shock and dismay at such a thing happening.

Others rush to Lawrence and me.

"Are you all right?"

"Can you move?"

"Can you see how many fingers I'm holding up?"

Lawrence is sitting up, though he still seems disoriented. In spite of all the chaos around him, he keeps his eyes fixed on mine. I squeeze his hand.

"You did it, Cassandra," he whispers. "You saved me."

The realization sinks in. It's over. It's really over. Inexpressible relief mixes with the residual adrenaline and fear, and I can't stop the tears spilling from my eyes.

"We did it," I say, gripping his hand. I need to feel the flesh and pulse of him. Proof that he's alive. That he's here. That we're really together.

"We need to get you a doctor," a woman says, coming to Lawrence's side. "You look pretty beaten up."

"I'll be okay."

A young man reaches for Lawrence's shoulders. "I'll help get you up. We got you, Lonnie."

But Lawrence holds out a hand. "No, Charles. Please…I

want to stay here for a moment. I'll come, but I need a minute. A minute alone with Cassandra."

The young man—Charles, I guess, is his name—glances at the woman, then at me. When no one moves, Fay comes over.

"It's all right," she announces. "Lon just needs to get his strength back. He's overwhelmed with all these people. Come on, everyone. Let's give him some space."

The lingering crowd seems reluctant. Fay sets her hand on Charles's shoulder. "Okay, everybody. Let's go."

The people shuffle away, glancing back at us with curious looks. Fay ushers them along. Just before she reaches the path, she glances over her shoulder too. I feel a stab of guilt. She loved Lawrence, that much I can see.

"Thank you," I say.

Fay manages a small smile, which fades as quickly as it came. And then she vanishes into the bushes.

Lawrence's hand comes to my cheek. His gaze is brimming with love. My heart bursts at the sight of it. I fall against his chest and his arms encircle me. Fresh tears fall from my eyes.

"I love you, Lawrence."

"And I you, Cassandra."

He pulls my face to his. The feeling of our lips joined together has never filled me with more happiness.

When we break apart, Lawrence strokes my hair. "I want to be with you for the rest of my life. It's time, Cassandra."

"Right now?" I ask, my voice trembling.

He nods. "When I go back to the house, I want you at my

side." He takes my hand. "Are you ready to come to nineteen twenty-five?"

CHAPTER 36

Cassandra

Lawrence and I rise carefully to our feet, hand in hand.

"You're trembling," he says softly.

I can only nod. Lawrence smiles and kisses me. "Don't be afraid."

Each step feels like scaling a mountain. Lawrence takes the first step onto the path.

"Wait."

He looks back at me. "What's wrong?"

"I'm not ready."

He smiles a little. "Why not? This is everything we've been working for. Don't you want to be together?"

"Of course I do, but…what if it doesn't happen?"

"What do you mean?"

"What if this beach, being able to see each other, really is just a freak accident? An anomaly. A random crack in the time-space continuum. There's no fate. No destiny. It just…is what it is. Nothing more. What if saving you changes nothing?"

"There's only one way to test that," Lawrence says. He holds out his hand.

The train of what-ifs roar through me again.

"Suppose it does work. What if we only get one free pass to move through time?" My throat feels tight. "I never really said good-bye to my mom."

"I'm sure that's not the case," Lawrence says, but I can tell he's trying to sound more confident than he feels.

"You don't know anything for sure." I stare at the pathway,. "What if saving you actually closes the portal or the gateway or whatever crazy thing has been letting us see each other? What if fate allowed me to see you only so I could save you? And now that I have…it will be over. What if when we leave this beach, we fade into our own times and never see each other again?"

The questions are enough to make Lawrence step back. He stares at the pathway, thoughts racing behind his dark eyes. I throw my arms around his neck. He holds me tightly.

"I can't lose you, Lawrence. I can't take the risk."

After a long pause, his words come. "But what other choice to do we have?"

I break from his grip. Lawrence touches my face.

"We can't stay on this beach forever."

"Yes, we can."

"Cassandra."

The lump in my throat burns. "I'm so afraid."

"And so am I. But the chance to spend forever with you is worth the risk. And the only way we can know is by trying."

He presses his lips to mine. I kiss him back hungrily. He starts to pull away, but I don't let him. He returns the passion.

And deep inside, I know that it is worth the risk. To have him forever. To have this kiss for the rest of my life.

I set my forehead to his. "If we don't see each other on the other side—"

He puts his fingers to my lips. "Don't even speak it. We will."

I release a trembling breath. "Okay. Let's do this."

Hand pressed to hand, we turn to the path.

One step. Then another. Lawrence keeps his face turned to me. He gives me a little smile. Pulling my hand, he runs into the path.

"Lawrence!"

For a blurred, breathless moment, we're flying hand in hand. And then…the definition of Lawrence's features start to fade. The strength of his grip seems to melt away. His colors fade, and like a ghost, he vanishes into the night air.

CHAPTER 37

Cassandra

He's gone.

I stand and stare at the spot where he vanished. This isn't happening. It's too cruel.

I stagger back to the beach. It's empty. Only dark sand and white-tipped surf.

"Lawrence?" I call out.

Nothing.

I scream as loud as I can. "LAWRENCE?"

Gasping, I fall to my knees on the sand. "No. No, no, no." It can't be over. It can't. I'll never forgive myself for letting Lawrence leave my arms. I'll never forgive the universe for not giving us a chance to say good-bye.

He bursts from the bushes.

His face is ashen, his eyes wide. I draw in a sharp breath, and we collide in a fierce embrace. There are no words. We just hold each other.

Lawrence finally steps back. Taking my hand, he leads me to our spot on the sand, overlooking the waves. The place we first met. Side by side, we stare out at the sea.

"I don't understand," he says.

"I do." The words hurt to say. "This beach is just an anomaly. A crack in time. Always has been, always will be."

Lawrence frowns. "But how could that be? Don't you think someone would have noticed in the nearly hundred years this house has been standing?"

I shake my head. "Maybe they didn't." But even as I say it, I realize how implausible that would be. Surely someone would have noticed.

"There has to be another explanation," Lawrence says. "Some sense to it all."

"Or maybe there's not."

Despondent, I lie on my back, wincing at the pain that still hangs over my body. My eyes are drawn to the moon. It's especially big and bright, hanging over the beach. Beautiful. Almost full, by the looks of it.

A sharp snap of realization clicks into place. The moon. The full moon. The full moon tomorrow night. I sit up.

"What is it?" Lawrence asks.

I set my hand on his knee. I need a minute of silence to put together the wild thoughts in my mind. That first night. The full moon rising out of the ocean. The pulse of light. Lawrence suddenly standing down by the water. The painting in the library.

The full moon. It has to mean something.

"What's going on, Cassandra? You're making me jumpy."

I turn to him. "I have an idea. A theory, really."

"Okay. So, tell me."

"First, I have to ask a question. On the night we met, did you watch the moon rise?"

He frowns. "I think so, yes."

"And did you notice anything…strange?"

He stares at me for a long moment. Then, slowly, shock spreads over his face. "The flash of light. You saw it too?"

I release a shaky breath. "Yes."

"I thought it was a trick of the eye. What was it, then?"

"All I know is, I was alone on the beach, and right after that pulse of light, you were suddenly standing down by the shore."

His eyes widen. "That's exactly how it happened for me. That has to be significant!"

"Lawrence. The next full moon is tomorrow night."

Lawrence perks up at the revelation. "Are you sure? Well, this could be our answer, Cassandra! This will be what allows us to travel into each other's worlds. Another full moon will open the portal."

"Or it could close forever." My words bring his enthusiasm to a halt. "Maybe this anomaly will only last through one cycle of the moon. And at the rise of the new full moon…it will be over."

Lawrence shakes his head, processing what I've said. "No."

"Think about it. If we were going to be able to move through time, it would have happened when we tried it. It's not going to last forever."

Lawrence's lips part to reply, but no words come. We're silent for a while, digesting the awful, sad truth of it. I glance over at

Lawrence, my heart still raw from everything I've gone through in the last twenty-four hours.

"They're probably all wondering what's taking you so long," I say.

Lawrence sighs. "You were supposed to come with me."

"I know."

He grips me by the shoulders. "We'll figure this out, Cassandra. There has to be a way. We will be together."

"You should go," I say. "The police have probably made it to the house by now. You'll need to tell them about your uncle."

His expression drops. "Yes."

"I'm sorry. I…can't imagine what that must have been like."

He only shakes his head. I touch his face.

"Everything's gone wrong," he says, his voice choked.

"You're alive. That didn't go wrong. And that's the most important thing. We changed the past. And probably the future."

A shiver passes through me. The old fear about messing with the time pricks at me, but I shake it away.

"Will you meet me here tomorrow?" Lawrence asks. "Will you spend the day with me, if it…"

His voice drops off, but I know what he was going to say. If it is our last day together.

"Of course," I say.

He rises, brushing the sand from his pants. His steps to the bushes are slow, conflicted. He turns just before going back to his own world. His beautiful brown eyes are flush with sadness.

"I need you, Cassandra. Now more than ever."

CHAPTER 38

Lawrence

The telegram from my father arrived early this morning. It lies flat on the desk. Like a wound. I try to ignore the neatly printed message and pour my pain onto the page.

I pause in writing for a moment, brushing my finger lightly over one of my wounds. The place where Ned's fists split my skin is hot to the touch. Overnight, an angry bruise has spread over the skin.

The police took Ned in last night. As it turns out, the Feds had been monitoring him from a distance, aware of his dealings with the Cartelli family. They were waiting for the announcement of the merger with Cooper Enterprises—another company they'd had their eye on—and they would have closed in.

After a restless night of sleep, it all feels like a bad dream or some sensational story I heard at a party. But then, many things have felt that way this summer.

I look back down at my writing. I've amassed several pages since I started. It's as if I'm searching for the answer to how to keep Cassandra in my own words. Nothing has come. Instead,

I flail in the deluge of sadness and anger and despair. The only way to breathe is to keep writing.

This telegram certainly doesn't help.

My father's words are written out in neat print:

> *Bad business, this situation with your uncle. Your Aunt Eloise is quite beside herself. She's purchased you a ticket home on the afternoon train this Monday, 7th of August. Don't be late.*

They're the first words I've had from my father all summer.

I close my eyes and set the telegram down. It's just as well. If Cassandra is right, if tonight truly is the last time I'll be able to see her, then I might as well be on a train back to Connecticut. If I can't see Cassandra on that beach, then I never want to set foot on it again.

I don't want to seem ungrateful after escaping the grasp of death, but at this moment, all I can feel is pain.

Tomorrow. I leave for home tomorrow afternoon. And tonight I say good-bye to my Cassandra.

CHAPTER 39

Cassandra

It's another perfect summer evening as I walk across the lawn to the beach. A warm wind curls through the air, and the blue of twilight almost sparkles. Hearing the familiar sound of the ocean as I draw near, I'm overcome by how beautiful the place really is.

Lawrence and I spent most of the day together and agreed to meet just after sunset. I'm a little early, despite the fact that I spent a good amount of time getting ready. I brushed my hair in long waves, perfumed my skin, and put on the green silk dress that's hung unused in my closet all summer. It's childish, perhaps, but I want his final image of me to be beautiful.

I find myself lingering on the path. I have the strangest desire to see if I can feel Lawrence pass through me as he comes to the beach. Will I be able to sense him? Even separated by a hundred years?

But then movement on the shoreline draws my attention. It's Lawrence. He's already there. He's wearing a dashing suit. Dark gray with elegant pinstripes, and a deep-crimson tie.

He dressed for me too. For some reason, this makes me want to cry.

Lawrence looks up. At first, his eyes widen with awe, and then a sad smile pulls at his lips.

"Come here," he says, holding out his arms.

I run to him. As his arms close around me, the threat of tears returns. This isn't going to be a cry-fest. I swore to myself.

We break apart, and Lawrence gazes at me. "You look…sublime."

He cups my face in his hands, resting his forehead on mine, and sighs. There's a hitch in his voice.

"I don't want to speak," he says softly. "I know anything I say will just be the beginning of good-bye."

"That's all there is left to say, Lawrence." I can't meet his eyes or I'll lose the tenuous grip I have on my emotions. "We know we have to say it. Why prolong the inevitable?"

"No," he says resolutely. "No, there's so much more I have to say to you before good-bye."

He pulls what looks like a large envelope from his inside jacket pocket. The pale gold paper is tied with a brown string. I can see the shadow of words pressed through from the other side. Lawrence puts the envelope in my palm and closes my fingers over it with both of his hands.

"For you," he says. "My very soul is on these pages. You can have something to remember me by."

Not going to cry. Two rogue tears escape and splash on the envelope.

"And there's something else," he says softly. He reaches into his pocket. When he opens his hand, a glint of light flickers off the object in his palm. I draw a sharp breath.

It's a sapphire ring. Blue and bright as the moon.

Wide-eyed, I look up at him. His expression is sweet and sad.

"It was my mother's. Father gave it to her when he went to Vienna for a summer, as a promise that he wouldn't forget her. She passed it on to me to give to the love of my life. I was planning to give this to you once we…once we were truly together. But last night I realized that no matter what, you are the love of my life. I want you to have it. And I make the same promise my father did to my mother. Whenever you look at this ring, you can know that I will be thinking of you."

I try to keep the swell of tears from spilling over, but it's no use. Setting my hand over his, I feel the ring between our palms. It cuts into me deeper than any blade ever could.

"I can't take it. It will break my heart."

"Please," he says, stroking my cheek. "It will break my heart to keep it. It belongs to you, Cassandra."

He lifts my hand and slides the ring onto my finger. It hangs loose, a few sizes too big. He twists his lips to the side and places it on my pointer finger. "I guess now you know where I get my fat fingers from."

We both laugh. I wipe a few more tears and kiss his hands fiercely. "I love your fat fingers."

He smiles and then holds my hand out to examine it. "This ring belongs here. It's perfect. Nearly as beautiful as you are."

"I wish I'd brought something for you," I say softly.

Lawrence strokes the skin on the back of my hand. "You don't have to. You've given me the greatest gift anyone ever could."

"I want to give you more than just my love."

"Cassandra, you gave me my life. And I don't only mean by saving me from Ned. It's more. So much more." He touches the envelope in my hand. "You've given me a voice."

I stare at the words on the page.

"Don't you see?" Lawrence says. "Loving you has given me the courage to do what I should have done long ago."

"What do you mean?"

"I'm not going to law school. I'm going to write. I'm going to go home tomorrow and say good-bye to my father. Then it's on to New York or Paris or anywhere my writing takes me."

His beautiful eyes shine, even in the fading light. His happiness fills me with a bursting, soaring joy.

"I'm so happy for you. You'll be an amazing writer, Lawrence. I know it."

"I may be a lousy writer. But I'll be a writer. And I have you to thank for it."

Meeting Lawrence may not have been some grand plan devised by fate, but it doesn't matter. Knowing him, loving him, that is enough. Even if I can't be with Lawrence forever, he's still made a difference in my life. I'm a different person, a better person for having known him, however brief that time was.

Love is its own reason.

I set my hand to Lawrence's face. We don't kiss. We just look into each other's eyes. Everything that's passed between us, every moment, every feeling of agony and bliss, surges from his soul to mine and from mine to his.

"I love you," Lawrence says, his voice heavy with emotion. "I wish there were better, more meaningful words to express how much."

"A kiss could be a good start," I say, smiling.

He obliges me. As the warm night envelops around us, we push away every other thought but our kiss.

We take our place at our favorite spot. It seems only fitting. Lawrence keeps his arms around me as we walk, as if he can't bear the thought of being apart even one second before we have to. We're quiet, but then he asks the dreaded question: "When does the moon rise?"

"In about fifteen minutes."

"So soon?"

I rest my cheek to his shoulder. "Try not to think about it."

"How can I not?" He sighs deeply. "This is agony, Cassandra. I'd almost rather we just say good-bye and part ways."

"Would you really?"

He closes his eyes. "No. Of course not. I want to spend every moment I can with you."

"Then just hold me."

The minutes pass without mercy. Each moment fills me with deeper and deeper sorrow. And then we notice the first gleam of light on the horizon of the ocean. The moon. It's here.

"I'm not ready," he says. "I can't let you go."

I can tell from the way his voice shakes that he's crying, but I don't dare look at him. The sight of his tears will break my heart forever.

"We have to let go, Lawrence."

He pulls away from me. His eyes glisten, and tears spill down his cheeks. I wipe them away, kissing the wet trail as I do. He takes my face in his hands and kisses me. Even as I try to just enjoy the moment, I can't help but think that I'll never again find a kiss as beautiful as this.

The glow from the rising moon grows brighter.

Lawrence draws a shaking breath, trying to compose himself. I know the words he's going to say. "Good-bye, Cassandra."

I can't breathe. Part of me wants to collapse right here. Even if we die here on this beach, it has to be better than watching him disappear forever.

"Good-bye, Lawrence."

"Know this. We may never be together again, but I will love you for the rest of my life."

I hold him with all of my strength. I press my face into his chest, willing him to stay a minute longer. Just a minute more. But as he holds me, the pressure from his grip softens. The colors of his body become muted. A glowing line of light rises from the dark water.

It's happening.

Lawrence pulls back from our embrace. He's fading into the sand around me, as I know I am for him. Our eyes meet—his so beautiful and sad. As I stare back at him, an unexpected wave of happiness rushes over me. I don't know what I did to deserve a love this beautiful, but for the rest of my life, I'll give everything I have to do it justice.

I set my hand to Lawrence's vanishing face. With tears spilling from my eyes, I press my lips to his in a final kiss. We stay that way, locked in a kiss that will endure forever, even if just in our memories. We stay together until Lawrence Foster disappears back into 1925.

CHAPTER 40

Cassandra

The next two days pass in utter blankness. I have no memory of what I did, what I said, what I felt. There was nothingness.

Then came the sorrow. In many ways, sadness that you knew was coming feels worse than the unexpected. I spend the first nights lying in bed, staring at the ring Lawrence gave me, and crying as I never had before.

Mom does her best to help. We talk a little about it, when I can manage. She knows that I've had to say good-bye to Lawrence. Her encouragement that we can come back next summer and see him again only sharpens the sorrow. But I know she's just trying to help.

And in many ways, it does help. Spending time with Mom and Eddie, even with Frank, reinforces something I knew all along: that as much as I loved Lawrence, I couldn't have left my family forever.

Little by little. Piece by piece. Hour by hour, the pain softens. It's still there, but more a dull, ever-present ache. Then, one morning I'm halfway through my first painting of the summer, and I know. I'll be okay. I'll make it through.

I'm finally ready to go back to the library. This time I don't need to search through boxes and boxes of microfilm. Just one. The one that started this all. I know the date, of course, and I'm sure I have the exact box because it has the same red smudge on the left side.

August 1925. I know exactly where to look. I scroll to where I first read about Lawrence's murder.

The article is gone.

It skips from the story above it neatly down to the next. It's done. Lawrence is truly safe. Now I'm ready to read the pages he gave me on our last day together.

I take them to the beach. It's the first time I've stepped foot on the sand since the day Lawrence left. I honestly never thought I'd be able to come here again, but there's no better place to feel close to his soul.

My fingers tremble as I untie the string. For the first few moments, I can only stare at the vague shape of his words. The curve of the letters and gentle indentations on the page, these are his. Maybe I'm not ready for this. I've worked so hard to heal in the last few weeks. Do I really want this to tear open the wound again?

But then, the first line sharpens into focus.

We may never be together again, but I will love you for the rest of my life.

As clearly as if he were still beside me, I can hear Lawrence speak those words, the final words before we parted. The sensation of hearing his voice radiates through me. Every inch of my body tingles with happiness.

Hungrily, I pore through the rest of the pages. I don't cry a single tear as I read. I can only soar with joy. I read every last word and then immediately read them again. I stay on the beach for hours, reading and watching the waves, reliving the time we shared. Sitting here in our spot, savoring his words, I can almost feel Lawrence beside me. I can almost feel his arms pulling me close, his fingers brushing my face. It hurts, but I feel happier than I've been in weeks. I feel close to Lawrence again, and that's worth any amount of pain.

As the sun starts to shift to afternoon, I reread the pages where Lawrence describes how important his writing is to him. He's writing fast. I can tell from the way the words slant and are pushed into the paper. He's excited to share his longest held, deepest dreams. As I read one line in particular, however, I stop.

I reread the lines.

> *I plan to fully abandon the carefully constructed life my father has laid out for me. I'm even going to shed his name. I'll take on my mother's name, Winthrop. I'll start my life fresh.*

I ponder the passage. A memory blossoms deep in the recesses of my mind. *Why is that name familiar?*

And then all at once I know. Winthrop. As clear as a flash of white light, I can see the large banner stretching across the wall in the library:

L. James Winthrop: Crest Harbor's Greatest Treasure.

I make it back to the library with less than fifteen minutes before closing. Panting and red faced, I run in from the parking lot and crash through the doors. The librarian at the front desk gives me a swift, disapproving glance. These people are probably sick of seeing me. But I don't care. Ignoring the desk lady, I head into the main lobby.

The banner and decorations are gone. Breathing hard, I scan the area. I need to find that librarian who helped me with the microfilm. I have to speak with her. I have to know.

I run through the aisles, looking down each length for her. Library patrons glance at me with varying levels of annoyance and curiosity.

I see her. She's shelving encyclopedia volumes in a tall, cherrywood display case. I'm so happy she's here that I literally have to keep myself from throwing my arms around her. "Can I help you find something?" she asks with a tinge of disapproval at my galloping approach.

"I need you to tell me about L. James Winthrop."

Her face immediately brightens. "Well, of course. What would you like to know?"

"Everything," I say breathlessly. "Everything."

❧

We sit at a table in the sunny courtyard. The library has closed, but Evelyn, my new favorite librarian in the entire world, seems to have no problem letting me stay. She sets a stack of books in front of me.

"His major poetry volumes," she says. "*Gray Coast* is his most popular."

The second book in the stack peeks out from beneath *Gray Coast*. The bottom part of a man's jacket glistens on the cover. I draw in a sharp breath. A picture of him?

Unable to resist, I set my hand on the top book. The ring Lawrence gave me glitters faintly in the sun. The sight of it gives me strength. Slowly, so slowly, I pull the book away. There he is. Lawrence.

He's much older but still achingly handsome. In fact, if possible, he looks even better with age. Either way, it's Lawrence, smiling his beautiful smile.

"Are you all right?"

I look up at Evelyn, and only then do I realize that tears are rolling down my cheeks. I wipe them away quickly.

"I'm just…a big fan."

She smiles. "I can see that."

"Did he live a good life?" I ask, trying to compose myself. "Was he happy?"

"From all accounts, he was. Very happy. He married, had three children. His later writings won him recognition by the Academy of American Poets three times. He's the most acclaimed poet to come from the state of Massachusetts, let alone Crest Harbor."

I close my eyes, too elated to speak.

"A remarkable man," Evelyn says. "You know, I met him when I was just out of college. Got to shake his hand."

"Did you? What was he like?"

"So charming," she beams. "And very kind. I actually attended his readings several times. He spoke with every person who waited in line for his autograph. He seemed to really care and really enjoy chatting."

"Yes," I say to myself. "That's Lawrence."

Evelyn nods. "You're right. His first name was Lawrence."

"And…he's not alive?"

"Sadly, no. But he is buried here in Crest Harbor. Near the end of his life, after his wife died, he came back here to finish out his days. He bought the mansion his uncle had built in the nineteen twenties, where he'd lived as a teenager. They say he went out every morning to the property's beach and wrote. He penned some of his most famous poems there."

She grabs one of the volumes and flips through the pages. "Here. This group here. His final poems."

Trembling, I take the book. The poems are listed by date. My eye falls immediately to the final one. The last poem of his life.

It's titled: "For Cassandra."

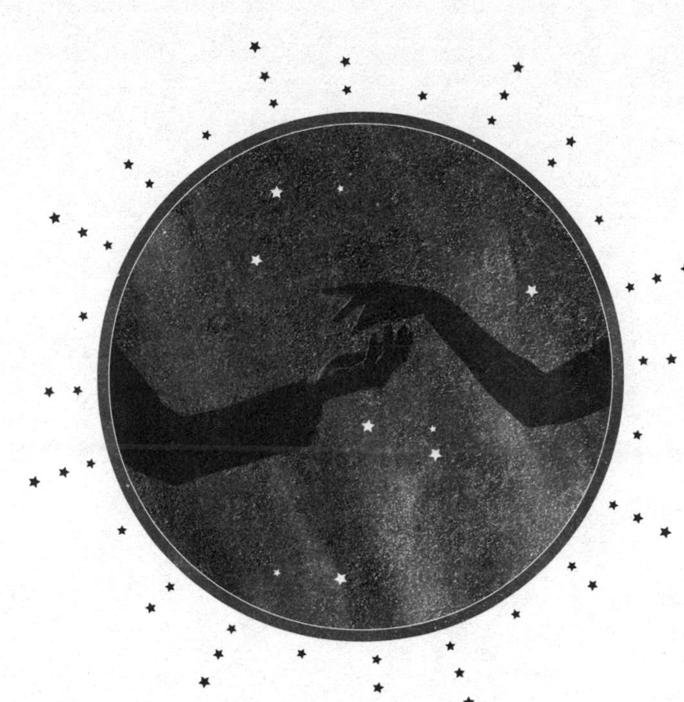

acknowledgments

I first have to thank my amazing agent, Mollie Glick. I feel so lucky to be your client. I owe you lots and lots of chocolate.

Hugs and thank you to Annette Pollert-Morgan. It has been an absolute pleasure working with you! You've helped me tell this story in the strongest way possible. And I love that the ending made you cry. Mission accomplished!

Thank you to the awesome people at Sourcebooks and Foundry Literary + Media. So many wonderful people have helped bring this book into the world. Seeing my story come to life like this is a dream come true that will never get old.

I also want to thank all of my amazing friends who have been here for me during the highs and lows of this crazy writer life. Natalie Whipple, Kasie West, Jenn Johansson, Candice Kennington, Michelle Argyle, and Sara Raasch. I love you all. And I don't see you ladies nearly enough! We need more Paolo in our lives.

A dozen doughnuts of gratitude to Tyler Jolley for being my local writer BFF. And a huge Dr Pepper to my previously local life BFF, Natalie Holmgren. You know this book wouldn't be what it is without your help and amazing ideas! Thanks for always being there for me. I miss you like crazy.

Thank you to everyone else who keeps me sane and happy and makes me laugh: Lisa, Susan, Aubrey, Mindy, The Best Book Club Ever, the Fruita Bike Chicks, and all my local friends! I am truly blessed to know so many amazing people.

Once again, I know that I couldn't be where I am today without my wonderful family. Mom and Dad, you have helped me in every way to make my dreams come true. I love you. I can never express my gratitude for all you have done for me and given me. When I stood on that cliff in Ireland, looking out at the most beautiful view I had ever seen, I knew I was the luckiest girl in the world.

Rebecca, Sarah, Jared, Amy, Rachel and all the in-laws: thank you for the support and good times! And, Diana, my story consultant, life coach and best friend, I know I can never express how much you mean to me. Thank you for always listening. For always talking with me. And for understanding me better than anyone else on this Earth. I love you, twin sister.

So many hugs to my beautiful children: Amber, Logan, and Ella. You guys are the light and joy of my life. I don't know how I deserve such delightful, loving, hilarious kids. And to my dear, Ben. I hope you know how truly wonderful your support has been. I love that you've been with me through all the greatest moments of my life thus far. I know we'll see many more together. I wouldn't want it any other way.